KONG
SKULL ISLAND

Also available from Titan Books

The Art and Making of Kong: Skull Island

THE OFFICIAL MOVIE NOVELIZATION

KONG
SKULL ISLAND

Story by JOHN GATINS and DAN GILROY
Screenplay by DAN GILROY and MAX BORENSTEIN
Directed by JORDAN VOGT-ROBERTS
Novelization by TIM LEBBON

LEGENDARY

TITAN BOOKS

Kong: Skull Island – The Official Movie Novelization
Print edition ISBN: 9781785651380
E-book edition ISBN: 9781785651397

Published by Titan Books
A division of Titan Publishing Group Ltd
144 Southwark Street, London SE1 0UP

First edition: March 2017
1 3 5 7 9 10 8 6 4 2

© 2017 Legendary

A CIP catalogue record for this title is available from the British Library.

Printed and bound by CPI Group (UK) Ltd, Croydon, CR0 4YY

KONG
SKULL ISLAND

PROLOGUE

This time, Marlow knew that he was going to die. It wasn't the first time he'd jumped out of a doomed aircraft. Indeed, this was his third time, and if it wasn't for the fact that he was his squadron's ace pilot, he might consider himself cursed. He accepted that always seeking the heart of the action meant that being the enemy's main target was inevitable.

But this *was* the first time he'd abandoned a plane without being in control.

He fell. His descent was no graceful drift towards the ground, nursed through the air by the comforting spread of a parachute. He was plummeting. Punched from the shattered cockpit of his P-51, he'd been forced back into the plane's holed and tattered tail, his left arm and shoulder bruised and numbed by the impact. Now he could hardly feel them at all. He'd succeeded in opening his chute but he was spinning, lines caught around his flailing limbs, air roaring past his ears, breath sucked from his lungs. At this speed the impact would kill him, if suffocation and fear didn't finish him beforehand.

His view was disjointed, images flashing past so that his panicked mind took a while to catch up and make any sense of things:

His damaged and smoking aircraft, gliding down and away from him in a large, lazy circle towards the land mass looming far below.

The island, remote and distant whilst he'd been engaged in the dogfight, now rapidly approaching and growing to fill his vision.

And half a mile away, the second parachute.

At least I got the bastard, he thought. *I'm going down, but so is he.*

Marlow took some small comfort in that news. This was the seventeenth Zero he'd shot down during his time in the Pacific theatre of war. His mother used to joke that number was unlucky for her, because she was that age when she met, fell in love with, and got pregnant by Marlow's father. Turned out that number really was unlucky for him.

Struggling to take control of the parachute lines, he experienced a brief, almost startling moment of peace and clarity that shocked him into immobility.

The scream of air rushing past his ears faded away, as did the spinning view of sky and island, sea and falling aircraft. He closed his eyes and saw his beautiful wife and the baby son he had never met. Saw them, loved them, knew them.

When he opened his eyes again the parachute gave a single hard jolt against his back and shoulders, then he was drifting rather than falling. He looked up at the opened canopy and grabbed the lines, experimentally tugging on the left and right.

Whatever he'd done, it seemed to have worked.

"Today's not the day!" he shouted. Though the relief was almost overwhelming, he couldn't spend any time celebrating the fact that his demise no longer seemed imminent.

If he didn't do *everything* right over the next few minutes, falling to his death might have been the kindest end.

Looking down, he was shocked at how close he was to the island. He could only make out a portion of it through a heavy tropical haze. The gentle curve of a wide beach might have looked inviting if it weren't for the dense, intimidating jungle that began close to the shoreline and extended as far as he could see inland. He could discern hints of a dramatic landscape—peaks and ravines, spurs of rock crowned with trees, dark shadows where valleys might hide anything from view.

The sea beneath him was a deep azure, its beauty almost hypnotic as its colours darkened and lightened again with each surging wave. A larger shadow seemed to pass along close to the beach, moving against the flow of water. Cast by a cloud high above, perhaps. A shoal of fish. As he saw what might have been the wave of a huge fin he tried to steady himself, look closer—

Something roared from off to his right, a huge, screaming rumble that seemed to shake the air and ripple his parachute. He twisted to look, and saw the blooming flower of fire rising from the Zero where it had crashed down onto the beach. Ammunition sparked and fired arcing tracers of flame through the air. The crashing aircraft had taken out a few trees, and big palm leaves burned as they feathered down through the flames. Smoke boiled skyward.

There was no sign of the Japanese pilot, nor his parachute.

Marlow prepared for landing. He was going to hit in the surf, just where the sea washed onto the beach, and though chance had carried him that way, he couldn't have planned it better. He hoped the sand would be softest there, and perhaps an incoming wave would also dampen the impact.

The shadow in the sea had vanished.

He bent his knees slightly, ready to perform a textbook parachute roll. If he did everything that he'd learned in training, he'd be up on his feet again within ten seconds, and ready to fight once more.

As he struck and his right foot sank into the sand, pitching him hard onto his side, and the parachute lines jerked his bruised left arm painfully upward, he heard and felt the massive impact of his own aircraft smashing down somewhere close behind him.

He waited for the surge of flaming fuel to wash over him, the flames searing away flight suit, skin, and flesh. Marlow had always sworn to himself that he'd never go out like that. He'd rather fall to his death or eat a bullet than let fire boil him away. He'd had too many friends die that way.

For a second as the wave struck him, he felt his skin blistering and boiling. Then water rushed into his mouth and he was rolling, up and down, left and right, becoming confused as the parachute lines became even more tangled around him.

The wave receded. Gasping, squinting into sudden glaring sunlight, he looked around to try and make sense of what had happened.

The P-51 had buried its nose into the sea two hundred feet from shore. Waves smashed against the aircraft, and steam billowed from places where fire might have taken hold. At least there was no explosion. Not yet.

To his right and further along the beach, the Zero burned.

Good. Hope the bastard parachuted into his own burning—

Then Marlow saw a shape beyond the burning enemy plane. Distorted by the heat and smoke, the running Japanese pilot quickly passed his downed aircraft and sprinted into view. He was screaming in fury. His katana sword swung on his belt.

Marlow struggled to release himself from the tangled chute lines, paused, changed his mind. There was no time. If he thrashed around he'd only get more tangled, then the bastard would have him pinned down, ready to cut his head off with one swipe of that blade.

He pulled his service revolver instead and knelt up, heaving against the weight of water dragging the parachute down. Aiming, he fired off six shots, certain that at least one would hit his enemy.

The Japanese pilot stopped fifty feet away, both hands pressed to his chest.

Marlow felt a cold sickness crawling in his stomach. He'd killed men before, shooting down planes and watching them spiral, crash, and burn. But he had never killed a man face to face.

The enemy pilot looked up at Marlow... and screamed, louder and more furious than before, as he started running again.

Missed! How the hell did I?

Marlow unclipped and hauled himself out of his

harness just as his enemy began to shoot back. Out of bullets and with no time to reload, he ran for the trees. Bullets zipped past him like angry wasps. At any moment he expected to feel the sting.

Nothing.

The sudden change from sun-baked beach to shadowy, still jungle was jarring, but Marlow knew he could not pause for an instant. He recognised the wild beauty of the place, and knew also that it would be a deadly environment if he didn't keep his wits about him. One clumsy step could send him sprawling. A move in the wrong direction might bring him face to face with a sheer rock wall, or a chasm that could not be crossed.

With his enemy close on his tail, any halt in his headlong advance would be the end of him. He was under no illusion that this was kill or be killed. They might both be marooned here, but they were still at war, and their blood was up. Their aerial combat had taken barely five minutes, but now their ongoing battle might last a lot longer.

He had to reach a place he could use. Somewhere he could hide, perhaps, and let the Jap pass him by. Then he could take time to reload his own weapon. Pursue. Stalk.

Either that, or he had to outrun him.

The ground beneath his feet soon started to climb.

That slowed him down, but it would slow his pursuer, too. He shoved palm leaves aside as he ran, dodging hanging vines, pushing through dense ground foliage and hoping he didn't step on a snake or feel the furry touch of a spider dropping onto the back of his neck. He'd never been anywhere like this, though they'd had basic training on board their aircraft carrier. He knew the dangers such an island could throw at him— dangerous animals, poisonous plants, disease-laden water. One mad Japanese pilot.

Another gunshot, and a bullet smacked into a tree several feet to his left. Marlow ducked right and forged ahead, arms sweeping plants aside as if he were swimming his way inland. That was too close for comfort. There was no time for caution. Whatever dangers might lay ahead were nothing compared to the one chasing him down.

The ground rose steeper and he dropped to his hands and knees, hauling on vines to pull himself upward. He couldn't see very far ahead through the dense undergrowth, and he hoped that the slope did not become too severe. Crawling across a cliff-face would make him a sitting duck.

From behind him he heard a triumphant shout.

Marlow paused and turned, looking back and down at the Japanese pilot twenty feet below, aiming his gun. His flight suit was torn and scorched across one shoulder, his hair singed on that side of his head. His face was lacerated in a fine web pattern from broken glass. He was a vision from hell, and a demon intent on killing him.

His enemy grinned as he pulled the trigger.

The grin fell as the gun clicked on empty.

Marlow uttered a hard, sharp bark of laughter, then started to climb again. He heard his enemy following, and he knew that he had to get to level ground. There, they could face each other and fight. He looked more wounded than Marlow, and he'd take advantage of that.

The slope continued for some time. Marlow soon became tired, the humidity and still air drawing the energy and strength from him. He cast frequent glances behind at the pursuing man, and could not help but be impressed at his tenacity.

Impressed, and scared.

The slope grew even steeper, and the trees and shrubs seemed more tangled and intertwined than ever. Huge leaves held deeply shadowed areas where anything might be hiding, ready to leap out and bite, sting, or assault him.

As quickly as it had begun, the steep slope ended on a clear ridge. Marlow rolled onto his back and stood, sweating heavily and exhausted. He looked around for something to fling down at his climbing enemy—a rock, a log, anything that might dislodge him or injure him enough to make him vulnerable. But the Japanese pilot was closer than he had believed.

He saw his sword first, the blade rising above the ledge and catching the blazing sun.

Marlow turned to run, sprinted ten paces, then skidded to a halt just in time. The drop on the other side of the ridge fell away into deep, impenetrable shadow. He could have made his way along the ridge, but the going was marred with sharp rocks, and dangerous falls to either side.

Here was where he would have to make his stand.

Hearing footsteps behind him he quickly turned, left arm held up to deflect the swishing sword. The blade never met flesh. He stepped in close and punched with his right fist, connecting with his enemy's throat. The man croaked and dropped the sword. It struck the rocky ground and bounced.

As the pilot glanced to the left after his fallen blade, Marlow kicked his left knee, hard. He screamed, fell, and Marlow dropped on top of him.

The impact shook the ground.

He punched again, again, and each time his fist connected with the man's cheek or jaw, the ground seemed to shake.

Weird... Marlow thought, but he had no time to wonder.

The pilot bucked beneath him, and Marlow heard

the clean *shush* of a knife being drawn. He rolled aside and went to stand, but only managed to rise to his knees before the man came at him, blade in his right hand, blood smearing his face red.

Marlow caught his wrist as the knife swung around towards his neck. The men struggled, a match of strength, face to face and close enough to smell each other's breath. Marlow stared into the man's eyes and saw something of himself in there.

For the shortest moment, both men felt the force of hate between them diminish.

A huge impact punched up through the ground into Marlow's knees, knocking him onto his side. Winded, he rose to his hands and knees, gasping as he struggled to draw in breath.

Struggled, too, to make out what had happened. Something had landed on the ridge with them. A huge object. A dark black boulder bristling with a mat of… something. Black cacti, perhaps. Thick, spiked, the stuff seemed to twitch and wave as the heavy thing it grew upon suddenly flexed and spread across the rocky ridge.

Another massive crash knocked Marlow onto his back, as another object landed thirty feet in the other direction.

Something rose from the dark valley beyond the ridge. *Earthquake!* he thought. *Volcano!* The steadily growing roaring sound could have been either. But this was no trauma of the earth. It was something else entirely.

The dark shape climbed higher and higher, the things that were its hands crushing rocks and changing the shape of the ridge as they applied pressure to lift the being even higher before them. It blotted out the sun, and in its shadow Marlow and the Japanese man were lessened. Its mere presence made a folly of whatever they were fighting for.

The roar settled into a grumble vibrating through the ground.

It was only when Marlow saw the two huge, impossible eyes regarding him that he began to comprehend. But comprehension did not bring understanding.

Marlow and his enemy waited for whatever would come next.

ONE

"The world's gone batshit crazy, and it's drooling on our doorstep." Bill Randa looked from the car window as Brooks drove, and if he closed his eyes and opened them again quickly, he might imagine that he was somewhere far different from the America he knew and loved. These weren't the streets he was used to, or the ones he wished to see. These weren't the times he had dreamed of when he was a kid.

"You should be more positive," Brooks said from the driver's seat. "Positivity's good for your health."

"Oh yeah?"

"Sure."

"Stay positive when you're stuck in that." He pointed along the road at a gas station ahead. A snaking line of cars was queued by the roadside, parked along the hard shoulder at least four hundred yards from the station. Several police cars were parked beside the line, and the cops were out of their vehicles, each of them confronted by drivers. Some were tired and bored, sitting on their bonnets and shielding their eyes from the sun. A few were angry. Arms waved, the officers remonstrated, and Randa imagined shouting and swearing beneath the steady rumble of traffic.

As they passed the forecourt, he saw just how chaotic it was. Only one pump seemed to be working, but after queuing along the road for so long, it seemed that any concept of waiting ended once entering the gas station proper. Randa was glad he wasn't involved. His organisation had access to government fuel supplies, and though that sometimes gave him a pang of guilt, he was also relieved.

"People are upset," he said. "Who can blame them? It's a sign of the times. And talking of which…" He pointed to the left as they passed a series of apartment buildings. More than one of them had banners slung from balconies, most of them reading PEACE NOW! or similar exhortations. "Vietnam, Watergate, riots in the streets. Cities burning. It's like the end of times."

Brooks glanced across at Randa and raised an eyebrow. Randa expected a smartass response, but his companion continued driving. He had quickly become used to Randa waxing philosophical, never more so than occasions like today, when the future balanced on a fine knife edge—rich and revelatory, or shady and unknown. With so much at stake, Randa was well aware that he was diverting his own extreme nervousness onto the unsettled masses around them.

"At least some of them have a sense of humour," Brooks said. He slowed at a set of traffic signals at a crossroads, and it took Randa a while to see what he was talking about. Across the street, on the crossroads' far corner, a movie theatre's announcement board had been vandalised. Alongside the title *DELIVERANCE*, someone had spray-painted, *FROM NIXON!*

Randa chuckled, but such public signs of dissatisfaction inspired a sense of deeper unease. The idea that society could not even take care of itself disturbed him greatly. What if it was confronted with some greater, deeper threat? Something cataclysmic? He liked to believe that the human race would step up.

He really *tried* to believe.

"They can hang banners and march, sure. But when the shit really hits the fan… what happens then?"

Brooks had no response. He drove, Randa sat in the passenger seat hugging his briefcase to his chest, and with every minute that passed he felt the stark future, and his true purpose in life, drawing close.

. . .

The congressional building baked in the scorching afternoon sunlight, and usually Randa would have taken a moment to admire the architecture, the grandness, and take in the atmosphere of this place, the heart of the country he loved. But not this time. Urgency drove him onwards, and an excitement and nervousness that was playing hell with his stomach.

He should have never had those pancakes for breakfast.

Eager to make his meeting, he hurried up the wide steps in front of the building, and Brooks worked hard to keep pace with him. He knew this was the young man's first visit here, and he'd have liked to give him time to take it all in. But there was no time.

"It's hard to imagine that there will ever be a more screwed-up time in Washington," Randa said. "Politicians are at odds. And even if they weren't, the boys on the Hill have their hands tied. They're directed to cut budgets, but they have no money for infrastructure and basic needs. With all the noise around them, they can't see how important our project is."

"So maybe it's not the best time to ask?" Brooks suggested.

Randa stopped three steps from the top and glared at the young man.

"I mean… we're hardly infrastructure or… or basic needs."

"Survival," Randa said. "That basic enough for you? Monarch is on the cusp of being shut down, Brooks. We're broke. Can you think of a better time to ask?" He continued inside the building and Brooks followed, both of them swallowed into the massive structure's cool embrace. It was a relief to get out of the sun, but Randa was too focused on his reason for being here to take much pleasure from it.

They crossed the large lobby area, Randa picking his route from memory. Passing through a wide corridor then taking a left, they came to a smaller open area and faced a wide, deep reception desk on one side. As they approached the desk, and their meeting loomed, a nervous Brooks started to express doubts that Randa had been struggling to allay for the past few days.

"I'm not confident in our presentation," the younger man said. "I mean, all our materials are loose leaf."

Randa was about to give their names to the woman behind the desk when a TV flickering in the corner caught his eye.

"In one day I could have it organised and bound," Brooks said, but Randa raised a hand to silence him.

Nixon's face filled the TV screen, and as they watched, one of the admin staff behind the desk also noticed and flicked up the volume.

"—a ceasefire, internationally supervised, will begin at seven p.m. this Saturday…" the president said.

"We don't have one day," Randa said. He tapped the desk to attract the woman's attention. Then he coughed, smiled, and tried to switch on his charm. "Hello there. Bill Randa, here to see Senator Willis."

The woman seemed to freeze, looking from Randa to Brooks and back again.

"Is there a problem?" Randa asked.

"Oh, well, Mr Randa. I think... Actually, sir, we were trying to reschedule today's appointment—"

A door opened behind her. She paused and glanced back, and Randa saw her shoulders slump. Perhaps she was seeing her job ending there and then.

Framed in the doorway stood Senator Al Willis. He was a big man, tanned, greying, and some might have called him fat. But beneath that fat was strength, and Randa knew more than most that he was definitely not a man to mess with. He looked agitated and angry, his face red and lips pressed tight. For a moment he didn't appear to notice Randa and Brooks, his eyes seeing something much further away. But a senator's preoccupations didn't concern Randa right then. He coughed, shifted from foot to foot, and then Senator Willis saw him and froze.

"Oh, God," he said.

"Al!" Randa said, putting on a big smile. "You're looking well!"

Willis stared at Randa and Brooks for a few seconds,

then seemed to dismiss them entirely. It was a trait that had always unsettled Randa in this man's presence— he held the room, however many people were there, and with one look or word he could make everyone in it feel about three inches tall. He held out his hand to his assistant, and she knew exactly what he was asking for. She pulled open a drawer, dug around, pulled out a packet of Rolaids and handed them over.

"Didn't you get my message, Randa?" the senator asked. He popped some Rolaids and swallowed them down. "To reschedule?" He continued looking at the Rolaid packet, as if far more interested in that than the two men standing less than fifteen feet from him. If he sought to disarm, he was succeeding.

"Reschedule for the fifth time?" Randa asked. "Sorry, I must have missed it."

Willis looked up sharply at the sarcasm—probably not used to being talked to like that, not by anyone— but that was just what Randa wanted.

"Senator, I wouldn't be here if it wasn't pressing," he said. "I know your plate's full, and that leaves precious little time for our small but hugely important cause."

The senator didn't answer, but his passive-aggressive bullying techniques switched target. He eyed Brooks up and down. "Who's this?"

"Houston Brooks, my colleague and an expert on Hollow Earth theory."

Brooks stepped forward and leaned across the reception desk, hand held out and a shit-eating grin on his face. Randa sighed inwardly. True, the guy was young, but he had a whole lot to learn about dealing with people like Senator Willis.

Willis didn't even look at Brooks's proffered hand, and he was left standing awkwardly with his hand held out. After a brief pause he stepped back and rolled his eyes at the senator's assistant. She threw him a quick smile.

"What is he, fifteen?" Willis asked.

"I'm twenty-two, actually," Brooks said. "I just graduated from Yale. I'm an intern."

When Brooks glanced back for Randa's support, Randa just sighed and shook his head. This wasn't going as he'd planned, and even though he knew the senator would have done anything to avoid meeting with him—last time, he'd seen the man hurrying away along a long corridor while his assistant swore blind that he was out of the country at a conference in Canada—he also knew that persistence would pay off. With Brooks acting like some starry-eyed kid on a movie set, they were giving Willis every excuse he needed to have them escorted from the premises.

Still, his naive air seemed to be hitting a chord with Willis's assistant. She was very pointedly *not* looking at Brooks, and the kid didn't seem to realise that this meant all of her attention was on him.

Yeah, he still had plenty to learn.

"Please, Al," Randa said. "For old times' sake."

The senator sighed heavily. True, they had a history, and its weight seemed to rest on his broad shoulders now, just for a moment. Recent history might have been regarded as rocky, but they'd gone to college together, played football in the same team, drank in the same bars, and mixed with the same crowd. It had only been for a year, before Randa's family moved away to South America and the exotic lure of the Amazon dragged him with them. But it was a year of shared experiences that neither of them could deny, and Randa knew for sure that in private the senator would hold fond memories of those times, just as he did.

He also held memories that carried a share of guilt and shame. Fear too, perhaps. Randa had never mentioned any of those more edgy moments from their past, not once. He hadn't even hinted at them. Yet Senator Willis knew that they were there, hanging between them like years-ripened fruits waiting to be picked, should the need arise. As it was, the need would only ever arise for Randa. His reputation was low enough, without revelations about drug-taking and decadent parties driving it any lower.

The senator, on the other hand, had plenty to lose.

Old times' sake was as close as Randa had ever come

to referencing the skeletons in the senator's closet, and the fact that he held the key.

"Jane?" the senator said.

"You really don't have long," his assistant said. She flipped a diary page on her desk and scowled at Randa and Brooks. "Really."

"We'll be quick," Randa said, and he was already skirting around the desk and approaching Willis where he stood in his office doorway. Brooks followed. "You're putting on weight, Al."

"You too, Bill."

"It's called getting old," Randa said.

"Speak for yourself. I'm sixty this year, but I feel forty." Willis turned and led the two men into his office, and Brooks closed the door gently behind them.

Randa had been here before, so he knew what to expect. He smiled as he heard Brooks draw in a sharp breath. This was the first senator's office he'd ever seen, and although he'd probably harboured some idea of what to expect, the truth was as surprising as it had been for Randa the first time he'd stepped foot in one. That had been sixteen years ago, another senator in a different age. The men changed, but it seemed their love of the finer things did not.

The office was almost forty feet square, with a large oak desk placed before two floor-to-ceiling windows, the chair facing into the room so that natural light bathed the desk. It held two phones, several stacks of bound reports, a writing pad, pots of pens, and a small statuette of a diving mermaid that Randa guessed was worth more than he made in a month. Across the office were two sofas set facing each other across a wide, low table. The glass table was strewn with magazines and newspapers, several used coffee cups, ashtrays and a crystal decanter and glasses, the decanter half-full of a deep bronze liquid that Randa knew would be a good single malt. It paid to know what the senator's tipple was.

Paintings hung on three walls, several more small sculptures sat on wooden pedestals, a large TV was placed before four chairs in one corner, and there was another well-stocked drinks cabinet beside one of the large windows.

Randa remembered just how much Willis liked a drink.

Behind the desk, the senator grabbed a jacket from the back of his high-backed chair and slipped it on.

"I'm already late for a meeting," he said. "You've got five minutes."

Randa sat in a chair before the desk and gestured for Brooks to do the same. He was still hot from rushing across town, every part of his journey haunted with the fear that they'd not get in to see Willis, he'd have security primed to turn them away, he might really not be here. Now with five minutes, Randa knew he could make it ten if he had to. Sitting and taking a deep breath helped prepare him for what he had to do.

If it came down to it, he was ready to plead.

Willis shrugged himself comfortable, then placed both hands on his desk and leaned forward.

"So, what imaginary monsters are you hunting this time?"

"I appreciate the humour, Al," Randa said. "Reduces tension. One sec…" He opened his briefcase on his lap and pulled out a cardboard file. Placing this carefully on the desk before him, he also extracted some loose sheets and a few illustrations, shuffled them together, leafed through them and handed one to Brooks.

While Randa took items from his briefcase, Willis packed his own, ready for his imminent departure. Randa noted the sturdiness of the senator's case, the metal corners, combination locks, and the reinforced handle able to take a pair of handcuffs if the need arose. Al sure had come a long way. For that, Randa was glad. He hoped that by the end of the day, he'd be happier still.

Randa half stood and held out a large photograph to Willis. The senator took it, glanced at it, then fixed his gaze on Randa. One raised eyebrow said, *Well?*

"This is a satellite photo of an uncharted island in the South Pacific, east of Kiribati," Randa said. "It has remained unexplored, and virtually unheard of, until now. Rumours of it persist through history, if you know where to look. Spanish explorers called it *Isla de Craneo*. Skull Island. There are also writings referring to it as 'the island where God did not finish creation'. It's notorious for the number of ships and planes that have gone missing in the area."

"Like the Bermuda Triangle," Senator Willis said, chuckling.

Brooks shifted in his chair, ready to retort, but Randa grabbed the sheet from his hand and nudged him in the process. *Shut up.* He knew how to handle Willis, and confronting his sarcasm with anger wasn't the way. The senator had to believe he was steering this conversation.

"In a way," Randa said. "But we think it's much more than that." He glanced at the photo he'd taken from Brooks, pausing for an instant, as he did every time he looked at this image. He'd seen it hundreds of times before, and would look at it countless times again. Searching for its secrets. Wishing, somehow, that by staring at those blurred lines, the out-of-focus waves and skin and spines, it would become clear to him.

He slid the photo onto the desk and pushed it across to Willis. The senator stopped it with one finger, turned it slightly, and looked. He smiled. He had also seen this image before, and Randa knew very well that his own take was very different.

"The nineteen fifty-four Castle Bravo nuclear tests weren't tests," he said. "They were trying to kill something on Bikini. I firmly believe that, and I think you do too, Al. I think you *know* it."

Willis glanced up, still smiling. Giving nothing away.

"To co-exist with these creatures, we need to know where they are. And where they are, we believe…" He glanced at Brooks. "*I* believe… is this island."

The room fell silent. Willis looked back and forth between them, as if expecting something more. Then he laughed, slid the photo back across the desk, and clicked his briefcase shut.

"Point one, Bill. That 'creature' has never been proven to be anything other than a whale blown up by the blast. It's a fairytale."

"Harry Truman didn't think these creatures were fairytales when he funded Monarch in nineteen forty-six." Randa held his briefcase up and tapped the Monarch design on its front.

Willis ignored his comment and did not even glance at the design before continuing.

"Point two, even if it *was* something unknown, we haven't seen it since. In terms of sheer waste, Monarch ranks right up there with the Search for Extraterrestrial Intelligence."

"Yeah, now those guys *are* nuts," Randa said.

"The answer is no." The senator picked up his

briefcase and strode from the office, leaving the door wide open and never once looking back.

Brooks raised his eyebrows. "Good try," he said.

Ignoring him, Randa stood and hurried from the room after Willis. He felt opportunity slipping away, and he couldn't help remembering those other times he'd been here with the same pictures, the same requests. He was certain that Willis knew more than he let on, and almost certain that he believed some of it, too. But how to get past the senator's shield of disinterest and scepticism was something he had yet to work out.

With Brooks behind him he paused by the reception desk, looking left and right. A few people were milling in the wide lobby or walking across it, but none of them were Willis. Randa's heart sank. He really had just shunned them and left them sitting there sucking their thumbs.

Old times' sake, he thought, and he remembered a couple of those old times that Al Willis would never want brought up again in private, let alone in public.

But Bill Randa wasn't that man. He'd never do anything to ruin the senator's career. Thing was, Willis knew that. In believing he was playing the senator at his own game, Randa was being played right back.

"Bill?" Brooks said. He was standing close to the assistant's desk. She was looking down at a blank sheet of paper in front of her, pen poised, fingers of her other hand drumming on the desk. Brooks nodded once towards a door tucked back in an alcove just a dozen feet from the office door. "Thank you," he said to the woman, then he headed off and Randa followed.

Through the door, into the wide corridor beyond, and he could see Willis walking ahead. He must have thought he'd shaken them, because he was hardly hurrying. It seemed his meeting wasn't that urgent after all.

They caught up quickly, and Willis only noticed when they were level with him. He cursed softly and shook his head.

"This is an opportunity that won't exist in a week," Randa said.

"You can quit chasing me, Randa. You're not getting any money for this."

"Who says I'm asking for money?" Randa said. It was a calculated response, designed to surprise the senator into stopping. It worked. They had his attention. "Well, maybe some, but—"

Willis started walking again.

"I got this," Brooks said, shoving past Randa and grabbing the big man's arm.

Willis spun around, glaring down at where Brooks held his jacket. But the young guy wasn't easily fazed.

"Listen, Senator Willis. NASA is sending a Landsat

mission to this island. They're geo-marking the area for further imaging. We can piggyback on their mission, cutting the cost and sharing some of the burden. With your permission, of course."

"And just what do you expect to find there?"

"Resources," Brooks said. *He caught Willis's attention with that one,* Randa thought. Every instinct told him to shut Brooks up and take over again, but he stopped himself. His young intern continued. "Who knows? Medicines, the cure for cancer, geological riches, possible alternate fuels, a new, strategically located outpost claimed by the USA…"

Willis was nodding slowly, and when Brooks trailed off he prompted him to continue.

"To be honest, Senator, we don't know for sure *what's* there. What we do know is the Russian NOVSAT is passing over this sector tomorrow night. In three days, they'll have the same images we have."

"And why haven't these images been available to either country before now?"

"Storm front," Brooks said. "The island's surrounded and covered by an almost permanent storm system, and as far as we can make out this is the first time it's cleared and broken. At least, first time since we've had satellites up there mapping the Earth's surface."

"So the Russians can see it too," he mused, almost to himself.

"Whatever's there, I'd prefer that we find it first," Brooks said.

Willis glanced at his watch, rubbed his chin. *He's thinking about it*, Randa thought, trying to withhold his excitement. He knew that once Willis started thinking about it, the cogs would begin turning and the idea would grow in his own mind. All he'd needed was one little nudge. Brooks had given it.

"I can't believe I'm saying this," the senator said, "but that *almost* makes sense." He looked at Randa. "Next time don't lead with the monsters, and let Yale here do the talking. I'll get you the piggyback, but this is it, Randa. Last favour."

Randa nodded. He was still nodding when the senator turned to leave.

"Oh, Senator, one more thing," Randa said.

Exasperated, the senator stopped and turned. His face looked like thunder... but Randa knew they had him.

"What is it, Randa?"

"I'm going to need a military escort."

"In case of monsters, right?" Willis asked, but neither man replied. He laughed. But Randa didn't think it was quite as heartfelt, or as honest as before. "Yeah, okay," Senator Willis said. "In case of monsters."

TWO

Warrant Officer Glenn Mills thought that his buddies might just love him and want to have his children. It wasn't that they hadn't already had enough beer. It's that they hadn't yet had *this* beer. Brewed by one of the 3rd Assault Helicopter Company (Sky Devils)'s most talented ground crew, using the finest ingredients and a filtration system ripped from the guts of an old Huey, this stuff might well be used as a substitute for napalm. If the war was still on, that was.

But it wasn't.

I'm going home! Mills thought again, the idea sitting uncomfortably in his own beer-addled brain. Home had been a calming concept for all three of his combat tours, but the longer he'd spent out here, the more alien a place home became. His last time back he'd spent pacing the neighbourhood and looking forward to his next tour. He knew that was twisted, and he'd never intended to become one of those guys, the sort who became entrenched in war and the camaraderie it entailed. He still didn't think he was. *I'm going home*, he thought again, and this time he pictured the good things—his mother's cooking; Jane Broderick's soft lips; sunset on the hill above town, where as a teen he'd gone to make out. *I'm going home, and I'll make it home again.*

He walked straight through the breaking yard. A dozen Hueys were parked here, most of them already in a state of being dismantled. Wrecking crews worked on the rest. Drills and saws buzzed, metal tore and screamed, and sometimes the sounds took Mills straight back into combat. He paused beside one aircraft and checked out the half-lion, half-eagle griffin that had become the Sky Devils' mascot. *Gotta cut that outta there.* He'd thought that before. He wanted to take one of these griffins home, but maybe he'd never get around to it. Could be that the only souvenir of his time out here would be the memories, good and bad.

He carried the heavy barrel into the old operations centre and booted the door closed behind him.

They were still partying. The room was large and now almost empty, apart from the group of Sky Devils over in one corner. They danced, spilled beer, changed records on Slivko's record player, and generally revelled in these new, post-war times. There was an air of hysteria about them that he'd never seen before. Usually the hysteria was because any one of them might be killed on their next mission. Now, it was because they were safe. Mills thought that fact might take a very long time to sink in.

He paused for a moment and glanced across at one long wall. It was still lined with photographs of friends they'd lost, along with their citations and medals ready to ship home to their families. Sometimes they were whole crews, pictures taken beside the aircraft that had gone down with them inside. Many of them were still missing, hidden out there in the jungle, rotting sculptures of metal and bone. Sometimes there was just one guy, unlucky enough to catch a bullet whilst airborne. Mills couldn't recall how many times he'd helped clean bodies and blood from a Huey's interior after an assault.

"Hey, Mills!" Specialist Joe Reles shouted. "You got your girl a present?"

"This is for you, numb-nut," Mills said.

"Oh, that's right. You think there's no point taking a gift home for your sweetheart." Reles helped him with the barrel and slapped him playfully around the shoulder. Other guys whooped and cheered as they popped the barrel and started filling their beer funnels. The brew even smelled toxic.

"All I'm saying is, we ain't exactly been angels while we were over here," Mills said. "So now that the war's over, don't go home expecting to find your women right where you left 'em."

"I left mine in bed, worn out and aching for my loving touch." Slivko laughed. He laughed at everything, though now Mills thought the young Detroit hipster's laughter carried a tint of desperation. He was a good soldier, but he'd lost it a couple of times, partaking too frequently of the drugs so easily come by out here. Slivko had believed that they'd numb him to the pain, but he'd learnt the hard way that they only brought another form of hurt. He was okay now, though. Mills hoped he'd take that level-headedness back home with him.

Cole just stared through his aviator glasses. Cole stared a lot and spoke very little.

"All except Cole," Mills said, staring back. "His woman's right where he left her, in the crawlspace under his house."

Cole didn't even raise an eyebrow.

"Smile, brother," Slivko said. "Pizza and hamburgers, man, and cold nights with warm girls."

"At least curl your lip so we know you're alive," Mills said, moving closer to Cole. They'd been on countless missions together, and on one memorable mission they had both saved each other's lives. You couldn't put a price on that. Yet he still didn't understand the guy. "You'll end up being shipped back on the wrong plane, in one of those coffins with the flag over it."

"Leave him alone," Reles said. "He's still in shock."

"Still in shock from being born?" Mills asked. "I ain't seen his expression change this whole war."

The sounds of the Sky Devils' aircraft being broken down for scrap increased as the hangar's side door opened. Mills glanced around to see Major Chapman enter, and behind him came Lieutenant Colonel Packard. Mills sighed. Just when things were about to get messy, here came the old man to spoil things.

"Atten-shun!" Chapman ordered. "Look alive."

Mills and the other guys stood and gathered to attention, swaying slightly in the heat. Mills's stomach churned. Damn, well, maybe he'd had enough to drink already, anyway. None of them really needed this new barrel of badness.

"At ease, you assholes," Packard said. "You look like idiots. This is a celebration!"

Chapman's stern face broke into a grin as he produced a big bottle of champagne from behind his back and popped the cork. Mills and the guys cheered and whooped, and Chapman came forward with a roll of paper cups and started pouring. A major serving champagne to the grunts. Mills grinned, but still struggled not to salute when it was his turn.

"I just want to say one thing," Packard said as the Sky Devils drank. "It has been an absolute honour to serve with you men. I know you're all happy to go home, but you'll realise in ten, twenty years… you'll look back at this time and miss it. The family we became out here. We're brothers. I know I'm gonna miss you. You all served in the most decorated chopper assault unit in air-cav history." Packard looked directly at Mills, and the barrel of toxicity he'd brought in. "If that doesn't rate tying one on, I don't know what the hell does."

Mills and the others cheered, even as Packard about-faced and walked towards the hangar's far corner. As he entered the small office there, Mills saw the smile drop from the colonel's face.

The sound of breaking aircraft increased again. Mills didn't think he'd ever get used to that, and with every crack or impact he felt a little bit of himself being broken off. It was like they were chipping away at his history. *Some things are best left behind*, he kept telling himself, hoping that one day soon he'd believe it.

The side door opened, and a couple of guys from the demolition crew looked in, as if searching for something else to take apart.

"Hey, man," Mills shouted, "can't you see we're in the middle of a meeting!"

The two breakdown crew retreated quickly and closed the door. Mills looked across at the small office, the door now closed. Then he turned back to his brothers and their party continued.

Packard leaned back and rested his feet on his desk. He stared. He wasn't even sure what he was staring at. Previously there would have been maps on the walls around him, marked up with red and blue pins, tape, marker pens displaying LZs and enemy targets. He'd known those places, even though much of the time he'd never flown there himself. He'd pored over those maps with Chapman and some of his better pilots, getting to know the lie of the land before sending his Sky Devils into combat. He'd always found it important to know as much about the missions as he could before committing his men, and that was why he often went against tradition and flew an occasional mission himself. Some believed that being in command was about giving orders from a place of safety, but he would never send his men to do something he wouldn't do himself. He knew that they appreciated that, but it was more about him than his men. It was because it made him feel strong.

Now there was only bare wood around him, snapped staples the only evidence of what had been there before. The office bore silent witness to the plans once made here, the deaths sanctioned. Buried in these wooden walls were echoes of conversations he might never have again. Most men would have been pleased.

Most men had more to go home to than they had out here.

The stripped-down office made him feel sad. If there were ghosts, they would surely inhabit somewhere like this. It was a place where violence, fear, and death were once planned, and now he could only sit and stare at an empty wall.

"Sir?"

The voice startled him, and Packard jumped. He didn't like being surprised, but this was his fault, not Chapman's. The major stood at the open door, one hand still on the handle.

"Chapman," Packard said.

"You need anything, sir?"

"What are you gonna do, Chapman?"

Chapman frowned, looking confused. He entered and closed the door behind him, cutting off the sounds of celebrating, drunken men. Maybe he'd seen some weakness in his colonel's face and didn't want the men to see that.

"Sir?"

"When you get back. What are your plans?"

"I'm all set up at Eastern Airlines. Grace and Billy are already moved-in in Atlanta. Ready and waiting for me." Chapman smiled, and it suited him. But Packard's stern mood drained the major's smile quickly.

"What about you, sir?"

"I don't know," Packard said, quieter than he'd intended.

"Home?" Chapman asked, moving from foot to foot. He seemed embarrassed and awkward, and Packard knew why. None of his men knew him. He was an enigma to them, and he liked it that way. They'd even been running a book on whether his wedding ring was real or not.

"Look at this place," Packard said, ignoring the word and pointing at the walls. "When these walls were covered in maps I'd think of myself as some sort of king, lording over all the lands around me. I could reach out with one hand and then the other, and touch places a hundred miles apart. Then sometimes, on those bad days… you know the days I mean, when someone came home in a body bag, or didn't come home at all… sometimes, I was a devil. So, home? I'm not sure where that is."

Chapman said nothing.

"Hell, I'm sorry," Packard said. "Get out there. Enjoy yourself."

"You're sure everything's okay, sir?" Chapman asked, and this time it was a friend asking a friend.

"Go on." Packard smiled and waved at the door, and Chapman turned and left. As he closed the door behind him, the smile fell from Packard's face.

Okay? he thought, and he had to really think about that. He had no real answer. There was no one waiting for him back in the States. Soon, there would be no one relying on him here. Sure, maybe he'd end up with a desk job somewhere, if he wasn't one of those destined to be thrown to the wolves for the way this war had played out. Heads were going to roll, he knew that for sure. He was old enough to remember the joy at soldiers' homecoming from the Second World War, and wise enough to know there was going to be nothing like that for this one.

Maybe the lucky ones were going home in a box. Maybe the luckiest ones, or the wisest, would decide to not go home at all.

Packard closed his eyes and listened to his men outside. He liked his own company, but he'd never felt so alone.

It was best to just go, and figure out where he was going when he got there.

With his kit bag slung over his shoulder, Packard stalked through the darkness, making his way across the base and towards the gate. He had no idea what might lay beyond. That would trouble some people, but not him. All he knew was that he needed to find a purpose in life once more, and the one place without purpose was here. The sight of choppers being decommissioned and taken apart broke his heart.

A dozen trucks were parked behind the guard shack, all loaded up and ready to leave. More would arrive tomorrow, ready to take his troops to the bigger airport seventeen miles away, and from there back to the USA. They'd still be together then, joshing and joking about what they'd do as soon as they got home—a beer, a burger, a woman. They'd soon learn. The joking would end pretty soon when they found themselves alone, and the time would come when they'd yearn once more for rain, thunder and bullets.

Packard knew that feeling so well.

He paused by the trucks, sighed, shrugged the pack higher on his shoulder, and took one more step towards his future.

"Sir?"

Packard turned to see a guard jogging towards him. He sighed, relieved. He'd thought it might be one of the Sky Devils coming to ask why he was leaving without saying his goodbyes.

"Colonel, there's a call for you."

"Thank you, Private." They swapped salutes, and as the guard left Packard stood wondering just who the hell might be calling at this time of night. The idea of ignoring the call and continuing on the beginning of this aimless journey crossed his mind, but he could not bring himself to do that. Duty called, and he was first and foremost a soldier.

He went to the nearest camp phone, set on a pole with a simple metal cover protecting it from the worst of the weather.

"Packard," he said into the receiver.

"Packard, it's General Ward."

"Sir," Packard said. It was the last person he'd expected, but he always felt a buzz talking to the General. He was a true military man as well, married to the army, a lifer who had told Packard that he hoped to die on duty rather than retire and wither away in some residential home for forces personnel. *A soldier too old or feeble to fight is no longer a soldier*, he'd once said.

"Word has it you're looking for a mission?" the General said. Packard froze with the phone pressed to his ear, staring out across the rain-dampened airfield towards the gate he had been readying to walk through. Perhaps the General had just offered a solution to passing through that gate.

"I wouldn't be opposed to one, Sir," he said.

"Why? Your orders to head home are already processed. I'm sure your men are anxious to get back to the real world."

This is the real world, Packard thought, but he said, "They are, sir."

"But you're not?" He was testing, pushing, probing.

He already knew the answer.

"You want me to lie to you, General?"

"You're sure about this, Packard?" General Ward said quieter, as if afraid his voice might carry.

Packard looked towards the gate once more. He tried to put himself in his men's place, walking away from camp with packs slung over their shoulders and diverse mementos of Vietnam tucked away in hidden places, ready to meet their worlds again—wives and girlfriends, families and jobs, friends and neighbourhoods where they'd grown up and to which they might now return, scarred and tired, to eventually wither and die.

"Yes, sir," he said. "I'm sure."

"Okay. Here it is. NASA has a gang of eggheads called Landsat. They need chopper transport to an island. Survey job. They need a half-dozen slicks plus pilots and support to get them in and out. A few days in paradise. I'll send the details, but you'll need to brief and prep your men immediately."

Packard smiled. It sounded fine. Non-combative, but that was okay, that was cool. He could spend another few days in the air with his men. The gate could wait.

"Sir?"

"Packard?"

"Thank you." Packard hung up and listened to the storm increasing in strength.

THREE

Where others would see the results of war, Bill Randa saw only opportunity.

The Saigon streets were buzzing. Motorbikes and scooters wove in and out of slower traffic, leaving behind clouds of exhaust fumes and the echoes of horns. Larger vehicles trundled along in chaotic queues, passengers blank-faced as if already resigned to never getting where they were going. Headlights splashed building facades with darting lights. Raised voices added to the hubbub, and although some of them sounded angry, Randa knew that was not the case. He'd heard such voices raised in anger. This was simply a typical street scene, and however out of place he and his companion Houston Brooks might look, they did not seem to be unwelcome here.

Randa led the way. He was more than twice Brooks's

age, and with those years came confidence. All his confidence was born of knowledge. He knew that to walk these streets would be relatively safe this evening because he'd researched the area to ensure that was the case. He knew where he was going, because he'd taken time to discover where the man he sought hung out. He was a man who came prepared, and that had always stood him in good stead. Now, more than ever, such preparedness would make what came next the success he had always desired.

Brooks followed with a natural and unspoken acceptance of Randa's superiority.

They turned down an alley. It was darker, quieter, and the stench of stillness hung heavy. Small shapes darted to and fro, keeping to the shadows so that it was difficult to make them out. Randa guessed they were dogs. At that size, he hoped so.

A group of Vietnamese men threw dice against a wall and exchanged cash. Their constant low-level chatter would set some people on edge, but Randa took comfort. It meant that they were immersed in their own activity and not concerned with his. As he and Brooks passed them by, a couple of them looked up and away again. He sensed no threat from them.

Further along the alley, a huge doorman blocked the entrance to the gambling den Randa was seeking.

"You sure we really need this guy?" Brooks asked,

looking around as if something smelled. In truth it did, but Randa hardly noticed.

"Is your Yale degree supposed to lead us through the jungle?" Randa asked without even looking at the younger man. "Besides, my father said never judge a man on where he drinks. Only that he holds it well."

Randa approached the big doorman and spoke to him. His Vietnamese was perfect and fluent. Yet another example of being prepared.

The doorman considered for a while, then nodded and opened the door. Randa glanced back. Brooks looked impressed, as well as uncertain about what Randa had said. He wasn't about to offer him the information. It was good to keep these youngsters on their toes.

The gambling den's interior was everything the exterior had advertised—dark, dingy, smoky, and filled with shouts and laughter, challenges and cheers. Dice and card games were the order of the day. A few card tables sat around the place, but there were also groups playing dice on the floor and on the bar. Any and every space seemed to be taken up with gambling men and women. Randa saw a small scattering of Westerners among the Vietnamese, just as he'd expected. Money was money, whatever colour the hand that dropped it on the pile.

Randa approached the bar, Brooks trailing behind him. A few people glanced his way, but no one seemed interested. At the bar, he shouldered his way in and nodded at the barman. Randa guessed from his bearing that this man was also the proprietor.

"Looking for Conrad," Randa said. The barman shrugged.

Randa placed his hand on the bar with a five-dollar bill beneath it. He tapped his fingers and the barman stared right through him. Randa lifted his hand and dropped another five he'd been holding folded between his second and third fingers.

The barman grunted, then nodded towards the rear of the large, low-ceilinged room. "Pool table," he said.

"Right." Randa left the cash and headed deeper into the bar. At the back of the room, almost hidden in a haze of smoke and noise, was a single pool table. It was poorly lit with one bare bulb hanging from the ceiling, and surrounded with several people watching the current game.

One of them was the man Randa sought, James Conrad. Perhaps he dwelled in these sorts of places because he wanted to fade away, but there was no hiding the colour of his skin, nor his military bearing. Though slight of build and unimposing compared to some of the men around him, it was all in his eyes.

"That him?" Brooks asked, but Randa didn't even bother answering. Of course it was him.

As if to prove the point, Conrad potted the black

to win and stood, stretching his back, and placed his hand on a pile of notes on the pool table's edge.

His opponent moved quickly. A big Vietnamese man, he slammed his hand down on top of Conrad's and pressed in close, almost nose to nose.

"You hustle me!" he said. Randa knew seven languages, and understood what the man was saying. "This money is mine."

Some men might have tried to talk it through. Some men would have drawn away, attempting to settle the sudden tension in the air with a measured response, perhaps some sort of mutual agreement beneficial to both parties. But those men would not have seen that this was a situation beyond saving by negotiation or grace. Even Randa could see that, in the bigger man's stance, his menacing air, and the sudden tension in those around the table.

Conrad saw it too.

With one hand he spun the pool cue and slammed its heavy end down on the thug's head. The man cried out and brought up both hands, but before he could press them to the pain in his scalp, Conrad had already poked him in the eye with the cue's thick end. He staggered back, tripped over a bar stool and went down. Bottles spilled and smashed. A few people moved out of his way.

One of the thug's friends was coming for Conrad from behind, wielding a bottle ready to smash it across his head. Without turning, Conrad swung the cue once more, holding with both hands this time to lever it back and up between his attacker's legs. He let out an explosive, "Oomph!" as the cue slammed into his balls, dropped the bottle, folded in half. Conrad placed his boot against the man's head and pushed. Still breathless and nursing his bruised genitals, the man rolled back and curled himself up against the wall.

Conrad barely seemed to have moved. He held the pool cue in one hand, end down, looking around the table at the other spectators. He caught Randa's gaze only briefly, then his eyes flickered aside, still checking for danger from elsewhere. The invitation was obvious, but no one took him up on it. As Conrad reached for the dollar notes now strewn across the felt, Randa delved into his pocket and threw a rolled wad of money onto the pool table. It rolled across and nudged against Conrad's hand.

He's dangerous, Randa thought. *He's killed. All that is obvious. And if he doesn't like being seen, doesn't want to be recognised?* He worried that Conrad might have another swing of that pool cue ready for him. But he had to try.

And the money had certainly grabbed the ex-soldier's attention.

"A moment of your time?" Randa asked.

"I'm busy."

Randa looked around the bar. The burst of violence had attracted only brief attention, and already the music was turned up again, chattering voices and the bustle of drinking and hustling flowing in to fill the silence like smoke.

"Doing what?" Brooks asked.

Conrad scooped up the money he'd won. "Spending this."

"There's more where that came from," Randa said, nodding down at the rolled wad of notes. Conrad looked from Randa to Brooks and back again, then pocketed the cash.

"Okay. You've bought my attention. But you have to drink with me."

"They sell decent whiskey in this place?" Randa asked.

Conrad smiled. "No." He nodded across to a table in the corner, raised his hand to the barman, and stepped over the man still nursing his balls.

Now it's time to buy his commitment, Randa thought. And suddenly, in the face of this gritty, grimy reality, the things he had to say sounded like a true flight of fancy.

Conrad stared at them both for a long time. He'd been right, they didn't serve good whiskey, but that hadn't stopped him from sinking a third of a bottle while Randa and Brooks set out their reason for being here and seeking him out. Randa ensured they kept to the scientific aspect of the expedition for now, holding back on the more outlandish Hollow Earth theories and what Senator Willis called his 'Monster Hunting Madness.' He was already afraid that Conrad might need only the smallest of reasons to say no. He could see that the soldier was far more complex than first sight would have people believe. Money drove him, and drink, but deeper down there was a whole lot more. Randa could not even begin to probe those depths. Not yet. But he hoped he would be given time.

Randa could sense Brooks thinking of more to say, greater ways to entice Conrad, but everything they were willing to reveal was out there. That, and the roll of cash in Conrad's pocket.

He viewed them over the top of his whiskey glass, then broke out into a huge grin.

"You won't last a day," he said.

"What?" Brooks asked. He was drinking as well, but slowly. Randa was worried that he'd blurt something about their real reason for going on this journey, because he knew the time for that wasn't yet. They'd push Conrad further away, not pull him in closer. He was a pragmatist, and little about Monarch and their search sounded rational.

"Untouched biodiversity?" Conrad said. "That's a fancy way of saying uninhabitable. Rain, heat, mud, disease-carrying flies and mosquitoes. Little shelter, rations at a minimum, no resupply. Sure, you load up on Atabrine for the malaria, but other bacteria? Ones we don't know about?" He drained his glass, leaned forward and poured some more. "And we haven't even gotten to all the things that want to eat you alive."

Randa put his glass on the table and nudged it towards Conrad, who poured in another two fingers.

"I sense that a negotiation is in progress," Randa said.

There was an envelope on the table containing more money. The cash he'd thrown to Conrad had been simply to grab his attention, but in the envelope was ten times that amount. Conrad had not touched it, but it sat there between them, a plea and a promise. *He could buy a lot of bad whiskey with that*, Randa had thought as he'd placed the envelope down, but he berated himself soon after. This image of Conrad—drinker, hustler, haunter of smoky dives—might have been accurate, but it was not who he really was. Perhaps now that the war was over he was in a holding pattern, just waiting to see what came next.

Perhaps he didn't want *anything* to come next.

"We'll double that," Randa said.

"Triple," Conrad said. "Plus a bonus if we all make

it back."

"If?" Brooks asked, looking at Randa wide-eyed. "Pay the man! I mean… I mean, I think we should fairly compensate Mr Conrad. For his expertise."

Randa grabbed his refilled glass and raised it for a toast. "To profit during peacetime," he said.

Conrad joined the toast and sipped from his glass. "One more question," he said. "You came here looking for a tracker."

Randa nodded. Brooks froze with his own glass tipped to his lips.

"So who, or what, am I tracking?"

"Mr Conrad," Brooks said, putting his glass down without drinking. Randa was glad, and he was also impressed to see that Brooks had hardly drunk anything. Young and green he might be, but he knew the value of keeping his head. "This is all the information that we have, okay? There is no map of this place. To our knowledge no one's ever been there before, or if they have they didn't see fit to chart the place and make that information available to the world. So we need someone with your skills and unique expertise in jungle terrain to lead our ground expedition."

"We're just scholars and scientists," Randa said. "We need someone with experience in case things go sideways."

"Sideways," Conrad said. "Right." He swigged

some more whiskey and slammed his glass down on the table.

Done deal, thought Randa. He should have been relieved: they were one step closer to their mission. But though he was excited, their reasons for hiring this man played on his mind. He was a tracker, true, but he was a killer as well. He knew the jungle, but he had no inkling of the things that might be waiting there for them.

The deception did not sit well with Randa, but for now it would have to stand. The time would come when he could tell Conrad of the true nature of their expedition. He only hoped that time was a moment of peace, not danger and threat.

The drinking den in which they sat suddenly seemed much less dangerous when he compared it to where they were about to go.

FOUR

Mason Weaver looked into the eyes of the traumatised child and wished she could not see. Photographs told so much more than *being there* ever did. She remembered seeing this young girl staring at her with the remains of her bombed and burning village in the background, feeling sad about it, taking the picture, then moving on. It was just a moment amongst many other bad ones, and a few minutes later she'd forgotten about the little girl.

Now, seeing the image forming and emerging in the tray of chemicals in the darkroom, Weaver realised that this was a picture that could touch nations.

You didn't want me there, she thought, looking into the girl's eyes. *You'd hate it if you knew this picture existed.* She saw that truth in the girl's eyes and recognised it so well, because it also existed in her own.

Weaver had only ever wished to live in the background, which was why she spent most of her life behind a lens.

It was probably her father's fault. She didn't think about the past too much, but when she did it was with a feeling of sinking sadness rather than anger or regret. He'd been a good man, but in his goodness he'd managed to give the young Weaver a sense of insecurity that had plagued her through her teens and into adulthood. He had wanted the best for his only daughter. Nothing was ever quite good enough for her, and that included the things she did as well as the things done by those around her. If she performed poorly in a school test he blamed the school, but she always read an underlying blame in his voice for her, whether it was really there or not. In his quest to create from his child the adult he desired her to be, he forgot to consider everything that she wanted. It was a benevolent dictatorship, and by the time Weaver was old enough to even begin to understand what damage such control was bringing down upon her, it was too late. The damage was done.

She was only sixteen when he died. At the funeral she'd felt invisible, as much a ghost as he might have been, drifting from room to room during the wake at their house with no one seeing her. Her mother had spent the day standing in the kitchen making endless cups of coffee for the mourners. She had no siblings. So Weaver had wandered the house, never finding comfort in any one place and constantly seeking something and somewhere she could not find.

She'd left home six months later, going to college and returning only for brief visits, and she'd spent from then until now still seeking that thing, that place. It was only through the lens of a camera that she started to feel close.

Weaver moved the photo back and forth in the tray, waiting for exactly the right moment to remove it.

The phone on the wall started ringing. She'd been waiting for a call all day, but now was the most pressing time. If she left the photo for too long it would overexpose and be ruined, and she knew already that this was one of the best shots she'd ever taken.

"Come on, come on," she whispered, nursing the photo towards perfection.

The phone sounded impatient.

When the exact time arrived she pulled the photo from the tray and slid it into the stop bath, lunging for the phone at the same time.

"Weaver."

"Mason, it's Jerry."

Her heart skipped. *This is the call I've been waiting for!* Jerry had come to report on the war for various European news agencies, but his talents had stretched much further than being able to get a story. It turned out that Jerry could get almost anything. He'd become known as something of a fixer amongst the journalistic family in the Far East—arranging interviews with generals, embedding reporters with Special Forces teams, extracting information from embassy staff; he also had a handle on where and when big announcements would be made, and he knew his way around military circles and society like no one else.

He also had contacts in the highest and lowest places, and he often teased that he was owed many favours. For what, Weaver had never been able to discover. Any enquiries into Jerry's life before he'd appeared on the scene had led to dead ends. Weaver assumed he'd been involved in something covert and very probably illegal, but she didn't care. Whether his was a good heart or bad, Jerry had his uses.

She tried to rein in her excitement, but as soon as Jerry started asking how she was, what the weather was like, and whether she'd seen the news about something-or-other, she almost leapt down his throat.

"Hey, Jerry, just tell me, okay?"

"Okay," he said, but the son of a bitch still paused for a second before saying, "You're in."

"Really? Oh God, thank you." She crooked the phone between her cheek and shoulder, keeping her eyes on the photo as she used tongs once again to lift it into the fixer tray.

"Here are the details."

"Okay, wait, let me grab a pen." She plucked up a pen and scoured the messy desk for a spare sheet of paper. In the end she wrote on the back of her hand. "Okay, go."

"It's the *Athena*, docked in Bangkok, eighteen hundred tomorrow."

"Got it. Seriously, I owe you." Dropping the pen, she rinsed the picture and hung it to dry. The little girl stared at her. *Where are you now?* Weaver wondered, and she hoped the girl was well. She always felt a duty to her photographs but, strangely, rarely to their subjects. Weaver was there to record and share, in the hope that her work might prompt understanding and action from those who saw it. It was curious now that this girl's plight returned to her with such an impact. It must have been her eyes.

It served to reveal the power of photography.

"What makes you think this is anything special?" Jerry asked.

"Huh? Jerry, when three sources tell you the same thing, word for word, you know they're lying."

"Not everyone's a liar," Jerry said, but she heard the smile in his voice and thought, *Takes one to know one*.

"There's something else going on about this op," she said. The girl in her photo watched with approval.

"Something nobody's talking about. This isn't just a survey mission, and I won't be on it just looking for nature shots."

"Just take care," Jerry said.

"You know me."

"Yeah. I know you. So take care." He rung off and Weaver was left in the darkroom, bathed in red light and staring at the information written on the back of her hand.

It was time to pack her kit.

FIVE

Captain James Conrad was wondering what he'd got himself into. Another mission, another paycheck, and while he had been happy with both, this was something bigger than he'd been led to expect. All that cloak-and-dagger stuff in the gambling house from the two civilians had painted a picture of a small, well-funded jaunt to some godforsaken island, with shovels, drilling equipment, and sample bags for whatever came up. A few people. Nothing major.

This was something else.

Bangkok docks was always a busy place, but this evening most of the hustle and bustle seemed to be directed around the ship he was heading for at Dock 62. The *Athena* was a huge weather-beaten transport ship, centre of a chaotic convergence of delivery trucks, swinging cranes, and people hurrying around

on board and across the surrounding dockside. Piles
of supplies and boxed goods were stacked on the dock,
gradually being carried up several gangways. Several
Hueys and a bigger Sea Stallion were parked on the
Athena's aft helicopter deck, rotors folded away and
landing skids being tied down. There wasn't a drill or
a shovel in sight.

Conrad was also surprised to see a good helping
of military clothing. It was hardly a surprise, with
the helicopters being used as transports most readily
available from the US Army. What was a surprise
was the boxes of military hardware he saw stacked
along the dockside. Others might not have realised
what they were looking at, but he knew ammunition
and weapons boxes when he saw them. He could
even tell what some of the weapons were from their
packaging. Someone here thought it necessary to
bring the big guns.

Conrad shrugged his backpack higher on his
shoulders and paused, trying to make sense of the
scene. He'd done and seen a lot in his short life, both at
war and at home, and he'd developed what he thought
of as a healthy cynicism. It was often a case of self-
preservation. Things were rarely exactly what people
said, especially when there was money involved. In
this instance, there was definitely real money behind
this expedition. Randa and Brooks had shown that

when they'd lobbed a wad of cash at him, and it was even more evident here.

Money twisted hearts and shadowed minds. Conrad knew that as well as anyone. He'd have to be careful.

As he headed for the *Athena*, an open jeep idled by. There were several military men in the back, and Conrad picked up from their insignia that they were chopper crew. He saw the griffin symbol of the Sky Devils. He'd worked with some of them before, although these guys were not known to him.

"A day away from going home," one of them said. "Oh man, one day away. And now another damn island, another damn jungle."

"Vietnam's not an island, Mills, you dumbass," another said.

"Key West is," Mills said. "That's where I should be right now, with a drink in my hand."

"Key West isn't an island either. It's a key." The man speaking caught Conrad's eye and held it as the jeep pulled ahead.

Conrad followed at his own pace. These were experienced fighting men, close to shipping home now that their war was over. If this was a private mission it must have government backing of some sort. Great. With money *and* politics involved, things could only go from bad to worse.

Closer to the ship he saw the final helicopter being

loaded, lifted by the heavy cranes, deposited on deck next to the others, and then quickly tied down and covered. There was security at the gangways, but as soon as he flashed his ID he was waved through. They were expecting him.

As usual, Weaver was late. Running along the dock, she saw that all but one of the gangways were already raised, tie ropes released, and the *Athena*'s smokestacks were billowing at the dark sky. Her kit bag banged against her hip as she ran, and across the other shoulder she carried her camera equipment bag. If she had to drop one, it would be the kit. She'd happily live in one set of clothing for several weeks if it meant she got the shots. It wouldn't be the first time.

It was all about the shots.

Approaching the one remaining gangway, she dodged past a couple of dock hands and went to run up the metal walkway. A man stopped her.

"Woah, no unauthorized people beyond this point," he said.

"I'm authorized… Steve," Weaver said, picking his name from a name-tag on his weird blue jacket. Not military, still it had the appearance of a uniform.

Steve's only reply was to hold out his hand. He held a clipboard in his other hand, and she had the distinct impression he was unused to bearing any sort of power. Well, if this was his idea of power, he was welcome to it.

She dug out her credentials and handed them over. While he perused her press card and letter of appointment, she checked out the ship. The *Athena* was already looking like a much larger operation than she'd anticipated. It was a big vessel, with a helicopter deck wide enough to house six Hueys and a Sea Stallion, and supplies tied down beneath tarpaulins. Sure, it could have been a science operation, and at its heart it probably was.

The fully armed Hueys seemed to suggest it wasn't only that. And the soldiers lounging by their helicopters spoke volumes.

"Mason… Weaver," Steve said, obviously finding the name on his clipboard. He looked up at her. "Is a woman?"

"Last time I checked, Steve," she said. "We good?"

He nodded. She plucked the documentation from his hand and stalked up the gangplank. She was used to the casual discrimination encountered during her work, and her first name often attracted raised eyebrows when someone finally met her. The fact that they assumed she'd be a he said an awful lot about attitudes towards people working in war zones. For many, women should be back at home keeping the bed warm. She sometimes took pleasure in their surprise, but more often it just pissed her off.

Another man stood waiting for her at the top of the gangplank, and as she approached she saw it was a colonel. This would be Packard, then. She'd already done her homework and knew he was a hardass.

"Can I help you?" he asked.

Weaver handed over her papers. If he was anything like she'd heard, he'd already done his homework on her, too. Still, he examined her papers. She was pleasantly surprised at the detail he picked on.

"Two years in-country. Where you been?"

"Embedded with MACV-SOG."

"Which detachment?"

"CCS out of Ban Me Thuot."

"You were in the shit." He nodded. "I respect that." He handed her papers back and she walked past him, pleased to be on deck at last. But she knew this conversation was not over.

"It's people like you that lost us support back home," he said.

Weaver sighed, stopped, turned around. She'd heard this before. Usually from the people higher up the ladder, not those on the ground and in the shit. Not those whose blood and stress and injuries and deaths she recorded, week after week. To them, she was telling the truth.

"You're blaming the people without the guns for losing you the war?" she asked.

"A camera's more dangerous than a gun," Packard said. "And the war wasn't lost. We abandoned it."

Weaver sighed, went to respond, then shook her head and walked away. She'd argued with too many men like Packard to think she could change his mind. His body was stiff and hard as if carved from stone, and his opinion would be the same. He might think a camera was dangerous, but men like him were the most dangerous of all. Men like him wanted to carry on fighting.

"Yeah, you walk away," he said softly. "Me, I have to live with it."

Weaver headed below decks to find her quarters. It was already becoming clear that this wasn't a simple scientific expedition. Having someone like Colonel Packard along for the journey made it even more obvious.

Once on deck, Conrad paused for a while to sense the ship beneath his feet. Even docked there was the subtlest of movements. It was a while since he'd been at sea, and despite the mysteries still surrounding the mission, he found himself looking forward to the voyage.

He spotted Brooks and Randa across the deck, accompanied by a man who was obviously the chopper guys' commander. Even without seeing the insignia, Conrad could tell that this was a man in charge. Tall, straight, confident, he stood slightly aside from the two civilians, as if wanting to keep his distance.

Crossing towards them, Conrad passed one of the tied-down choppers. It was a Sea Stallion, and it was fully loaded. Gatling guns hung suspended under its belly, .50 cals fixed at the side doors, and inside the open doors were stacked napalm canisters.

Conrad paused, his skin prickling. He'd seen the results of a napalm attack on a small village and the enemy troops using it as a base, and he hoped to never see anything like that again. The sight of the shrivelled, blackened corpses had been bad enough, especially when it became clear that many of them were civilians being used as human shields. It was the stench that had made it unbearable.

A research and survey trip, they said. Yeah, right.

Randa saw him and gestured for him to join them. Conrad's trust for the big man was already filtering away, and he'd hardly trusted him to begin with.

Conrad made a good show of examining the Sea Stallion's weaponry, just so that they all knew where they stood. It didn't seem to bother Randa. As Conrad walked across the deck, Randa took the colonel's arm.

"Colonel Packard, this is Captain James Conrad."

Conrad was the first to reach out. Packard held back for just a moment, then he offered his hand and they shook. A good strong handshake, but not too strong. Conrad smiled.

"Commander in the sky, commander on the ground," Randa said, already drawing lines.

"I'm a commander wherever I am," Packard said.

"No argument here," Conrad said. "I'm just along for the ride."

"What outfit did you serve in, son?" Packard asked. He might only have been ten years Conrad's senior but was already acting the father.

"Special Air Service, until a few years ago. Then I was brought in to train the Army Combat Trackers."

"'Who Dares Wins' huh? Trained the jungle lost-and-found guys? I'm happy to say we never needed your services."

"No man left behind. Your combat record is well known, Colonel. It's an honour to meet you."

"What kept you around?" Packard asked, voice softer. "War's over."

"I heard something about that," Conrad said.

"We do what we know, I suppose."

"Try as we might," Conrad said. He gestured back at the Sea Stallion, then turned to Randa and said, "You told me this was a civilian operation."

"Oh, those? We just ordered the aircraft. The guns came extra."

Conrad saw Brooks's reaction—a slight widening of the eyes, then turning aside so that he was looking elsewhere. They knew about the weapons, and had likely ordered them. You don't hire a man like Colonel Packard if you're going on a leisure cruise.

"Fair enough," he said. It wasn't worth getting into now, and he wouldn't likely change his mind about coming along. All it meant was that he'd approach the whole voyage with a lot more caution, and that was no bad thing.

"Briefing soon, main wardroom," Randa said. "Why don't you take a look around?"

Conrad bid the men good afternoon and walked to the railing to watch the rest of the loading operation. If they were going to be at sea for the next week or so, he wanted to make the most of this view of dry land.

It was at times like this, with a new mission dawning, that he thought about Jenny. She'd been seven years old when he'd gone in to find her. Kidnapped by a rogue unit of Indonesian troops and held to ransom, the Malaysian government had refused to pay. They'd turned to the British Special Forces for help, and Conrad and his team—already used to liberally interpreting the border between the two countries— had gone in to find her. Their orders had been to bring her back alive at all costs. She was, after all, the illegitimate daughter of a British embassy worker and a local woman.

Their mission had been troubled from the beginning. Conrad had quickly begun to suspect that while their efforts were expected, their success was not necessarily desired by some of those in power. A high-profile rescue would have been more troublesome than the simple discovery of a body, but he and his men knew that there was a little girl's life at stake. Huddled one night around a camp fire close to the heavily jungled border, the six of them had made a vow that whatever new orders might come through, the girl's life came before the mission.

It was a vow some of them had died for, and others had lived to regret.

They'd gone in hard and fast, spending the first few days discovering the girl's kidnappers' whereabouts, tracking them to a remote mountain stronghold, assessing the situation, making plans, then launching the rescue operation just seven days after entering the country.

They knew what they were doing. Conrad and two others formed a distraction, destroying a hidden arms dump a mile down the valley from the rogue troops' base. The other three members of the platoon made their way into the stronghold, killed the guards, and extracted the girl.

She was brave and sweet, and frighteningly intelligent. She'd known that they were there to help her, and did everything she was told. She hadn't started crying, shaking in fear and terror, until an hour later when they were away from the stronghold and heading back towards the border.

Their mistake had been radioing ahead.

The ambush took them by surprise. It happened a mile into Malaysia, in an area supposedly safe from border skirmishes between the troubled nations. Still alert, still cautious, they fought back, but in the crossfire two of the platoon were killed.

When the shooting died down and the ambushers disappeared as quickly as they had arrived, Jenny lay dead with a bullet in her head. Conrad had examined the wound and identified its cause as a sniper's rifle. This was no accidental death in a heavy crossfire. It was an assassination.

He had lost a vital part of himself that day—trust in the country and government he worked for; and trust in himself. It was the first time he'd ever lost someone he'd been sent in to find. It was also why he chose his freelance missions with the utmost caution. Conrad didn't take jobs where the odds were already stacked against him.

That had been his last mission as a soldier of the Special Air Service. The rest of his life had begun on that day, and almost eight years later he was still trying to decide how that new life would be built.

Looking out over the dock and contemplating the journey to come, he tried to assess these odds. Without knowing the specifics of the mission it was difficult. Yet he still felt that familiar frisson of excitement about this new undertaking. Cautious though he was, there was still that part of him that craved adventure, and this looked like it had the makings of an epic.

He guessed it was like Packard said—they did what they knew.

SIX

Randa felt his excitement building. This had been a long time coming, but now the expedition was underway. So much organisation, so many arrangements to be made—above board, and a few under the table—and now they were sailing.

Sailing for the island.

A chill went through him, and he looked around at the rec room filled with sweaty, uncomfortable men and women. The chill was nothing to do with the temperature. It was everything to do with this, history in the making.

Some who knew him would say that he'd been working towards this for five years, but in truth it was all his life. He had always felt the need to push boundaries, lift the veil of reality and generally accepted science, and look beneath. Beyond the veil lay wonders. He had always known that, and finding such wonders had been the driving force in his life ever since he could remember. As a boy he'd been the one with his nose in a book. While his friends were out on their bikes or exploring old mines in the Arizona hills, he was at home or the library, reading Jules Verne and Jack London and imagining his own, even wilder stories.

He'd never written them down. From a young age he'd sworn to himself that his own far-fetched tales would find their way onto the page only when they were known to be true. He enjoyed his flights of fancy, and they fuelled his desire to travel and discover. But reality was always his play space, science his mentor.

During World War Two he'd been posted to North Africa and then Italy. Even though he wasn't the oldest in his unit he'd quickly attracted the nickname Prof. While the rest of the men enjoyed the local wine and women, Randa tracked down books about the blasted areas they passed through and consumed their histories, as if to discover what those places had been like before bullets, bombs and blood had changed their landscapes forever.

More accurately, he soaked up the local myths and legends. Always searching. Always seeking that kernel of truth that he knew existed in most tales. Occasionally he'd found a seed and nurtured it, but more often than not they were moved on from one battle to the next, and those ancient tales never germinated into something he could touch.

Then he was shipped to the Pacific and his whole world opened up. Hopping from island to island, seeing horrors and trying to save himself by filling his mind with unknown, impossible wonders, he'd sensed the vast scope of untold stories that endless ocean contained.

The gradual focus of his efforts had begun. He'd remained there after the war, travelling as much as he could and never settling down for more than a few months at a time. There had been women. Once or twice, he'd even fallen in love. It was his deeper love that always won through, and while he remembered the tears in their eyes when he left, he was already looking ahead to a wider, more fascinating world.

Slowly, surely, he'd begun to find it.

Perhaps this was the time when his life would begin to make real sense. He was going to record this journey, and when he returned he was going to commit his adventures to paper at last. Because those wild imaginings would be true, and he'd present the wide scale of his dreams to the world in a series of scientific papers that would shake history to its roots.

Randa smiled as he looked around the room. It was good to have ambition, and he'd never compromised on his own.

There were around thirty people in the room, and

the place was filled with a low hubbub of curious and excited conversation. Many here already sensed that this was no ordinary voyage. At one end of the room, several display boards had been set up with sheets draped over the contents. That only added to the sense of expectation.

There were twelve people in the Landsat team, all of them sporting blue Landsat windbreakers. Randa knew that only a couple of these guys had been in the field before, and most of them exuded an almost childlike wide-eyed excitement. This was a true adventure for all of them, and he appreciated their enthusiasm. He saw in some of them how he'd been thirty years before.

Sat apart from everyone else were the Sky Devils crews. There were a dozen pilots, co-pilots, and support personnel, including Packard, the hard-faced colonel. Randa didn't like him. He wasn't sure if it was purely because he found the man intimidating and resented that, or for other reasons. Packard was a career military man, and Randa had the impression that he always looked down upon anyone not in uniform.

At the back of the room, alone, Conrad leaned against the wall and observed his fellow travellers. He was someone else who intimidated Randa a little— knowing his background, and some of the things he had done—but he couldn't help liking the ex-SAS captain. He was quietly spoken most of the time, and unlike Packard he did not appear to look down on anyone out of uniform. It might have been because he considered everyone beneath him. Now, Conrad took in everyone and everything with a quiet intensity. He calmly flipped a lighter open and closed as he did so.

Randa had already decided that Conrad was a good man to have on their side.

Randa and the other six members of his team also sat apart, close to the front of the room. It gave the whole place a cliquey feel, but he hoped that might lessen over the course of their voyage. Nine days at sea together might help break down boundaries between disparate groups.

He was especially pleased to have San Lin with them. Not only was she a brilliant scientist with some startling theories, but speaking with her also helped him brush up on his Chinese. He was always looking to improve his education in any way that might aid his lifetime's work.

Randa saw Brooks approaching, and knew instantly that the young man would go into auto-flirt mode. He headed directly for San Lin and held out his hand.

"Hi, Houston Brooks."

"You two haven't met, have you?" Randa asked. "San, Brooks wrote that dissertation at Yale I was telling you about."

"Yes, the geologist." She and Brooks shook hands.

She smiled. "I'm San Lin. Biologist. I've been in the field since you were hired. Looks like I'm still there."

"She's been in the Brazilian jungle," Randa said. "You should see her findings. Very impressive."

"Yeah, I read the report," Brooks said. "Interesting speculation."

San raised an eyebrow. "You're sceptical?"

"Don't take it personally," Brooks said, glancing at Randa. "I'm not sure I believe any of this. It just makes for a good paper."

"Please forgive the new guy," Randa said, enjoying taking Brooks down a peg. He was a nice guy, but too casual sometimes. Not committed enough. "He's got a brilliant mind, but he doesn't yet appreciate the beauty of the unknown. Your work was sound, Mr Brooks. This expedition is going to prove it."

There was movement from the Landsat team, and Randa noticed Victor Nieves moving to the front of the room. He stood behind a table that had been set up there, glancing at the covered display boards, shuffling a sheaf of paper and looking nervously around the room. At first Randa thought he was nervous. Some people weren't built for public speaking. Then it hit him—Nieves looked just like an excited teacher about to impart some treasured knowledge.

"Show's about to start," Randa said quietly, and his own excitement thrummed in his bones.

"Hello and welcome," the man said. "I'm Landsat field supervisor Victor Nieves. Sitting just there is my colleague Steve Gibson, our data wrangler."

Gibson raised a hand in greeting. The room had fallen silent, and remained so. Expectation was heavy.

"For those of you unfamiliar with Landsat One," Nieves began, "it's a satellite that views the exact same surface of the Earth every sixteen days, and provides an unbiased image using a multi-spectral scanner and return beam vidicon to provide eight-bit data..."

Shit, how to lose a room before you've even begun, Randa thought. Glances were exchanged, eyes rolled, and when Nieves looked to him, Randa shook his head. Someone laughed. One of Packard's soldiers swore softly.

"Oh... er... well, it gives us pictures of the Earth from space. Since Landsat began, our team has surveyed a dozen untouched land masses discovered by the satellite imaging, with the express purpose of travelling there and exploring. We believe that this island, our destination on this voyage, will be the most challenging of the dozen we've found. All our images show the island surrounded by a near-constant storm system. That said, we've never had helicopter transport, so to the third helicopter attack squadron, a hearty thank you!"

Packard and his men nodded, and a couple gave soft *whoops*.

Nieves continued. "We're also pleased to be joined for the first time by the resource exploration team, led by Mr Randa. Our main focus as map-makers will be on the island's surface. Mr Randa's team's interest is in what lies beneath." He smiled at Randa, then nodded at Brooks. "Mr Brooks?"

Brooks stood and walked to the front, tugging a couple of sheets from display boards as he did so. All very theatrical, Randa thought, but it was a good way to grab people's attention. One revealed a large map. Beneath the other was a projector screen, and Brooks switched on a projector and stood back. The larger map was a composite from many satellite pictures, and the slides displayed more detailed, smaller sections of that same large image. Some areas were outlined, others marked with arrows.

Randa took in a deep breath and thought, *I only hope Brooks doesn't mess this up.*

It was time to lay their plan on the line.

Too many cooks, Conrad thought. He'd been carefully surveilling the room, and he'd already come to the conclusion that there were too many independent parties involved in this effort, with disparate aims and each with their own leaders. Landsat, Randa's team, the Sky Devils, the reporter. Him. And even within these smaller groups, there were those who didn't seem familiar with each other. Brooks didn't know the Chinese woman, a fact evident from his clumsy flirting. The Landsat guys seemed like nervous school kids out on their first big trip.

The reporter, Mason Weaver, didn't seem to know anyone else in the room. She intrigued him, and he wondered what she thought of all this. Hopefully soon he'd have a chance to ask.

The whole set-up felt wrong, and from the moment he'd boarded the ship he'd begun to question the wisdom of coming along. Conrad wasn't in the habit of making bad decisions, and rarely considered that he'd swung the wrong way. It was uncomfortable thinking that now.

What Brooks started to say next grabbed his attention once more and made him like things even less.

"We'll be performing a full geological survey of the island's subsurface," he said, pointing at a slide. "We'll fly in over the south shore and drop ground sensors in this zone. They'll measure data generated by the seismic charges we'll drop on our next pass."

The room went quiet and still.

"You're dropping bombs?" Conrad asked.

"Scientific instruments," Brooks said.

"You don't approve?" Packard asked.

Conrad shrugged. "When has science ever steered us wrong?"

"You heard that boys," Packard said to his troops. "We're scientists." They laughed, clapping each other's backs.

The slides moved on, displaying waves from seismic charges travelling underground to the red-dotted sensors. A simple animation then showed data transmitted to monitors set around and within the survey area.

Nieves took over from Brooks.

"After the survey, we'll land and make base camp for ground excursions, led by the entertaining Mr Conrad."

"Your humble guide," Conrad said. "Tips encouraged."

Nieves nodded to Major Chapman, one of Packard's team. He stepped quickly to the front to address the room. Conrad admired his military precision and efficiency, but yet again he found it troubling. This was a civilian operation with gunships, seismic bombs, and napalm canisters.

"Once on the island," Chapman said, "the storm's magnetic field will block all radio contact with the *Athena*. That means we'll be on our own. After three days the refuelling team will meet us here." He pointed at the map. "North shore, thirteen-hundred hours. This may be the only safe departure window for an unknown time. We *cannot* miss it."

Across the room, above the worried chatter rising from virtually everyone there, Conrad caught Weaver's eye. She threw him a frosty smile and looked away. She didn't seem anxious, and he thought he knew why—she still didn't know what she'd come to find.

There was more to this trip than anyone had yet revealed.

SEVEN

Randa grabbed a drink from the bar and dropped into a seat beside Nieves and the rest of his team. At least the ship had an officers' lounge. On this voyage, it had been reserved for the passengers, no crew allowed. Randa had expected Packard to attend on his own, perhaps bringing Major Chapman along, but it seemed that the colonel was happy with his grunts drinking here too. Randa didn't mind. It gave the place some much-needed atmosphere.

Now, though, he hadn't come for fun, and Nieves knew it. He was here because there was a stranger on their ship, and all his thorough planning and secrecy might be under threat.

"So?" Randa asked. Nieves knew exactly what he was talking about.

"Bill, look, it seems the guy we hired dropped out at

the last minute. I wasn't made aware until now."

"She hasn't been cleared. No background check."

"I don't see what the problem is," Nieves replied. "It's our standard protocol to have a photographer on these expeditions."

Randa sighed heavily, trying to hold in his anger. Everything could be put at risk by Weaver's arrival. Chim had been in Randa's pocket, as reliable as a journalist could be. The woman was not. He didn't like having a wild card on board, and this was his party.

"Her resume is impressive," San said.

"I don't care how impressive it is, she's a journalist!" Randa said, and when San and Nieves looked past his shoulder he knew that Weaver was standing right behind him. He didn't really care. His skin was too thick for him to be guilted by social *faux pas*. Nevertheless, he tried on a smile as he stood and turned around. "Ah, Miss Weaver. I'm Bill Randa, leader of this expedition. Glad to have you along."

"So what government agency are you with exactly?" she asked. No preamble, no greeting. Straight down to business. "Didn't catch the acronym."

"I didn't drop one," Randa said, smile slipping. "We're explorers."

"Exploring." Weaver looked around at them all, as if taking pictures with her eyes. She'd probably already researched background on most of them. "I thought that ended with the pioneers. The ideals of Manifest Destiny aren't too highly regarded anymore."

"We live in a cynical age," Randa said, meaning every word.

"After five years of military briefings, your bullshit meter gets finely tuned."

"Listen, Miss—"

"*Ms* Weaver."

"Right, Ms Weaver. Did the Europeans set out into unknown waters in search of gold? Or was it the mystery that was more enticing."

"Gold, I'm pretty sure," Conrad said. He raised his beer from where he'd been watching and listening at the bar, then quickly downed it and walked off, Weaver watching. Randa so wanted to spin around and berate him. But he knew what the man could do—it was why he'd hired him, after all—and the last thing he wanted was to piss him off. If things went south once they got on the island, Conrad was the person he wanted by his side.

Packard approached the bar and poured himself another whiskey, his presence forcing his way into the conversation.

"Colonel, have you met Ms Weaver?" Randa asked.

"I know her work." The soldier joined them, his expression unchanging. "I don't like it." He downed the whiskey in one, touched his brow, then stalked from the room.

Weaver leaned in close to Randa and muttered, "Nice party you put together." Then she walked to the bar and grabbed herself a drink.

Conrad liked being on a ship. He sometimes thought it was the isolation, cutting him off from all the things he had done and promising new experiences over the horizon. Or sometimes he guessed it was the idea of looking back along the ship's wake, phosphorescence glimmering in the waves left behind like the remnants of past deeds.

He saw the little girl Jenny in that wake. He often saw her face.

It had taken a long time, but Conrad was quite at peace with his life. He'd chosen his paths, and even when he'd killed, it had always been essential in some aspect. Either kill or be killed, or kill because to not do so would put others at risk. He'd killed men fighting. He'd murdered a man in his sleep. He'd burned a woman alive in a car. All bad people.

His choices were all his own, and he lived with them well enough. The only choice that had not been his own had been the death of the little girl, and he had taken many years to put that in a place where he could deal with it. Perhaps it was selfish, or even cowardly, but he had come to accept that it had not been his fault. He couldn't save everyone. Every time he saw her face or remembered her sad voice, he tried to offset the memory with the face or voice of someone he'd saved. Downed pilots, lost soldiers, inept civilians getting into situations way over their heads there were many people alive today who would be dead if it were not for him. It was ironic that a death he had not caused troubled him much more than those he had.

Yet today, steaming across the endless Pacific Ocean towards a new, unknown future still felt good. Even though he knew he was being deceived.

Snooping around to uncover that deceit felt good, too.

The hold wasn't as dark as it could have been. A few small lights remained on, diffusing a soft glow here and there that helped him navigate his way through the stacks of tied-down boxes, crates and piles of equipment. There were no guards that he could see, yet he remained low and quiet, just in case. He'd already checked to make sure there were no cameras covering the hold. Security was lax, and he hoped that meant there was little to hide. But he thought not. It was more likely that those hiding secrets didn't think that anyone would come looking.

Beside a pile of crates he flicked on his lighter. The two closest to him were heavy wooden constructions marked with the Monarch name. He moved on to the next pile. SEISMIC CHARGES was stencilled on the side of one box, and beside that another read EXPLOSIVES.

Conrad extinguished the lighter. "In case things go sideways," he whispered. Explosives? Were they actually mining for something? He liked this less and less, but to pry open the boxes would reveal that someone had been investigating.

Right now, it was probably best to leave things alone. See how all this played out. He was being paid well, after all.

He heard a click and spun around. Weaver was aiming a camera at him. She shifted position, focused, snapped another picture, then lowered the camera.

"This trip's getting more interesting by the mile," she said.

"What are you doing down here?" Conrad asked. She'd surprised him, and he didn't like that. He'd let his guard down.

"I could ask you the same thing."

"Just killing time," he said.

"Me too." She aimed her camera at the crates behind him and took a shot. "Why does a geological mapping mission need explosives?" she asked.

"You weren't listening in class," Conrad said. "Seismic charges for the geology survey."

"And you believe that?" She swung the camera and snapped a shot of Conrad, casual, matter of fact. The camera was almost part of her, an aid to communication. Perhaps some sort of shield, too. Even in the briefing she'd had it slung around her neck, though she'd taken no pictures.

"I'm not a geologist," he said.

"Doesn't take one to know something doesn't smell right." She looked around the loaded hold as if deciding what to photograph next. The ship rocked and groaned, never silent. Conrad kept half of his attention on their surroundings in case someone came to check on the cargo. If they were caught down here, he'd have to confront the truth of this mission before he was quite ready. Maybe it was Randa, maybe Packard, but whoever was running the show, there was definitely more to it than appeared on the surface.

"Says the eager photo-journalist. So who hired you for this?"

"Nieves. Landsat guy." She came a step closer and looked him up and down. Examining him with her reporter's eye. Conrad wondered what she saw, what conclusions she came to.

"Meet Colonel Packard yet?" she asked.

"Yeah."

"He's wound pretty tight."

"The man's a decorated war hero. That's the package they come in. So, isn't shooting a mapping mission a step down for you? I get the impression you're someone who's seen real action."

"I begged for this gig," she said. "The war's over but there's a sudden interest in a remote Pacific island and we're going in with military choppers, machine guns and explosives? I see dirty Pentagon fingerprints all over this op."

"And you want to expose it and win a Pulitzer?"

"If you're not there you can't get the shot," she said. They were standing closer now, and hidden down in the hold it felt to Conrad like they were having the most important conversation on the ship. "The right photo can alter the course of things. It can shape opinions."

"And win you a Pulitzer."

She smiled. "So what about you? How did a British Special Forces legend get dragged into this?"

And there it is, thought Conrad. *Of course she knows who I am.* He'd suspected it anyway, and she'd probably followed him down here to corner him for this talk. He didn't like the idea of someone stalking him like this without him knowing, but he guessed he wasn't the first person she'd followed. She was as serious about her work as he was. He could only respect that. He was also pretty certain that they were on the same side, whatever side that was.

"You know more about me than I know about you," he said.

"I'm a journalist. I ask questions, Captain Conrad."

"Just Conrad. I'm retired."

"Sure, it looks like it."

He shrugged.

"So when I ask questions, more often than not people give an answer, even if they're lying." She waited. Conrad looked around, listened—still alone.

"They offered me money," he said.

"Really? That's it?"

"A lot of money." She raised her eyebrows. Conrad continued, "I don't get too invested in outcomes."

"You don't strike me as a mercenary," she said.

"You don't strike me as a war photographer."

"*Anti*-war photographer."

That surprised him. He'd rarely heard such distinctions from the correspondents he'd encountered, and he was about to ask her more about that when he heard the soft, regular tread of footsteps.

Conrad and Weaver crouched down between the crates. They were close now, so close that he could smell her subtle perfume and faint perspiration. He sensed that she had plenty of questions for him, and she intrigued him, too. She'd worked hard to get on this expedition, and was already more ahead of the game than him. He'd work hard to catch up.

Hidden in shadows, Conrad peered around the edge of a crate and watched two soldiers enter the hold. They seemed casual and relaxed, chatting and laughing. One of them picked up a small box, and after a quick look around they left the hold.

"They gone?" Weaver asked.

"Yeah. Don't worry. We're just killing time."

Weaver smirked and left, stealing away across the hold, through shadows, and out through a different door.

EIGHT

"I could so get used to this."

It was almost like a holiday. Mills had soaked up plenty of sun during his time in Vietnam, but getting scorched whilst lying next to your chopper, waiting for the call to get skyborne and possibly fly to your death, was far different from this.

This was almost luxury.

The Sky Devils were splayed across the *Athena*'s deck. Mills sat with Cole and Reles, shirts off, playing cards and drinking beer that Slivko seemed to be able to find just about anywhere. Reles was ten bucks down, and Mills knew from experience that playing poker with Cole was never a good idea. The guy probably had a poker face when he was coming. Maybe he'd smiled once, but few of them could recall when, or under what conditions. Mills guessed even his mother would have trouble remembering.

Weaver was taking photos of the men at play. They all pretended not to notice her, but Mills could see guys drawing in their guts, tensing their muscles, whenever the camera looked their way. She sure was hot. They all agreed on that. Mills also silently suspected that she could take on any one of them in a fight, and probably come out pretty good the other side. A reporter like her didn't make her way through the war without being hard as nails and twice as sharp. She'd already proven that she took no bullshit.

He'd noticed how she often sat with the camera close up to her face, even when she didn't appear to be taking pictures. Weird. Lots of things were weird about this trip.

"Oh, man!" Reles said when Cole revealed his hand. He'd won with two sevens. He swept the notes into his small pile, face barely changing.

"Hey, Major!" Mills called. Chapman was leaning back against a pile of kit, writing pad balanced on his knees, pen in one corner of his mouth as he thought about what to write. "Another letter to Billy?"

"Yeah, Mills. What of it?"

"Nothing of it, Major," Mills said. He smiled and stood, hands slapping and drumming his stomach to get everyone's attention. "Dear Billy!" he said, loud enough for all the guys to hear. A few were already chuckling. "I know I promised you I'd be home by now, but the world is too big, and the smell of sweaty men too damn irresistible."

More laughter greeted him, and Chapman offered his usual patient smile. Mills said no more. He left the major to his letter-writing. They knew how important it was to him, and that made it important to them all.

"Hey, Mills," Cole said. "Another hand?"

"Sure," Mills said. "I've got seventeen dollars you haven't stripped me of yet." He sat back down and glanced across at the reporter. She hadn't moved, and had barely seemed to notice his quick performance. She kept the camera to her face, focused on Chapman where he sat writing. Waiting for the perfect shot.

Once, he'd spent a couple of days with a sniper from the Marines, a middle-aged guy who'd just volunteered for his third tour. The guy was called Max, and the VC had nicknamed him Viper because of the snakeskin he wore around his hat. With over forty confirmed kills under his belt, and by his own calculation over a hundred unconfirmed, Max had become something of a legend on both sides. Mills had been fascinated, but quickly came to realise that Max was not a well man, nor a happy one. On a mission, with a target in mind, he was utterly focused on everything around him—the sky, the grass, a leaf, a spider, his quarry. Everything came down to the mission. He'd told Mills that the only life he could ever really, truly live was viewed through his scope. Anything else was just waiting.

On parting company, Mills had been profoundly unsettled. He'd seen the result of war on many men, but never quite like this. Max, the Viper, had lost the ability to see the world through his own eyes.

Mills wondered just what Weaver saw through her lens.

When the *Athena* hit the first rough patch of ocean, the mood changed aboard ship. Much of the team became seasick and went below, taking to their bunks, but finding little respite there. Randa was surprised that even some of the Sky Devils turned green and disappeared to puke in private. He'd have thought that helicopter crews would be used to lurching, jumping, and leaping stomachs, but only Packard and Mills seemed immune, standing on deck close to their moored birds and watching the magnificent views.

Randa loved the sea. He liked it when it was millpond flat, and he loved it even more when waves broke over the bow and smashed against the hull. It gave the ocean character and texture, and was a reminder that humans were only passengers here. He was not superstitious, and did not attribute any real emotion to however the sea was behaving. But he liked when it was rough. It seemed more natural, more honest, like a giant beast writhing to shed parasites from its hide.

He loved the tumultuous ocean even more from high above.

The crow's nest offered fantastic, unhindered views. Down below, the ship rolled and dipped through the waves, bow slicing through the swell and throwing spray back across the foredeck. The sea flexed and shone like the scaled skin of the world, and sometimes that was how Randa thought of it—the Earth itself was a giant beast yet to be discovered. They travelled across its surface, dived beneath to explore its riches, but did not yet fully understand that the ocean was part of a living, breathing thing. This high above it he could look with objective eyes, and what he saw sent shivers of anticipation down his spine.

Giant beasts had been part of Randa's imagination since he'd been a child. Growing up, he had started learning more and expecting less from the humanity he was part of.

Maybe that was why he liked being up in the crow's nest so much. The ship rocked, the ocean roared, the whole mast shook, and he held in defiance of the planet's casual fury.

Randa brought the binoculars up to his eyes again and scanned ahead of them. The seascape close by was ridged with breaking white waves, swells the size of mountains, troughs like bottomless valleys. Further away, the horizon was obscured by vast banks of clouds. They flashed with lightning deep within their mass, too far away to hear. From this distance they resembled a solid wall, but as the *Athena* drew closer he knew that more details would begin to stand out. Tough, intimidating details. No one had ever said this would be an easy journey.

He thought of Brooks lying below and spewing up his guts, and smiled. *You ain't seen nothing yet, kid*, he thought. The sea right now was a breeze compared to how it would be when they drew closer to the storm.

He heard a noise from below and glanced down. Conrad was climbing up to join him. Randa was pleased. He'd seen the ex-SAS man quietly and unobtrusively inspecting the whole ship, as well as observing every member of the team and ship's crew. He might have claimed to be along for the ride, but he was ensuring that the ride was as safe as possible for all involved.

"Weather's looking pleasant," Conrad said, joining him in the crow's nest and looking ahead to the storm front. He seemed unaffected by the weather, quiet and calm as ever. "How far out are we?"

Randa handed him the binoculars. "Barometer's dropping. We're near the centre of the Ring of Fire."

"Skull Island, Ring of Fire. You pick the loveliest vacation spots."

"It's the most volatile geologic region on the planet," Randa said. "Magnetic anomalies, radio outages, whirlpools. Hundreds of aircraft and ships have vanished here. It's even more deadly than the Bermuda Triangle, though for some reason far less known. There's even talk of a movie crew disappearing out here in thirty-three. I've been studying it for decades. This must be how Magellan felt!"

Conrad was staring through the binoculars, scanning the stormy horizon.

"Magellan was killed before he made it back," Conrad said. He lowered the binoculars and handed them back to Randa.

"We're being watched," Randa said, smiling at Conrad.

The ex-soldier didn't need telling. He glanced back and down at Weaver, who stood against the railing at the ship's stern aiming a zoom lens up at them.

"Yeah, well. She's got a job to do, too."

From far ahead came a flash and the first rolling growl of distant thunder.

A little over an hour later, Randa was on the bridge along with Nieves, Packard, and Chapman. The

Athena's Norwegian captain had already talked about turning around, and Randa would not, *could* not allow that. They had come too far, and not just on this boat. The voyage was the culmination of years of research and planning, and…

And it's important! he thought. *None of them knows how much. Not yet.*

"That storm does look a lot nastier in person," Nieves said. Randa threw him a withering look. The captain didn't need any more excuses to turn his ship and flee from the beast before them.

"How far are we from the island?" Packard asked.

"Fifty miles, maybe more," the captain replied. "Can't get exact bearings on a place that doesn't exist."

"Take us closer," Randa said, tired of the captain's bullshit.

"*Nei*, not this ship! You want to launch, you do it from here. I'll hold position, but I'm going no closer to that."

Randa pursed his lips and stared at the captain, but the Norwegian wasn't backing down. It was not cowardice, Randa knew. He'd been a captain for over thirty years, and he knew what his ship could and could not handle.

He'd also heard stories about this place, as had any captain who sailed this part of the Pacific. So no, not cowardice, but fear.

"Can you punch through that, Colonel?" Randa asked Packard.

"Those thunderheads must top twenty-thousand feet," Chapman protested.

"I'm aware of the storm, Major, but our window is now," Randa said.

"What about that opening?" Packard asked.

Chapman grunted and shook his head, tapping a small storm-eye on one of the satellite photos splayed out before them.

"It's a rare low-pressure pocket," Randa said. "Part of a pattern in the weather here. I've been studying it for years, employing climatologists to give me their predictions, building data models of the whole area."

"And we all know how much we trust the weathermen," Chapman said.

Randa fisted his hand, breathing heavily, calming down. If he lost his temper now it would achieve nothing. "The hole is there now," he said. "And we *will* have another opening to fly back out in three days. After that, the gales will force this ship out of the area."

"We knew this was a possibility," Nieves said. "The window is too tight."

"Nonsense!" Randa said.

"I appreciate your passion, Randa," Nieves said. "But as field supervisor of the controlling agency, I say we abort."

"Wise call," Randa said. He faced up to Nieves. "I'm sure the Landsat director will be inspired by your courage."

"This is just a map survey!"

"To one of the last uncharted areas on earth!" Randa felt the last few years falling away, leaving nothing in their wake but broken dreams. He couldn't afford that. Not after so long, and so much work. So much dreaming. "Do you really want to call it off on account of *rain*? Stay on the boat if you want."

He turned to Packard who was watching quietly, expressionless. "I was told your unit was capable of handling inclement weather, Colonel." He didn't think Packard was a man open to such a blatant challenge, but it was worth a try.

Packard stood even taller and straighter than before.

"That storm's a cool breeze compared to what we're used to. Isn't that right, Chapman?"

After a slight pause Chapman said, "Yes, sir."

"Let's spin 'em up," Packard said.

Randa closed his eyes briefly, then looked at Nieves and the ship's captain. Their concern was still evident. "We're good," Randa said. He smiled. "We're good."

NINE

As Cole called out the pre-flight safety procedures, Mills performed the checks. He was excited and a little nervous. They were all surprised that the old man had agreed to take the birds up in this weather, but they'd flown in worse. Just about. Although right then, he couldn't quite remember when.

"Battery. Generator. Cold start."

Cole was their pilot. The word 'Outcast' was stencilled on his helmet, and Mills didn't think anything could be more appropriate.

His own nickname was Love Child. It was probably less apt, from what little he could remember of his parents. When they weren't fighting they were fall-down drunk, and often both at the same time. This was his real family, here and now, and he had never belonged anywhere more fully.

The turbines powered up, and Mills peered out at the storm still battering the ship. "What'd the old man get us into this time?"

"Nothing he wouldn't do himself," Cole said, nodding to their left. Packard was pacing around and performing pre-flight visual checks on his own Huey, helmet already on and ready to fly.

"Yeah, well," Mills said, "there's probably a lot of stuff that man would do I want no part of."

Mills watched deckhands loading the final crates and supplies onto the choppers, then retreating from the flight deck. Most of the crew were already strapped into their allocated aircraft, and Randa sat behind them, their only passenger. He nursed a film camera in his lap. He seemed excited, and had already filmed the men going through their flight preparations. He said very little.

Packard was the last of the Sky Devils to board his bird.

"Ship's turning into the wind," Cole said. Waves smashed against the ship's starboard side, then slowly started breaking straight over the bow as the captain turned the vessel to face the storm. Each wave impact shuddered through the ship, and they could even feel the judders on board the choppers.

"We're really doing this," Mills said.

"It's easy," Cole said. Mills thought he was probably trying to reassure himself.

• • •

Randa strolled quickly towards his waiting helicopter, Brooks on his heel. This was it. Against all the odds, this expedition was about to lift off, and once they'd punched through the clouds to the island there would be no turning back. It felt like all his life had come down to this.

"We did ask to arm those helicopters," Brooks said. "Shouldn't they know why?" Randa felt a surge of anger towards the younger man for breaking the moment, but he didn't let it show.

"And raise an alarm? It's purely a precaution, Brooks." He slapped Brooks's back and climbed aboard the chopper, turning to watch him, San and Nieves boarding another chopper piloted by Slivko.

He was relieved that at least he could enjoy the flight without Brooks complaining in his ear.

As deckhands untied the last of the securing lines, Conrad and Weaver ran crouched low towards Slivko's chopper. Conrad spied Randa on the Huey with Cole and Mills, while Brooks, San and Nieves were on the Landsat aircraft. He realised that he and Weaver were late, the last two to board. That would likely raise suspicions.

Weaver pointed her camera everywhere, recording the departure even though the storm threatened to wash them all overboard. He had to admire her determination.

Once on Slivko's helicopter they strapped themselves in and slipped on headsets. Weaver ensured her camera bag was stowed and secured beneath her seat, and she kept one camera in her lap, strapped around her left wrist.

Conrad checked his seatbelt several times.

"Come on," Weaver said, "this is the fun part."

"I have a preference for solid ground," he said. "Water, at a push. Open air…?" He waved his hand from side to side.

Packard's voice came over the radio. "Time to put on another show for the ants. Hold onto your butts, and follow my lead."

Through the chopper's windshield, Conrad saw Packard's aircraft lift off, shake a little in a sudden gust, then drift away to starboard, climbing all the while. Slivko's chopper shook as it lifted from the deck, buffeted by high winds and with blown spray and rain strafing the fuselage like machine-gun fire.

Conrad clasped his seat arms until his fingers hurt.

Six years before, he'd been in a chopper that had gone down after striking a flock of birds over Malaysia. He was the only survivor. He'd lain there for three days with the remains of the crew slowly rotting around and onto him, before rescue came. A regular soldier would have received a citation or medal for that. All he'd had was a debrief and four days' medical leave before heading back into the field. Just because certain behaviour was expected of you didn't mean it came easy.

"Fox Leader to Fox Group," Packard's voice crackled. "Grab some altitude and let's get in formation."

"He's in his element," Weaver said. She was right, Conrad could hear it in the colonel's voice. This was his world.

"Combat spread," Packard said. "Keep visuals. Fox Five, let me know when you're closed."

"Fox Five in the slot," Cole's calm voice replied.

"We're gonna lose visuals, but hold course. It's nothing we haven't done before."

"Comforting," Conrad said. Looking from the side windows he could see the cliff face of the massive storm front as they approached it. Rain slashed across the windows, and twisting in his seat, he could just see the *Athena* behind them and below, slowly performing a wide turn as it headed away from the storm to hold position in calmer seas. Part of him wished he was still on board.

A bigger part of him—the part that kept him out here even though the war was over, the part that sought to tease death again and again for reasons he had never been able to explain—looked forward to what was to come. Once they were safely down on land, that was.

He turned back in time to see Weaver undoing her seatbelt.

"Weaver, what the hell—"

"Places to go, people to see," she said, pushing forward between the pilot and co-pilot's seats. They both glanced back at her. Slivko rolled his eyes and turned his attention forward again, scanning instruments and bracing himself as they approached the intimidating storm front.

It grew darker, and the chopper began to vibrate. It was a disconcerting sound and feeling, and Conrad was about to comment when they plummeted as if into a deep, dark hole.

Then the aircraft started to dance and shake through the air.

Weaver was taking pictures. Not of the outside, Conrad noticed, but of Slivko and the pilot as they nursed and jockeyed the Huey, recording their treacherous journey in stills that would speak volumes. Just visible for brief periods through the storm-lashed windscreen, he could see the flashing lights of the rest of the formation.

"You must have lived through worse than this out in the jungle," she shouted back to Conrad.

The helicopter hit another downdraft. Conrad clasped his seat even harder.

"'Lived' being the operative word."

"Dear Billy," Slivko said. "Today I saw a hurricane and flew right into it."

"Dear Billy," Mills's voice continued over the radio, "have you ever looked into the darkness and felt the cold hand of death squeeze your guts until you can't feel your legs?"

Conrad tried to get into the jovial mood but he couldn't. He knew this was battlefield humour, brother humour, and he was no part of this tight-knit group of warriors. The 'Dear Billy' thing was a private joke between them, part of the bonding gel that kept them close even when they couldn't see each other and there was a storm striving to force them all apart. It would have kept them close in battle, too, while bullets and rockets flew.

He sometimes wished he had someone he could 'Dear Billy' with.

He glanced at Weaver, but she was trying to frame a photo through the windshield with the pilot's face and helmet also in view. Looking for the shot no one had ever taken.

Maybe she'll find it on this expedition, he thought, and a strange, gloomy foreboding settled over him. He didn't think it was anything to do with his nervousness in the air. It was all about what might be waiting for them ahead and below, down on the ground that no one had yet explored.

"Compass is all over the place," someone said in his ear.

Packard replied, "Fox Leader to Fox Group, switch to inertial navigation. And remember the story of Icarus, whose father gave him wings made of wax, and warned him not to fly too close to the sun. But the exhilaration was too great, and Icarus flew higher and higher until his wings melted and he fell into the sea. Gentlemen, the United States Army is not an irresponsible father. They have given us wings of white-hot, cold-rolled Pennsylvania steel."

"Very poetic," Conrad muttered, not sure if anyone heard him.

Moments later they broke through. The buffering and battering ceased as quickly as it had begun and fresh sunlight streamed through the windows, diffracted through streaking rain and dazzling Conrad for a few moments. His grip on the seat handles lessened.

"Hey, Conrad. Our holiday's begun," Weaver said.

"Now let's take it down, low and level," Packard said.

Conrad opened the Huey's side door and air rushed in, thunderous and loud, but the views it revealed were staggering.

The ocean rolled below, a deep blue and shaded

with varying depths. Jagged white lines marked where reefs hid below the surface. Ahead of them, the waters broke against the shores of the massive island appearing out of the mists.

Conrad caught his breath. It was so strange, entering a storm and emerging on the other side to be confronted with such a scene. Stunningly beautiful, an untouched and unknown place exuding wilderness, it was almost intimidating. If everything Randa said was true, then this was a secret place, perhaps never before visited by humankind.

Sweeping beaches ended where dark jungle began, and inland there were tree-covered hills and mountains, sharp ridges, and the wounds of deep ravines, hidden from sight and immune to sunlight.

Weaver leaned across Conrad, paused for a moment to look, and then started snapping some photos. She glanced sidelong at him and grinned.

"Aren't you afraid of anything?" he asked.

"Clowns."

"I'll keep that in mind."

The helicopters roared over the coastline, and below them the jungle might have been a million years old. This was primeval. There were no signs of mankind's influence anywhere—no roads, clearings, buildings, or power lines. No indications of deforestation, footpaths, or communities. Conrad glanced behind them and saw leaves shaking in their wake, flocks of birds rising and scattering in shock at these new, noisy invaders. The ground rose sharply, then fell away again into a deep valley, its bottom marked by a dark channel that might have been a river, might have been an even deeper drop into darkness.

The island extended to their left and right, and ahead it rose inland towards a range of mountains and ridge lines. It was massive. Conrad had no idea that a place like this could have existed in the world without anyone knowing about it. The realisation made him feel small and insignificant. It was a feeling he often welcomed and revelled in, because being lost in the world was the place that he found most comfortable. But a location like this could make you feel lost in yourself. He was not a spiritual man, but he suspected some prayers were being whispered amongst the soldiers and civilians on this expedition right now.

"Fox Leader to Group," Packard said. "Split into two groups. Survey your zones. Let's get to work!"

Conrad held on tight as his Huey tilted and split to the right, dropping with two others into a valley and following a roaring river upstream. The sound of their rotors was even louder here, bouncing back from the steep valley walls to make a haunting echo. He couldn't help thinking that they were disturbing somewhere tranquil and quiet.

Weaver seemed entranced, framing photos through the open doors. He wondered what she saw through the camera that he could not, and he promised to ask her about that when they had a chance.

Over the radio Chapman said, "Stick one prepared for landing."

So this is when they start dropping bombs, Conrad thought. *Now we'll see what this place is really like.*

TEN

As the Landsat Huey settled in a small clearing beside the river, Randa filmed their arrival from his hovering bird. This was a momentous moment, the culmination of years of dreams and hope, but he was also aware that they had work to do. Below, Brooks and San jumped from the landed Huey, and the Landsat crews started unloading monitors and other equipment. It was a slick, much-rehearsed process, and soon Randa waved as they lifted away.

He held on as the chopper rose and headed further upriver. The valley grew wider and deeper, and soon they broke left towards the first of the target zones.

"Ready for the seismic sources," Nieves said over the radio.

Randa ensured his straps were secure and leaned closer to the open door. He knew they had to keep a safe distance, but he was eager to film what came next. It was a purely scientific endeavour, but it was also going to look spectacular.

Ahead of them he saw a Huey circling a pre-designated drop zone. Inside, the soldiers would be readying the first of the seismic charges. Sure enough, a few moments later he saw a cylindrical object drop from the door, small parachute fluttering open behind it, and heard the static-filled voice of a soldier saying, "Welcome to the world of man."

Filming, Randa frowned at that. A curious choice of words. Revealing. *We're not typical men*, he thought. *We're here to discover, not destroy.* But these were soldiers, not scientists.

He followed the floating object as it disappeared into the jungle canopy below. His heart beat faster in anticipation. Moments later, the first charge exploded.

Trees bent with the force of the blast. Smashed trunks and branches were thrown aloft on a boiling mass of flame and smoke. A shockwave passed through the jungle canopy like ripples in water, startling birds into flight and shimmering far across the jungle.

Randa continued filming, his dawning sense of wonder giving way to a strange, niggling foreboding. Whatever they called these things—seismic charges, scientific instruments—in reality they were bombs.

Their helicopter circled the explosion site, and he

continued filming the resultant smoke cloud. The blast zone soon settled back into jungle, and it appeared almost undamaged. It was as if the trees had swallowed the explosion and hidden it away. His low dread was fed by this sense that the jungle could shrug them off so easily. He had no wish to destroy, but he *had* come here to make his mark.

What came next brought that feeling of triumph he'd been craving since breaking through the storm front.

"Randa, the bedrock!" Brooks shouted into his ear. "You gotta see this. It's practically hollow!"

Randa smiled, still filming the smoking site of the first explosion. "So how does that feel, Brooks?" he asked.

"Commencing second pass to drop charge number two," a voice said from one of the choppers circling lower down.

Brooks had not replied. He was probably eager to absorb as much data as he could, he and San watching the monitors and ensuring that all recording devices were accurate and fully operational. But Randa could imagine the man's mixed emotions. He was glad. Brooks should never have doubted him.

Cautioning himself, more than aware that they had only taken readings from one blast zone, nevertheless Randa felt a growing sense of excitement. He made himself more comfortable as he watched history being made through his film camera.

• • •

Weaver wished she was piloting this thing. With three more blasts shredding the canopy and throwing flaming, then smoking fingers skyward, there were far better angles she could be getting on this. Still, she did her best. A series of shots through the cockpit with the pilots framing one huge explosion. Another of the impassive-faced pilot with an explosion reflected in his aviator glasses. More snaps through the open doorway, catching some of the shockwaves tearing through trees, up slopes, and losing themselves down in shadowy ravines. She couldn't help thinking it was like throwing rocks into a lake—the initial eruption, then ripples spreading, and finally a gentle lessening of the repercussions, until there was little evidence at all. It was as if the island was swallowing the explosions, and she hoped her series of photographs would illustrate this strange effect.

She felt excited, not scared. For her, lately, that was an unusual experience on a photograph assignment. There was something very liberating and freeing about taking pictures of explosions not designed to kill, but to discover.

She glanced back at Conrad, still sat in the doorway and staring down at the blasts. He looked worried. Maybe his fear of flying went deeper than she thought.

He sensed her watching and looked at her.

"Gonna make a nice brochure," she said, lifting her camera and taking a shot of him.

Another explosion erupted outside, but this one was different. It started low and grew, rather than fading from an initial loud blast to mere echoes. She saw in Conrad's reaction that he sensed the same difference, and both of them leaned closer to the doorway, Weaver hanging onto one of the straps swinging from the ceiling.

"What the hell…?" he said, but if anyone heard him they did not respond.

The roar continued, swamping echoes from the seismic charges, growing, loud and primal like the island shaking itself awake and angry at their intrusion.

Looking down towards the drop zones, and at the three Hueys circling the smoking remains of the initial explosions, they both saw the shape flung from deep down in the jungle canopy.

Conrad tensed beside her, and Weaver heard a pilot's panicked shout: "Incoming!"

The massive splintered tree trunk struck a Huey head-on, shattering the cabin, spearing the chopper and making minced meat of the pilot, sending the aircraft into a spiralling, deathly spin.

"Delayed explosion?" Weaver asked.

"That was no explosion," Conrad said, and that

made no sense, she couldn't comprehend what he meant. No explosion? Then how?

Frightened voices merged over the radio, a chaos of confusion that sang the chopper down to its fiery, terrible end.

"Fox One is hit and down!" someone shouted.

Weaver felt Conrad grasping her arm as if keen to hold onto reality. She held onto her camera.

The thing she saw rise from the jungle canopy and smash down a second Huey looked like a giant black hand.

The chopper span from the impact, one rotor spinning off into the air. Weaver saw a shape fall from the open doorway and plummet, limbs waving as it disappeared into the suddenly deadly jungle. The out-of-control Huey ploughed its way down towards the canopy. The pilot struggled to retain altitude, but it was a lost cause.

"Mayday, mayday, we're going down!" he shouted over the radio.

Conrad clasped her harder, half-standing and pulling himself closer.

"You seeing this?"

"Yeah, but not believing."

The Huey jarred to a halt, as if held upright above the canopy by heavy tree limbs. Watching from their own circling chopper, Weaver dared to hope that the survivors on board might be saved. One man clung to a landing strut, arms and legs wrapped tightly around the support, probably trying to make sense of his miraculous escape.

The jungle beneath the halted helicopter burst apart as a huge, dark shape rose up from below the trees, standing from a deep crevasse and thrusting the crippled aircraft aloft in one giant hand. Smashed trees and a million shed leaves floated around it as Weaver tried to make sense of what she was seeing. Some sort of sense that might pin her to the world, the reality she knew.

But she could find none.

The shape was a massive, impossible gorilla, perhaps a hundred feet tall. It shook the stricken Huey it held in one mighty hand, and as she saw the man tumble from the landing gear and drop into the beast's open, roaring mouth, she felt a cool flush of utter terror go through her, chilling her heart and flooding her stomach with ice.

She sat down heavily next to Conrad, camera forgotten, everything forgotten other than what she was witnessing at that moment. She had no history and no future, only this dreadful, impossible present.

Weaver struggled to remember her name.

• • •

Conrad knew what would happen next. A year ago he'd have done the same. But this was not a war, and this was not an enemy. At least, nothing like any enemy man had faced before. He didn't know *what* this was. But he had to put the fear and confusion in the background if they were going to get past this moment in one piece.

Packard and the rest of his Sky Devils went into combat mode.

The colonel shouted from his Huey, "Fox Six on guard! Fox Five is down, Fox Four is down! Respond, Fox Three!"

Conrad saw several Hueys scatter and twist like panicked birds, their pilots taking classic evasive manoeuvres. Trouble was, no one knew exactly what they were trying to evade, or what that giant thing was going to do next.

As Cole dropped into formation with the other Sky Devils and flew towards the towering beast, the creature seemed to rise and rise, so high that it eventually blocked out the sun.

"What the hell is that?" Mills asked, saying what everyone else was thinking. None of them knew. None of them could know.

It's a gorilla, Conrad thought, but to say those words

would be to admit a staggering, impossible truth.

They were closer to the behemoth now, and Conrad began to appreciate its true size and power. It was a mass of muscle and anger, fury emanating from it in waves, and why not? They had been bombing its territory, after all. As they approached, it threw the wrecked helicopter aside like a child discarding a broken toy.

Then it turned to face them.

"Shut up and fire!" Packard ordered. Even through the radio, Conrad could hear the sounds of door machine-guns being cocked and readied for the attack.

He pushed past Weaver, feeling able to take action at last, shoving aside the disbelief and letting his survival instinct engage. It had brought him through many situations, mostly whole. He had to trust it now.

At the cockpit he started to shout, "Don't engage! Pull out! Tell everyone to pull out!"

"Ignore that man!" Packard shouted. "We're going in to rescue our downed men, and we need cover."

Conrad leaned between the pilot and co-pilot and searched down towards the crash site. A Huey hovered, a man lowered down on a rope. He dropped the last few feet and raced towards the crashed chopper.

"Move fast!" Packard called. "Hurry."

"Yeah, hurry," Conrad said quietly, because he'd already seen what was about to happen.

The giant beast seemed to crumble like a falling cliff as it bent down low and brought its fisted right hand down onto the crashed copter, the survivors, and the man who'd gone to rescue them.

He'd seen many men killed before, but never wiped from existence like that. Crushed to a smear. Swept away with a flick of a hand.

"Fox Leader to Group," Packard's voice came, low and steady. "Cleared hot. Fire at will. I say again… fire at will!" A pause, and then behind his own firing weapons they heard Packard mutter, "You son of a bitch."

The open radio channels were suddenly filled with the *rat-rat-rat* of heavy machine-gun fire as the .50s opened up. Hueys swung into attack, and Conrad had to grip the seat backs as his own aircraft swung down and around, door gunner opening up.

He looked back at Weaver. She had her left hand wrapped in a ceiling strap, right hand nursing the camera as she clicked off photos. She caught his eye and stared, wide-eyed. Neither of them knew what to say, even if they could hear each other above the cacophony.

Conrad turned around again, just in time to see the beast leap aside from the gunfire, agile and fast considering its unbelievable size.

"Colonel, pull left, we're going to—" someone shouted, and then two Hueys attacking from different directions struck each other a glancing blow. These were experienced, battle-hardened pilots, but the situation had stolen their caution and concentration.

"The colonel's going down!" Slivko shouted.

Conrad could only watch in horror as Packard's Huey span lazily groundwards. It smashed through a copse of trees and hit the ground, rolling and bursting into flames. He wasn't sure anyone could have survived that. He wasn't sure it mattered.

The huge beast was running, several survivors from the first crash site sprinting ahead of it. It leapt onto the first chopper brought down and stamped, moved back, smashed its fisted hands down. The Huey exploded, scattering burning debris. If the giant did feel any pain, it only served it enrage it even more.

It roared at the sky, and it might have been thunder splitting the air asunder.

"Give it all you've got!" Slivko shouted. Theirs and another Huey closed formation and unleashed all their firepower, bullets and tracers tracking across the monster's furry hide. The gunners shifted their aims across its chest and neck and up towards its face, blooms of blood opening all across its body.

Drawing its attention.

The beast swung both hands at the ground, fingers splayed now, and Conrad saw what was about to happen.

"Slivko, pull back!" he shouted, but too late.

A hail of rocks, soil, and broken trees were flung skyward at the two attacking choppers, rising in a spreading cloud that quickly enveloped the helicopters. They struck the fuselage, rattling like bullets, and exploded into shards as they entered the rotor space. Ricochets cracked the windshield and zinged through the open door, scoring a bloody line across the back of Conrad's hand.

Something else hit the rotors.

None of them could know who it was. The body was diced in a second, bloody innards, bones, and flesh scraps splattering across the cracked windshield. A spray of blood splashed through the broken glass and spattered across the instrument panel and Slivko's chest.

Their chopper banked away, warning sounds chiming as their rotors started to fail and power dropped.

"Brace!" Slivko shouted. He looked back over his shoulder at Weaver and Conrad. "We're going down."

Conrad dropped back into his seat and struggled with his belt. He was breathing hard, and with every blink he remembered that other chopper crash. This would be different. If even one of them survived the crash, the thing they'd made furious would ensure that their survival did not last for long.

Weaver clasped his hand, and he was grateful. Whether it was her need or his, they gave each other comfort.

"Fox Three going down!" Slivko shouted into his headpiece. "Getting as far away as I can," he said quieter.

The engines were sputtering, and through the blood-smeared windshield Conrad saw a tree-covered hillside approaching. The pilot somehow nursed the stricken aircraft over the ridge, landing gear slicing through the canopy. He could smell the fresh tang of torn leaves.

"LZ ahead," Slivko said. "If we can just…"

Tree limbs smacked at the Huey, as determined to bring it down as a giant's hand. A branch slapped through the open door and scored Conrad's thigh. He and Weaver leaned forward, heads down and hands wrapped around their head, and he tried to remain loose as he braced for impact.

It was like flying into a wall. Breath was knocked from him, his insides mixed and stirred, straps tugging so hard against his stomach that he vomited, once and hard. The world exploded around him, and Conrad had the very definite sense of everything coming apart. In that moment he thought of Jenny, the little dead girl, and was glad that her death had been instant. At least she had been spared the sense of unravelling he was feeling at that moment.

Blood splashed across his face, warm, sticky, rank. And not his own.

ELEVEN

Mills could see the chaos around him and he knew what they had to do. Packard was down, Slivko was down, and the thing they'd awoken was running amok. This was not a fight they could win.

"Take evasive action!" he shouted into the radio.

Chapman's Sea Stallion drifted into view alongside. The bigger aircraft was carrying much of their ordnance, and Mills wished they could use it now. He looked across and saw Chapman, and the two men swapped a glance that registered their disbelief at what was happening. Among it all, it was the loss of Packard that had hit Mills the hardest. The colonel had always been there, solid and indestructible. Seeing him go down had been like hearing God was dead.

Just as Mills was about to talk to Chapman, the monster leapt a hundred feet from the ground and grabbed the Sea Stallion's tail. It clasped hard and pulled the aircraft down as it fell, shaking it, and the helicopter's rotors slashed through its hand and arm. Bright red blood sprayed across the sky like an early sunset.

Got you! Mills thought, relishing the idea that the beast was in pain. But it shook the Sea Stallion as it let go, hard, rupturing the fuselage and throwing it high into a spinning, helpless course…

…directly towards Mills's Huey.

"Look out!" he shouted. Even though Cole had already seen and was trying to lift them above the spinning Sea Stallion, its rotors caught their Huey directly amidships. Metal screeched. Their door gunner was slashed in two. Reles was thrown from the far side of the chopper and out into open air, falling just as quickly as them.

Mills closed his eyes as they crashed down into the tree canopy of this damned island.

Packard had never lost a chopper before. He'd been shot up, had a bird stall on him but landed safely, and had even flown home with his co-pilot and two passengers blasted to pieces by a lucky shot from an enemy RPG.

This had always been his nightmare, and the greatest nightmare for any airman was being burnt alive.

He was hanging upside down. His co-pilot, Nova, moaned somewhere to his left, but Packard couldn't see him. There was too much blood in his eyes, and branches and leaves had intruded into the cockpit of the downed Huey. He assessed his wounds, hoping that he'd find nothing that might cripple his escape. His shoulders both hurt like a bitch, but that was okay, he could still flex and move them. He was bumped and bruised all over, and he felt blood running up into his nose from his mouth. He spat a thick wad of blood and phlegm. He'd bitten his tongue on impact, but he was pretty sure he hadn't lost any of it.

The smell of burning singed through the blood. Aviation fuel had a very specific stench, and he could smell that, too. Once the flames reached the spilled fuel, he was done for. He reached for his sidearm, comforted that he could touch it. He only hoped he wouldn't have to use it.

The radio crackled, reminding him of the chaos he was only a small part of. It was Chapman's voice.

"Fox Six losing fuel! Tail rotor assembly's cracked and failing, nominal control… trying for north end of the island…"

Packard reached for the harness release, but there was a heavy splintered branch in the way. He crawled his hand around his hip instead, plucking the combat knife from his belt.

He heard the soft *whomps!* of flames taking hold.

Nova groaned some more.

"Anyone alive back there?" he shouted. It hurt his chest, but he liked the sound of his own voice. He sounded in control.

No reply from behind. His gunner was unconscious, dead, or gone completely.

Packard worked his knife out from its sheath, turning it so that it rested against the harness across his chest and hips. He started to saw in short, hard slashes.

When the harness parted he tucked in his head, dropping and landing on his shoulders, rolling, emerging from the Huey's wreck, sheathing the knife and rushing around to the other side.

"Nova, I got you," he said, reaching in and taking the co-pilot's hand. He was still alive, but badly hurt. If he could only get him out, maybe he'd be able to administer some first aid.

He squeezed his hand.

Then he was ripped away as the Huey was hauled skyward by the giant beast, debris raining down on and around Packard. He shielded his face then looked up again, just in time to see the mountainous monster flinging the stricken Huey into the air, watching it spin, then punching it hard with one closed fist. It disappeared from view, and moments later landed some distance away and exploded.

Packard drew his pistol and started firing. It was like shooting into a black hole.

The thing looked down at him and caught his eye. Packard's finger froze on the trigger.

Machine-gun fire rattled across the monster's face, flicking thick fur and spattering blood into the air. The operation's single Chinook was roaring in, its familiar *wacka-wacka* sound a strange comfort. It was a heavy, slow-moving bird, carrying two jeeps and other equipment. Surely too large for the monster to take down.

Packard felt a sense of doom closing around him. Unreality bit in, and he looked around at the strange jungle, trees cracked and shattered by the crashed Huey he could no longer see. It was as if he'd been dropped here into a nightmare, and the glimpses he caught of surviving helicopters, the sounds of machine-gun fire, the roar of the beast, were all snippets of his damaged mind.

He shook his head and slapped himself across the face. Blood smeared his hand. That was real, and the lives of his men were real, too. Those that the animal had not yet killed.

That thing's no animal, he thought. *That beast is something else.*

With one giant leap the monster closed the distance between it and the attacking Chinook. The ground shook as it landed, and it clapped its huge hands together, fingers splayed and palms closing on the Chinook's top and bottom. Rotors sliced into its arms and hands and it roared, the sound echoing in the Chinook's destruction. The big aircraft's back was broken, and the beast clasped the two halves and smashed them together, threw them to the ground, trampled them underfoot.

Packard watched aghast. *If he remembers me…* he thought. *If he comes back…*

Packard did something he had never done before in his life. He started running from the enemy. Not because he was scared, but because he wanted so much to live.

To fight another day.

Conrad surfaced. Maybe he'd been knocked unconscious, or more likely he'd just blanked at the moment of impact, his body and mind protecting him from the trauma. He needed to be back. He had to be fully functional, all there, and ready for anything. For a brief, ridiculous moment, he wondered whether it had all been a terrible dream.

Then he smelled smoke and someone started coughing.

"You okay?" he croaked. He tried to look at Weaver

but his eyes stung from the smoke. He wanted her to answer. He tasted blood, instinct told him it wasn't his, and he wanted her to answer!

"Weaver!" he said, louder. He reached for her, hand closing on her thigh. She was still seated beside him, still strapped in.

"I'm okay. I think."

Conrad rubbed blood and smoke from his eyes and released his straps. He looked across at the other door. The door gunner was gone, as was the .50 machine gun. A smear of blood was all that was left behind.

"Slivko, stay where you are," Conrad said, not knowing if either of the pilots were even still alive. "We've come to rest in the trees."

Weaver was trying her straps but they were stuck fast. Conrad didn't want to waste any time. He whipped out his combat knife, leaned across her body and cut her safety belt. They edged together towards the door, then started clambering down. They were only ten feet above the jungle floor, the Huey suspended almost level on two trees that had splintered and cracked beneath its weight. They had likely saved it from a harder impact.

As they reached the ground Conrad sniffed. No spilled aviation fuel, at least not yet. He called up to the cockpit.

"Slivko! How's the pilot?"

"Dead."

"Can you get free?"

There was no answer.

"Slivko!" Weaver called.

Slivko's face appeared through the pilot's-side doorframe. He looked down, both terrified and elated at being alive.

"Down here," Conrad said. "We've got to go."

Conrad had survived the crash, and with solid ground beneath his feet once more, so came a sense of control. Ridiculous as it seemed—with dozens probably dead, and every aircraft seemingly taken out by the monster—he felt completely at ease once again. In the air, his destiny was in another's hands. Here and now, he was his own man.

It was time to see just what the hell was going on.

Slivko started shimmying down the broken tree. He was covered in blood.

"Help him down," Conrad said to Weaver. "I need to get to higher ground."

"What? Really?"

"I won't be long." He took one step, then she grabbed his arm.

"Conrad…" Everything she wanted to say was in her eyes, but there was no time right then. Disbelief, shock, grief could come later.

Terror, too.

"I know," he said. She nodded and let go, and he stalked off through the trees, dropping down into one of the huge depressions left by the beast's foot. He paced across it and clambered out the other side, smelling something distinctly animal. Like wet dog, unwashed for some time. A heavy, damp, almost overpowering aroma. *Unwashed gorilla feet*, he thought, and he had to suppress a giggle.

There was blood, too, spattered across the ground and the leaves of surrounding undergrowth. Lots of blood. No wonder that thing was pissed.

Conrad ran, following rising ground where he could, pushing his way through dense undergrowth. His senses were alert, and he realised without pausing that he did not recognise some of the plant species around him. He'd served in jungles on three continents, but this was like no jungle he'd ever seen before. Creepers and vines hung from large trees. Wide swathes of heavy leaves hampered his movement, the rubbery growths slick to the touch. Parasitic flowers blossomed from low-hanging branches. It was beautiful, but also disconcerting.

He came to a steeper slope and began climbing. He rushed, fearing he didn't have much time, driving himself hard and fast even though exhaustion already threatened. Adrenalin kept him moving. He was used to the pain of exertion, and he relished it—it made him feel alive.

So many of the soldiers and civilians he'd left *Athena* with were not.

As he approached a ridge line, he reached a much steeper piece of ground. Too sheer to scramble, the rock surface too obscured by undergrowth to climb, he had to hold onto plants and creepers and haul himself upward. He continued moving quickly, arms burning as he hung on, legs screaming, adrenalin pumping. He might not have much time, and—

A creeper moved beneath his hand, slipping down the rock wall. He paused and held his breath, ready to jump if the plant stem started falling. Then it flexed. Conrad paused, not certain what he'd felt, and then the creeper started moving before him, sliding up the sheer cliff face and pulling him with it. He loosened his hand and slipped, scrabbling for purchase and closing his hands around other clinging plants smothering the cliff's surface.

Above him, something curled out from the cliff and dipped down towards him.

The snake's head was as large as his own, and with jaws open wide it could easily have surrounded his body and swallowed him down. He could not see its tail. It must have been far below him, maybe thirty feet, and with the curl of creature even now dipping down towards him, he feared the monstrous snake was at least sixty feet long.

He reached for his pistol and slipped some more, hooking his left arm around a dried stem that instantly parted from the cliff, swinging him out over the sheer drop. He heard the ominous sound of crackling, dried wood.

The snake hissed. Its head dipped towards him, fangs dripping venom, eyes dim then bright again as a protective film flickered back and forth across them. Its body stiffened and prodded him, swinging him even further out on the old plant that was now the only thing holding him up. Ahead of him, the cliff face and the snake's looming head. Below, a drop that would almost surely kill him.

Conrad tried not to panic. His pistol was on the wrong side, so he reached down with his left hand and pulled his knife, taking his time, knowing that if he panicked and dropped the blade he would be out of options. He'd have to let go and fall. If he was lucky and the impact didn't kill him, or if he managed to grab hold of other undergrowth to arrest his fall, the snake would arch down and swallow him whole.

He brought the knife up and around just as the serpent went for him. Gripping hard, his hand passed into its mouth, knocking its head aside, blade slashing through its darting tongue and severing it at the root. A lucky shot, but one that pained the serpent so much that it thrashed and coiled, shoving itself out from the wall and almost taking Conrad with it. The creeper he was grasping tore from the rock, and as he fell he leapt for another plant, gripping it with one hand just as the writhing snake smashed into the wall beside him.

He bit the blade between his teeth, almost gagging on the taste of the snake's blood. Then he started climbing.

Whatever pain it was in, the serpent still focused on its prey. He felt the tail loop around him, circling his stomach far quicker than he believed possible. Two loops, three, and then it started constricting.

Conrad tensed his muscles, fighting the snake's powerful grasp. He groaned through clenched teeth, still holding on to vines covering the cliff face. Just as he let go with one hand and went for the knife, the snake pulled him away from the cliff.

For a terrifying moment he was suspended out over open air, with a long drop beneath him and the cliff too far away to reach. The snake was curled around several heavy branches, holding him steady as its head extended out towards him. It was shaking, a heavy shiver that passed all along its body and transmitted into his core as it began to draw tighter, tighter. He could no longer hold out against the pressure, and when he exhaled and tried to draw in another breath, he was not able. Darkness grew around the edges of his vision. The snake's head was feet away, those fangs as long as his fingers, edging closer, closer…

Conrad grabbed the knife from his mouth and slammed it down into the top of the snake's head.

Its coils loosened instantly and he began to slip. Tugging his knife free, he grabbed one coil of its body and felt himself dropping as the snake began to slide from the cliff. At the last moment he leapt, pushing off from the snake's heavy body and striking the surface, scrabbling for purchase, nails clawing at stone and vine stems until his left hand lodged between a creeper and the cool rock. It jarred his shoulder and brought him to a halt, and he hugged himself close to the steep surface, curling his leg around another creeper, gasping for breath as the snake fell away from him and out into open space.

It landed several seconds later, a heavy, meaty thud that he felt through the cliff. He looked down, but already it was lost in the undergrowth growing below. Bushes rustled and trees shook as it made its escape.

Breathing heavily, trying to ease back the delayed panic, Conrad sheathed his knife and pressed close to the cliff face. He took a few moments to catch his breath. He'd been close to death many times, but never that close.

After a while he started climbing again. This time he was careful to ensure that whatever he grabbed hold of was plant, not animal.

Three minutes later he reached the ridge line. He rolled onto his back, panting heavily. His hands were shaking.

Control, he thought, *take control, breathe, it's just you, that's all, take charge of this time, this place and you'll survive.* His heartbeat calmed, and when he opened his eyes his vision was clear. He was staring up at streaked white clouds and a blue sky that could have been anywhere.

Standing, Conrad looked north and saw what he had climbed up here to see—a wide, uninterrupted vista of the island's interior.

The island was even larger than he'd suspected. To his right he could see the sea, but ahead and to the left it was only land, the mountainous horizon quite close but with the suggestion of more island beyond. It was a vast, heavily wooded terrain, with plenty of places for huge things to hide.

He pulled the compact binoculars from his belt and started searching.

He soon found a narrow river that snaked from his right towards the island's interior. It was visible in places, but where it wasn't he could follow the course of its valley, rising and skirting the foothills of the central mountains, losing itself in the far distance. From here and there, several columns of smoke still spiralled up from the seismic charges and the sites of downed helicopters. The beast had done a good job on the Sky Devils, wiping out one of the US Army's most efficient attack squadrons in the space of fifteen minutes.

They needed to head inland, then north across the central mountains. Their extract point was to the north of the island. How to get there without any serviceable aircraft or a boat was a problem they'd have to face when the time came. For now, at least he had an immediate plan in mind. Reach the river, track it, cross the mountains.

It looked so very far away.

He shifted his view left and right, looking for any trace of—

His view went black.

Conrad lowered the binoculars so that he could see a wider scope, and there it was. The monster had just crested a hill in the distance, still snarling and spitting, beating its chest and causing a sound that reminded him of aircraft breaking the sound barrier, again and again.

He watched the big beast scramble down the hillside, trees bending and breaking before it, piles of rock tumbling down. It seemed to be in a rush, and he soon saw why. It was making its way to one of the craters created by a seismic charge. A fire still blazed there, consuming the jungle in two long, uneven lines. Smoke billowed skyward, the oily colour of living things dying, both plants and animals.

The monster stared back in Conrad's direction and roared. His blood chilled, and he couldn't help but think that the scream was for him alone. He ducked down on the ridge line, pressed flat against the ground. He was too far away for the giant gorilla to see him, he was certain. Yet he felt its eyes upon him, and sensed its hate.

It stopped roaring and stood still for a moment. It stared down as if examining the crater. Then it started trampling the fires, scooping up huge handfuls of soil and smothering the flames. It worked until just a few wisps of smoke curled skyward, then it sat, snorting and exhausted, touching wounds on its arms, chest and face. Quieter now, less threatening, Conrad saw something painfully human about the giant beast.

He was entranced. This thing had killed so many, and yet it had done nothing wrong. They had come here and dropped the first bombs. The beast had attacked in self-defence.

He turned and stalked back the way he'd come, taking more care on his descent of the cliff. At the bottom he paused every few steps to make sure the snake was not still there, in truth enjoying these last few moments when he could be alone.

Soon, he would meet with Weaver and the others

again. He already knew what their next move should be.

Go home.

TWELVE

Packard and the few survivors he'd found moved quickly through the jungle. They had discovered many bodies at the several crash sites they had visited. A couple were still alive, bleeding out, horribly wounded and doomed to die. His men. His comrades of war, slaughtered all around him, crushed like insects into the soil. In all his years, he had never seen such carnage brought down upon the men he loved.

As the beast had fled, Packard imagined that they had locked eyes. In that moment he had silently vowed revenge.

The beast had roared laughter at him and then walked away, dismissive and aloof. A mocking departure. A challenge.

Bastard, Packard thought. *I'll get you, bastard.*

They found Reles beneath a tree. He was battered

and bleeding but alive, even though he did not appear eager to accept the fact. As he saw Packard and the others approaching, his smile broke into a grin.

"Reles, come on, your heart's beating," Packard said, waking him with a slap to the face. "I can hear it from here. Get up. That's an order."

"Colonel." Reles clambered to his feet, groaning and wincing.

"You okay?"

"We were just attacked by…" He couldn't bring himself to finish his sentence.

"Yeah, I know. You're okay. See if you can get me a radio that works."

Packard looked around at the men he had left. There weren't that many. Shocked, bloodied, wide-eyed, he had to rally them and lead them. That's what he was here for, and they'd be looking to him for comfort.

He couldn't give them that. Maybe he could give them something else.

Reles appeared by his side, shaken but pleased to be with his companions again. He handed Packard a survival radio.

"Group, this is Fox Leader, request situation report. Group! This is Fox Leader… any station! Radio check, over!"

"Leader… this is Fox Six… Chapman…"

"Chapman!" Packard said. "Come in. Say again

your last position."

"Leader... Flores KIA... I'm lone survivor. My location at crash site... four klicks west, highest mountain peak. November Alpha, bearing three-zero-zero."

Packard tugged a grid map from his pocket. Formed from Landsat photos, it displayed some of the landforms known, and also contained the codenames allocated to them by his team.

"Roger your last, Chapman. West, highest mountain peak. Over."

"Roger," Chapman confirmed. "November Alpha three-zero-zero."

"Fox Six, stay put," Packard said. "We will come to you, Chapman. There's enough ordnance in the Sea Stallion to kill that thing. Survey your radius and scout for an ambush site."

"Fox Six confirm," Chapman said. "Scouting radius. Holding near Sea Stallion. Heading—" His transmission broke into a series of crackles and white noise.

"Fox Six, come in," Packard said. He tweaked the frequency control. "Chapman, come in. Jack?"

The signal was gone.

Packard glanced sidelong at Reles, standing close by with his pistol drawn. Despite the shock at what had happened to them, he and the rest of his men were acting like the professional soldiers they were. Three had taken defensive positions around the crash site.

Others were searching the wreckage for ammunition and supplies. One of the men gathered dog tags from the dead.

"Looking for an R and R day, specialist?" Packard asked Reles. "Or are you ready to move?"

Mills sat on the ground with his back against a tree. He had his M-16 resting across his legs, but every time he looked at it he laughed. He'd once killed a man with this gun, gut-shot him from a distance and then moved in closer to put a bullet in his head. It hadn't felt good. There had been none of that gung-ho bravado that some men displayed, and Mills firmly believed that few people could kill a man without dying a little themselves. Kill or be killed was never an all-or-nothing exchange.

He'd had nightmares about that killing ever since.

He looked at the gun, thought of shooting the beast that had brought them down, and laughed again.

Cole approached from the crashed Huey. He'd been rooting among the still-smoking wreckage, even though it had burned and exploded soon after they'd got away. He had a ration can in his hand. It must have been thrown clear in the blast.

Mills could hardly believe that Cole was actually eating tinned fruit.

"What the hell is wrong with you, Cole?"

"Eating's for the living," Cole said.

"We just got taken down by a monkey the size of a building!"

"Ape."

"Huh?"

"It was an ape. And yeah, that was an unconventional encounter."

"That's it? That's all your brain is doing right now?"

"There's no tactical precedent," Cole said, shrugging. He spooned in another mouthful of fruit. "We did the best we could in the situation."

Mills stood and was about to say more when he heard a sound behind him. A rustle in the undergrowth. *That thing wouldn't rustle*, he thought, but he crouched and span around, bringing his M-16 to bear.

"Hold your fire," Packard said as he pushed into view from behind some hanging branches. Reles and some other guys were with them, lugging arms, survival kit, and other supplies.

"Jesus, sir, I'm glad to see you made it," Mills said.

"Unless this is heaven and your ugly asses are the angels," Packard said. "How many other survivors?"

"Seven from our squad," Mills said. "Three confirmed KIA—Hodges, Saraf, Galleta. A few others missing, but I saw some of their Hueys hit and go down, and…" He held out three dog tags. Packard took them and shoved them inside his jacket. *More letters for the colonel to write*, Mills thought.

"What about the civilians?" he asked. "Where's Randa?"

Mills jerked a thumb over his shoulder. "Back there. Sitting on a rock. He's gone kinda quiet."

"Quiet," Packard said, and Mills had never seen such an expression on the colonel's face before. He hoped he never would again. "That's okay, Mills. I'll make him talk."

Weaver hated breaking her camera equipment. These were her tools, and cracking a lens felt like losing a limb. She saw her world through the camera, and sometimes she wondered whether true reality existed only on the other side of the lens. Perhaps it was a buffer between her and the cruel truth. A safety system, like a heavy glass screen between a watcher and a wild animal enclosure. She felt confident only when she was behind the camera, and that was when she was at her best.

She didn't like to think about what might happen if that shield was ripped away.

She sat to assess the damage. The lens must have been cracked in the crash. It was ruined, but she was lucky that she carried two spares in her strengthened and waterproof camera bag. The rest of the camera seemed in good working order, and she changed the film and pocketed the used one. It was precious. It might already grace the future cover of a *National Geographic*.

She noticed that her hands were shaking, and she rested the camera on her legs and clasped them into fists. She was stronger than this. She'd proven that again and again in the field.

"You okay?" Brooks asked.

"I'm fine."

Brooks, San, and Nieves had joined them at the crash site, arriving dazed and dragging their equipment. She guessed that none of them had witnessed violent death before. Or if they had, certainly nothing like this.

No one had witnessed anything like this before.

They stood close together, huddled like kids waiting to be told what to do next.

Where the hell is Conrad? she asked herself yet again. He was the most able among them, and she'd seen a change in him since the crash. Quietly and without fanfare, he seemed to have taken control. He was also the only person among them who she felt comfortable with. She wasn't used to feeling like that with a trained killer. It was strange, but she didn't question her instincts.

Slivko had been fiddling with a handheld radio since the crash, checking batteries, searching channels, turning it up and listening for voices in static. She could have told him half an hour ago that the radio was toast.

"All units, is anyone airborne? I say again—"

"They're all down," Conrad said. He emerged from the trees, breathing heavily. He swapped glances with Weaver as she stood. "Every one of them." He nodded to Brooks, San, and Nieves, and assessed the equipment they'd brought with them. Weaver saw something different in him, but she wasn't quite sure what it was. He'd seen or experienced something out there. She'd ask him later.

Everyone remained silent, waiting for him to speak. He was that type of guy.

"Right, listen to me. We're on the south side of the island, and the place is bigger than we first thought. There's a river, couple klicks from here. If we stick to the banks it should lead us to inland, and from there we'll make it to the northern shore."

Slivko was staring at him, mouth open. He looked around at all of them.

"So that's it?" he asked. "We're not gonna… talk, or anything?"

Conrad was already approaching Brooks and San. "You two. What was that thing? What do you know?"

Nieves was staring past all of them. He had been since they'd arrived at the crash site, and Weaver was surprised to finally hear him speak. She thought perhaps he'd gone into shock, and she knew that could be a deep, dark place.

"I… I should be sitting at a desk…" he said. "I've got pictures of my family. My own pencil sharpener. Sometimes, I link paperclips together until…" He smiled at the memory, then the smile dropped at more recent ones.

"You all right?" Conrad asked Weaver.

"Yeah," she said. "That was… I've never…"

"Yeah. Nor me. And there's more. I just had a run-in with a snake. Fifty feet long, maybe more. This island's like nowhere we've ever seen before. The ape, the snake, that means there's plenty more here, too. Stuff that just wants to kill us or eat us, or both."

Weaver stared at him wide-eyed.

"Looks like your suspicions have been confirmed," he said.

"In all the wrong ways."

"If you're not there you can't get the shot, right?"

"The money they paid you," she said. "I hope it was a lot. And I hope you're worth it."

THIRTEEN

Randa had a cut on his finger. He was focusing on it. The wound was not too deep, and to him it looked something like a question mark, curved at one end and long and straight at the other. A question mark or a crook. Perhaps a scythe. The skin was neatly sliced, not ripped. Probably a shard of glass had caused it, and he hadn't even felt it until he'd noticed blood dripping onto his shoe. It was his only wound from the crash. That was so unlikely that it bore deep consideration. The cut. It was his whole world right now, because to expand his horizons beyond the cut—to see and hear further, to think on what had happened and what was yet to happen—would invite in madness.

I invited it myself, he thought, *when I knew what we were*—

This was what he had always wanted. His whole life

had been working towards this. His childhood years had been filled with disappointment and bullying. As a teenager he'd been troubled, bookish and distant when most of his contemporaries were playing sport or considering their career options. Later, as an adult, he'd constantly searched for something he knew was out there, some place where he could be himself and triumph. And then when the *Lawton* had been hit…

Here, at last, he had found triumph. But triumph had also brought tragedy.

He shook his head and stared at the cut again. A bubble of blood formed. It was almost perfect, its colour quite beautiful. The stuff of life. His life.

He still had a life. He remembered those choppers going down, crushed by the beast, beaten to pulps, and thought of the blood that would be bubbling and burning and squeezing through wounds in flesh and metal right now across the jungle, this jungle that—

A shadow fell across him, darkening his blood. Heart fluttering, fear chilling him, he looked up.

Packard was standing right before him.

"Are you okay?" the colonel asked.

"It's a deep cut, but yes, I'm fine."

"Oh good, that makes me feel much better." Packard pulled up a crate and sat close in front of Randa. He made himself comfortable. Randa smiled at him, but Packard did not smile back.

The colonel drew his pistol and aimed it directly at Randa's face.

"You're going to tell me everything I don't know, or I'll blow your head off."

Randa forgot his cut. Fear burned in his throat, tears welled in his eyes, but he was afraid that if one spilled then Packard would go through with his threat. Weakness wasn't what he needed to show now, nor was a need for pity. The soldier would respect neither.

"Monsters exist," Randa began, trying to ignore the gun's dark barrel.

"No. Shit."

"Before today nobody believed that," Randa continued, warming to his subject. "Yesterday I was a crackpot, but today…"

"This was never about geology!" Packard shouted. "You dropped those charges to flush something out."

Randa only stared at him.

"Who the hell are you?" Packard asked.

"Another man on the front line, just like yourself. My agency is known as Monarch. We specialise in the hunt for Massive Unidentified Terrestrial Organisms." He tried a smile, but it felt strained.

"You knew that thing was here," Packard said, sitting back, lowering the pistol, aiming it at Randa's stomach.

"Not for sure. But… I was hoping. Not for this outcome, of course, but for evidence. Evidence that we could use to determine the threat. Evidence that might help us understand that the world is a much bigger place than we ever imagined. The holes on this island are more than just entryways to a hollow earth. They are portals for creatures beyond imagination."

"You put my men at risk. Some of my men *died* because of you."

"I did, and I'm sorry. This was a reconnaissance mission, and now it's a battlefront far more important than the one you left behind." Randa looked at his finger. The wound had stopped bleeding. Still, he applied the bandage. "The world doesn't belong to us. Ancient species owned our planet long before mankind, and if we keep our heads buried in the sand, they will take it back."

Packard stood, holstered his pistol, and turned to walk away.

"Get us home, Colonel," Randa said. "I'll take care of the rest."

Conrad was assessing the people with them, and he was doing his best not to get too pessimistic. But other than Slivko and Weaver, he thought the others were added weight. Brooks, San, and Nieves weren't like any field operatives he knew. They might be good at digging holes and taking samples, but he was pretty sure that if he asked them to build a fire or hang a hammock, they'd be screwed.

And believing themselves screwed meant that they'd already given in to the Big Guy. That was how he'd started thinking of the giant ape. For all he knew it was a female, but Big Guy still seemed to suit it.

They were readying to move out and head north through the jungle, searching for the river he'd seen. He had to keep his wits about him. As ever, they were looking to him for words of advice before they headed off. He could think of many, but he wasn't sure any of them would save lives. Not in such a place, with such things threatening them.

"We need to stay tight and move fast," he said. "Slivko, divvy up those weapons. One per person."

Slivko dug around in his pack and offered a pistol to Weaver. She shook her head and held up her camera.

"I'm happier with this."

Slivko shrugged, saying nothing, and handed out rifles to Brooks and San. When Brooks reached for the weapon, Slivko kept hold.

"You led all of us into a trap, man."

"I didn't know. Didn't believe. I've never seen anything alive, just million-year-old fossils, but—"

"Randa believed," San said.

"Believed what?" Weaver asked. She was still quietly snapping pictures. Conrad thought she probably did so almost without knowing.

"The Hollow Earth theory," Brooks said. "Randa hired me because I wrote a paper substantiating what most people think is a crackpot idea. I postulated that there are massive spaces underground, hollow zones, isolated from the surface world except for certain spots."

"Passageways to the surface," San said. "Randa believes this island may be one of them."

Brooks and San were getting more animated, talking about what they knew, or at least suspected. It sounded ridiculous to Conrad, but then so did a giant gorilla fighting machine-guns and helicopters.

"He believes there's an emergence point here, somewhere on this island, for everything that lives below. Ancient species… like what we just saw." He shook his head. "I thought he was out of his mind."

"He is," Nieves said. "You are. This is insanity."

"Well, we'll all hash that out over beers," Conrad said. He was keen to start moving. "Right now, we're stranded in an unknown wilderness with less than three days to reach the northern shore, and who knows what between us and there. We'll track the river inland. Follow its course."

"Inland?" Nieves said. "Are you nuts? You said it yourself, we have no idea what else is out there. I'm heading back the way we came." He grabbed a weapon from Slivko and started for the tree line. Conrad could tell by the way he carried the rifle that he probably hadn't even held one before, let alone fired one. Chances were he'd shoot himself in the foot or kill someone else.

"Might want to take another route, then," Conrad said. He nodded at Weaver; she was photographing him now, and he felt strangely vulnerable beneath the camera's impersonal gaze. It was as if it stripped her of personality.

"Why?" Nieves asked.

"That rubbed bark on the tree beside you," Conrad said, pointing. "About waist high?" He walked past Nieves to the tree, ran his fingers over the scored marks. Then he knelt and examined tracks on the ground. They were confused, churned up, but he saw enough to take a good guess. For what he intended, it didn't need to be accurate. "Staggered tracks, diagonal walker, clawed, maybe feline, but probably canine. A meter and a half in length, at least. This is likely its feeding run." He stood and gestured for Nieves to pass him by. "Oh, and when I was out there I saw a snake as long as the Sea Stallion, head as big as mine. Beast like that will swallow you whole, alive. Digest you slowly. But go ahead. Enjoy the stroll."

Nieves seemed flustered. The others moved over to stand by Conrad, and really there could have been no other outcome. Strength in numbers, Conrad knew, even if some of those number were ineffectual at best.

"I'm next in the chain of command!" Nieves said. "Not you." He sounded like a petulant child.

"Do you really want to be in command?" Weaver asked, frustrated.

Nieves glared for a moment, then looked down at his feet and shook his head.

"Then we're moving." Conrad headed out, not looking back. Time was ticking. He listened, counting the footsteps of those following. It was all of them.

One of the Landsat guys looked like he was about to piss his pants. Packard thought his name was Steve, but he wasn't sure. These civilians all looked the same to him. They sat around binding their wounds, some of them shaking their heads, most of them surviving alone in this mess even if they sat next to one another. There was no brotherhood here for them, no sense of being part of a team.

It was Packard's surviving team members who were taking action. They'd salvaged as many weapons and as much ammunition as they could from the crashed 'copters and were going through the process of checking it for working order. Two of them stood guard while this happened, eyes and ears scoping beyond the rocky slope where they were gathering themselves.

They were trying to shake off the past, but it was too immediate and too horrific to forget.

Packard could smell burning. Smoke still drifted across the jungle from the crash sites, and he knew the warm tang of cooking flesh well enough to recognise it now. He could tell by the looks on his men's faces that they could smell it, too. That was the stench of their dead friends.

Randa and the Landsat guys were too wrapped up in their own small, disastrous worlds to notice.

"They're gone..." the guy whose name might have been Steve was saying. He sat on his ankles, rocking slowly back and forth. "They're all gone..."

"What do we do now, sir?" Mills asked. He stood close to Packard, keen to keep their conversation unheard. There was a network of cuts on his face from smashed glass. He didn't seem to notice. "How the hell do we get out of here?"

"We don't," Packard said. "Not without every last man in this unit. We'll head south for Chapman's position at the Sea Stallion, rally up with any others on the way."

"What about that thing out there, Colonel?" He nodded towards Randa and the moaning guy, Landsat Steve. "What about the civilians?"

"You know what a civilian is?" Packard said, louder

so that everyone could hear. Heads turned. Randa stared at him as if afraid of what he might say or do next.

"Sir?" Mills asked.

"A man without a gun." Packard nodded to one of the soldiers guarding the pile of salvaged weapons. "Hand them out, soldier. But not to him." He nodded at Randa. "He's done enough."

The Landsat guys accepted the weapons offered to them. From their faces, Packard could tell that none of them had ever fired a shot or held a gun before. If he had time he'd have taken the opportunity to give them at least a crash course, but they had none to spare. This was kill or be killed, as much for his men as these civilians. They'd have to learn the hard way.

"Isn't anyone gonna show me how to..." Steve said, holding up the pistol he'd been handed like it was a hot rock. His voice trailed off when no one acknowledged him. He looked lost, forlorn, and Packard felt a surprising pang of sorrow for him. It was only small.

The colonel climbed up onto a large moss-covered rock and turned to face the assembled men. They were a ragged fighting force by any stretch of imagination, but they were all he had. A soldier's training had taught him to make the best out of the resources he had available, and Packard was determined to do just that. He had his men, his soldiers, his family, who were the real fighters.

Everyone else was bait.

"Settle down," he said. "And listen up. That monstrosity took us out from the air and killed our brothers and friends. But from the first sharpened rock, the first spear, all the way to napalm and the cold judgement of a mounted M-60, it's been us, and our fathers, who have asserted our dominion over this planet and all that inhabit it. Whatever that thing is, it's still an animal and we're still men. And with chrome-plated staffs, chemical lightning, and fifty- caliber fury from heaven we will kill everything that comes at us and send any soul it may have straight to hell. You hear me?" He scanned the faces staring up at him and chose to see only agreement and respect. "So pull yourselves together and move out!"

The survivors seemed boosted by his brief speech, and the soldiers mobilised, ready to head out.

Packard grunted in satisfaction. His hate burned deep, smothering fear and giving every sense an edge. He imagined that beast down and dead by his hand.

It felt good to be taking action.

FOURTEEN

Conrad moved gracefully, swinging his machete as he hacked through the jungle, leading their way. Like him, Weaver had been in the field for a long time, constantly on the move. Looking for the next story. Seeking a greater truth through her lens than war, conflict, death, and the inevitable descent from civilisation into chaos. She witnessed it everywhere she looked. There was nothing to be seen that could convince her that humankind was heading in any other direction.

As they moved forward, sweaty and dirty, exhausted, still scared, Slivko continued to monitor the radio. The static sang, fading in and out. There were no voices. It was as if the island was whispering about them in mocking tones.

"Save it for when we get closer to the others," Conrad said. "If anyone else is even still alive."

Slivko clicked the radio off and slung it across his back. Weaver took a snap of him, dejected and defeated. She wondered what that momentary image would show if and when she developed it. That was what she loved the most about taking photographs. She witnessed life through the lens, animated and constantly moving, but truth lay in those frozen images she caught. Sometimes reality was too fast or too deep to see with the naked eye.

Just ahead of her, Conrad froze. He turned and pressed his finger against his lips. Then he pointed ahead at a clearing in the jungle. It contained a wide pool of water fed by the river, its surface relatively still and speckled with large lily pads and clumps of rushes. At its centre was a hillock, an island of sorts that was scattered with logs and long, grassy water ferns. Colourful birds flitted back and forth from the island, digging at the ground and fleeing with large winged insects in their beaks.

"What is it?" Weaver whispered. Conrad only shook his head and pointed at the island. She looked closer, but it was only as she brought the camera up to her eye that she saw the subtle movement.

Ripples were breaking out from the island and travelling across the large pond. Lily pads rode the ripples, and gnarled frogs leapt on and off the pads, adding their splashes. She clicked a photo.

The island began to move.

Weaver lowered the camera as the island began to lift from the water. It was disorientating, as if the ground was dropping beneath her feet. She swayed but remained upright, then gasped as she recognised the shape in the pool.

A huge, majestic water buffalo slowly rose from the water and muck. Weeds and plants trailed from horns that must have been fifteen feet in length. Its head was an island in itself, lifting from the water and turning as it stared at them. It chewed slowly, each grind of its jaw making a wet, dull *thud* that echoed across the clearing. Water poured from its back. Birds landed on its exposed horns and starting plucking small creatures from the plants drooping from them.

Slivko lifted his M-16, but Conrad placed his hand on the barrel and pushed it back down. Slivko did not resist. Weaver was glad.

She sensed no threat from this beast. It did not seem as fascinated with them as they were with it, dipping its head back down and scooping another mouthful of foul-smelling muck and plant from the pond's bottom.

"That's… big," Weaver whispered. Conrad smiled at her, and she was pleased to see the sense of wonder she felt reflected in his eyes. *Maybe it's not all struggle and fight*, she thought. *Maybe what I've been looking for all this time is wonder.*

"We'll pass on slowly," he said to all of them. "I don't think it's a threat. But we take it slow and cautious, and be ready for anything."

The water buffalo snorted, and it reminded Weaver of the sound a whale made filling its lungs on the surface of the sea. She could smell it now, a heavy dank odour mixed in with something altogether more spicy and sweet. It watched them as they moved around the edge of the large pool, head turning slowly as it continued to chew. Slivko and Conrad moved ahead, and behind her came Brooks and San, both staring at the amazing creature as they passed. Nieves brought up the rear. He seemed more alert to their surroundings, less engrossed in the creature they had disturbed. That comforted her. While their attention was on it, something else might be focusing its attention on them.

Seeing the huge buffalo was not the first time she'd considered what else might be on this island with them. The ape, the snake that Conrad had encountered, and now this buffalo, all meant that the island would be home to countless other unknown creatures. Fascinating animals, she was sure, and horrors too.

The terrain grew more challenging, and soon the pool was lost in the jungle behind and below them. The ground rose and fell, plants grew thick and spiked, and Conrad worked hard to clear a route. Some of the plant life around them she recognised, much of it she did not. She was no botanist, but she knew for sure that some of this undergrowth was found nowhere else on the planet. She'd heard of carnivorous plants before, and knew that there were several species that trapped and digested insects. When they saw one with large upright cups filled with water, it was Conrad who investigated the dark shapes contained inside.

"What is it?" Slivko asked. Conrad grabbed the stem and snapped it so that the bulb spilled its contents across the ground. There were several birds in there, a lizard, and a wasp the size of Weaver's hand, all in varying stages of decay.

"Don't touch," Conrad warned. "Acid." Weaver took a picture.

They moved on in single file and remained alert, Nieves and Slivko pausing frequently to look around and take stock. Jungle sounds and smells assailed them. Weaver knew from experience that it was when the constant sounds lessened and faded that they would have to take care. The jungle seemed to know when something bad was about to happen.

In such situations attention could wander. Weaver walked into Slivko where he'd come to a standstill. He barely seemed to notice the impact.

"What?" she asked, immediately on edge.

"Conrad?" he whispered. Ahead of him was the path Conrad had been cutting through the undergrowth, trailing creepers dripping sap where he had sliced them through. A snake hissed and curled away up a drooping branch. The scurrying shadow of a large spider disappeared into a carpet of trampled leaves. "Conrad?" Louder. No answer.

"What's happened?" Weaver asked.

"I lost Conrad."

"What do you mean, lost him? He was right in front of us."

"And then I looked around and he was gone," Slivko said. He nursed his M-16, sweeping the undergrowth ahead of them. "Conrad?" he called, louder than before. Then as he drew a breath to shout Weaver caught movement from the corner of her eye. She span around and crouched, wishing she had accepted a weapon from Slivko after all.

Conrad emerged from the jungle, looking from Weaver to Slivko.

"Keep your voices down," he said. "Wouldn't want to wake up anything with teeth."

"Where'd you go?" Slivko asked.

Conrad pointed back through the trees he'd just emerged from. Deeper in, Weaver could just make out a patch of depressed foliage.

"Combat boots did that. It's fresh, maybe only fifteen minutes."

"The others must be close!" Weaver said.

"No one can move quickly in this jungle," Conrad said. He eyed the whole group, assessing their condition and obviously satisfied, for now. "Come on. This way."

They followed him again, shifting direction and heading up a steep slope towards a tree-smothered ridge line. There was little to be seen, even from that high up, because the foliage was so dense. They took a quick breather, then continued down the other side.

Weaver was fascinated watching Conrad work. He was clearly tracking the other group, although most of the time she couldn't see what he did. He paused frequently, checking branches and leaves, crouching to look at the ground, touching scuff marks on tree bark, sniffing the air. She was close behind him, observing but not wishing to interrupt his flow, when he froze.

She sensed his tension as he looked across the valley that suddenly opened out before them.

They had reached the edge of a tree line, and now another startling truth hit home.

"This island was inhabited!" Brooks said.

Ruins filled the valley, vast structures of angular grey rock, almost chalk-white in places, some vaguely pyramidal and some more like long, high walls. Creepers and undergrowth had smothered some of the lower reaches, but the higher ruins remained relatively plant-free. They protruded from the jungle in several places, and Weaver could make out a pattern that connected all the ruins into one huge settlement.

There was writing on the stonework in no language she had ever seen. It was bright red, like blood.

That's not ancient, she thought. *The sun would have bleached it, rain washed it away. That's recent.*

"Not *was* inhabited," Conrad said. "It *is* inhabited." He drew his pistol and held it down by his leg, and Weaver felt a deep pang of unease.

Something about the whole scene changed. It was a fluid motion, something that almost fooled the eye and made Weaver sway and feel queasy. The constant heat that stuck her clothes to her body with sweat seemed to fade, and a chill pulsed through her veins.

People were appearing as if from nowhere. Close to them, men and women manifested from the jungle, their movements the only sign of their existence. Their camouflage paint was perfect, blending them into the jungle in shades of green and brown that made them almost invisible. Further away, other people were moving towards them from the buildings, their bodies also camouflaged with pale paint and coloured shapes that blended them in with the edifices.

Their clothing was similarly decorated, hoods and swathed skirts matching the colours splayed across their exposed skin.

They came with strung arrows and heavy spears aimed at the small group.

Slivko raised his M-16, and Weaver saw Conrad lifting his pistol, his body tensing into the beginnings of a shooting stance.

No, she wanted to say, but she also realised the danger this situation presented. She became the observer, raising her camera, dreading what she was about to see and record. And in that moment—one of a thousand when she had been preparing to witness and document violence from the outside, rather than from within—she realised that she was *always* the observer. She'd believed all along that the camera brought her closer to the truth.

In reality, it insulated her from it.

"Woah!" a voice shouted. "No need for that! Everybody keep your wigs on, now." A bearded man emerged from the jungle and ran towards them through the painted men and women. He was taller, paler, so obviously not one of them, yet none of the tribespeople even looked at him.

He was dressed in a torn and tattered Air Force jumpsuit that had been patched and sewn multiple times, a parachute harness fashioned into a belt, and well-worn combat boots.

"What the…?" Brooks said from behind Weaver.

Quite, she thought.

Conrad shifted his aim to this new target. The man skidded to a halt with his hands held out, and then he smiled, poor teeth grinning through a mass of beard. It was his eyes that really defused the situation. Weaver could see the joy there, the honest delight at seeing them all. She already knew that he would have such tales to tell.

Conrad slowly lowered his gun and gestured for Slivko to do the same. The soldier only half-lowered the M-16, and the two groups stood facing each other, weapons to hand, with this wild bearded man the only thing between them.

"Combat boots," Conrad said, as if that might explain something.

"Look at you!" the man said. He was almost dancing on the spot. "I didn't believe it when they said you were coming! I was up all night just thinking about how many times Gunpei and I dreamed of this moment, and now here it is! Twenty-eight years, eleven months, and eight attempts to get back to the world, and instead it comes to me. Not that I'm complaining. I never saw anything more magnificent in my whole life. You're more beautiful than a beer and a brat on a summer day at Wrigley. And you're real." He came forward and touched Conrad's shoulder, flinching back as if expecting him to disappear in a puff of smoke. "Yes you are! Hey, that was a hell of an entrance. What were you bombing out there? Not smart." He grew even more excited as he suddenly remembered something else. "And what are those wingless planes with the eggbeaters on top?"

"Helicopters," Conrad said.

"You crashed here?" Weaver asked.

The man seemed to gather himself, realising that this small group were staring at him with shock and surprise.

"Oh, yeah, sorry. Lieutenant Hank Marlow of the Forty-Fifth." He raised his eyebrows, grinning. "I even put on the old flight suit for you." He nodded at Slivko. "You can put that down, now. You really should. The Iwi won't hurt you."

Slivko lowered his M-16. "There's something out there, man."

"Oh, there's a *lot* out there!" Marlow said. "Come on, we gotta get back home."

"Home?" Conrad asked. He glanced at Weaver. She shrugged.

Then she raised her camera and Marlow posed for her with a wild, delighted grin.

FIFTEEN

Conrad let Marlow and the tribespeople lead them down towards the valley floor. Their footsteps were loud and clumsy compared to these island people, who seemed almost to flow rather than walk. Even Marlow made barely a sound as he moved. Conrad could only marvel at how good they were at not attracting attention to themselves. If this island proved to be as dangerous as he was beginning to suspect, that was an essential survival instinct.

They passed through the ruins that were not really ruins, and Conrad had a chance to observe more closely. Some of the buildings did appear abandoned, or meant for some obscure purpose he could not identify, although he guessed they were still maintained to some extent. There was no telling how old they were.

They emerged close to the river, and there were more tribespeople waiting by several skiffs moored at the bank.

"We need to find our people," Conrad said.

"You will. I'll help you." Marlow gestured at a skiff. "For now, though, you're safest with us. Who knows what the hell you've woken out there with your noisy arrival."

Conrad considered for a moment, then climbed into the skiff, followed by the rest of their small group of survivors. Marlow joined them in their boat, and for that he was glad.

Their skiff was pushed from the bank and into the river's gentle flow, and several others joined them, tribespeople using long poles to shove them along. It was almost peaceful, serene, and Conrad risked a momentary lapsing of his guard. He closed his eyes and lifted his face to the sun, enjoying the heat on his dirty, sweat-streaked skin. A moment like this was valuable in recharging his batteries.

He had a feeling that he'd need them fully charged before long.

He heard the familiar shutter clicks of Weaver taking more photos, then the sounds of her changing the film in her camera.

Marlow watched her taking pictures. He could see her fascination with the silent tribespeople, as well as with Marlow himself. Conrad saw a man who had been waiting to tell his story for a long time. That very soon proved to be the case.

"Don't worry about their silence," he said. "They didn't speak to me and Gunpei for the first two months."

"Who was Gunpei?" Conrad asked.

"The Japanese pilot who shot me down. I shot him down, too. Both great shots! We both parachuted out, landed on the island, tried to kill each other, and then…" His eyes grew distant.

"The villagers found you?"

"Yeah. We weren't sure if they were gonna eat us or treat us like kings."

Conrad glanced around at the tribespeople he could see in this skiff and others. Their faces were harsh and impassive, both men and women. He'd become adept at reading expressions, realising that the eyes and face told so much about a person's intentions long before their actions revealed themselves. That had saved his life more than once.

These people were inscrutable. They looked capable and calm, but their eyes and decorated faces gave nothing away. They might as well have been wearing masks.

"I'm hoping it's the latter?" he asked Marlow.

"Somewhere in the middle," Marlow said.

"That's reassuring," Weaver replied. "I think. So you and Gunpei became friends."

"Over time, he became the best friend I've ever had."

"Did you say you were told we were coming?" Nieves asked.

"Yep. Two days ago," Marlow said.

"They told you?" San asked, and when Marlow nodded she said, "How?"

"Truth be told, it was over my head like most everything that goes on here. These folks live on top of the trees, and compared to them we live down in the roots. Some of them don't even seem to age. Listen, I'm like the janitor around here." He shrugged, seemed content with what he'd said. "Yeah. That'll kinda put it into context for you."

"What's that?" Conrad asked. They were approaching a cliff face, tall and imposing, and the river disappeared into a wide cave mouth at its base. He didn't like it. They were being steered somewhere unknown, and once in the cave darkness would descend. He had a small pocket torch, but these tribespeople would be able to do whatever they wished.

"Beyond that is home," Marlow said. "Hey, trust me. You'll want to see this. All of you."

Conrad looked around at the others. Although nervous, most of them also seemed excited. For the first time on this journey, the unexpected inspired curiosity over fear.

They entered the cave mouth, the soft shush of the river echoing into a greater roar, light quickly fading away. But it was not total darkness in there. Creatures scurried across the low ceilings, beaming with a bright phosphorescent glow that gave a soft background illumination, like ever-moving stars. The river was flat and even, the walls steep, and Conrad had the distinct impression that some of it had been carved rather than eroded. Yet another unanswered question about this mysterious place.

"You're okay with this?" Weaver asked, leaning in close to whisper to him.

"Not really," he said. "But if they'd been a threat, I think we'd know by now."

"I hope so."

"They know the island and what's on it," he said. "They've been here for... forever? So if they can survive here, so can we. We've got to learn everything we can from them if we're going to get away."

As he spoke their surroundings grew lighter, and eventually they emerged from beneath the hillside into another valley.

This one seemed steeper-sided and more enclosed than the wide valley they'd just left. The river was narrower and faster moving, and they quickly drew close to the left bank. Stone columns stood beside the river, topped with pedestals upon which stood strange statues. There were other structures all across the valley, some of them similar to the ones they'd seen before, yet with less of an abandoned look. There were more patterns and symbols painted on these buildings, differing in colour and shape. It lent them an alien, ethereal beauty.

A few minutes later the river widened into a lagoon. The expert boatsmen steered the skiffs around a small headland and towards shore, and the village that sprawled there. The structures were quite different from the larger stone buildings they'd seen, and included many homes built on stilts. Incorporated into the village, grounded on the curved lagoon's bank, was a wrecked ship. Its superstructure seemed to be part of the village, with homes built against it and rope ladders slung from its upper decks down to the ground. Its rusted metal hull was also decorated with the colourful, angular lines that also appeared on the other buildings.

The vessel was so out of place that Conrad blinked a couple of times, shaking his head to clear his vision.

Drawing closer, he could just make out its name. *The Wanderer*.

"Looks like we're not the first people to never, ever leave this island again," Slivko said.

"We'll get away," Conrad said.

As their skiff ground against the shore and many more tribespeople came to meet them, he began to have his doubts.

Chapman was the only survivor from the downed Sea Stallion. He'd checked on the co-pilot but Warzowski was dead, his neck broken in the crash. As for the door gunner, Muller was nowhere to be found. The heavy machine gun still hung from its mounting, but the door surround was torn and slashed and several streaks of blood were drying across the walls and ceiling of the passenger cabin.

Chapman's radio was glitchy, and his brief communication with Packard had been fragmented at best. He was certain that every other chopper had been brought down. He'd debated his alternatives and decided to remain with the ruined chopper, for now. At least here he had some food, shelter, and enough weapons to start another war.

He was exhausted, suffering from heat stroke, and his dressed wounds were causing him pain. He was most worried about the deep laceration across his left forearm. It should have been stitched, but he'd made do with gluing the pouting edges of the wound together.

He needed water. Several storage drums had been holed in the crash and the water leaked away, and he'd already drunk his way through the canteens that had survived. He'd assumed that the jungle would have abundant water sources. Now was the time to find out.

After just fifteen minutes trekking downhill he came to a blue lagoon where the river widened into a bowl-shaped valley nestled between three mountains. He collapsed in the shadow of a rock on the bank, hoping and praying that this was fresh water, and not fed from the sea.

He crept forward through the mud of the riverbank, leaning out, cupping his hands and letting them fill with water. He sipped. Clean, fresh water. He sighed with relief, then scooped another handful.

An impact punched up through his hand and knees, sending a shimmering ripple all across the surface of the lake. Water dribbled from his mouth as he froze, breath held. *What the hell was that?*

Another impact, closer, and a shadow fell over him, blocking out the sun as completely as an eclipse. As the surface of the water shimmered and then stilled again, Chapman saw what looked like a mountain standing behind him.

That thing! His heart fluttered and then pounded. The ground shook once more. Turning his head slightly he saw the giant ape kneeling close to the lagoon bank less than a hundred feet from him.

It'll see me it'll know me it'll eat me and then—

Chapman breathed deep and slow, trying to compose himself. It hadn't seen him yet. The large rock he'd sat against was shielding most of his body. He still had a chance. *Just stay still, stay quiet…*

The ape scooped a huge handful of mud and water from the lagoon bank and began slathering an open wound on its forearm. Chapman froze in surprise, looking at his own arm, and the wound there that was troubling him. Something about that moment bit deep.

We did that to him, he thought, and for the first time since arriving he saw the beast as something other than a monster, and an enemy.

The ape paused, then looked directly at him. Its eyes changed. Its face wrinkled as it drew in a huge, snorting sniff. It reached out the mud-covered hand, crawling closer along the bank, reaching past Chapman's rock—

—and then plunging its hand into the lagoon, right up to its elbow. Waves splashed and washed against the shore, and Chapman took the opportunity to push himself backwards, hugging the rock and desperately hoping it would shield him enough.

The beast withdrew its hand clasping a massive tentacled limb, suckers puckering at the open air. Water thrashed as more tentacles lashed out from the deep and wrapped around its arm, then the ape stood to its full height, pulling with all its strength.

A squid partially emerged from the water. This was

a true giant, far larger than any Chapman had ever seen or even heard of before, perhaps eighty feet from tip of tentacles to the end of its tail. It was a powerful creature. Several limbs remained hooked onto something beneath the surface as the ape tugged and wrestled to haul it out. Water churned in the violent struggle, turning dark as the squid released sprays of thick black ink that spattered down around and over Chapman. It stank, a heavy viscous fluid that stuck to his clothes as thick as tar.

One of the squid's tentacles lashed out across the rock Chapman was hiding behind. Even the tip was as thick as his arm, and it whipped him across the legs, a heavy wet impact. He cried out, voice lost amidst the fight between these two behemoths. Then he heard a sickening crunching sound, and risking a look around the rock he saw the ape chewing down on the squid's head. Its skin ruptured, head burst, spilling a sick stew of rank fluids, sticking in the ape's fur and forming a thick slick across the lagoon's surface.

Chapman curled against the rock and waited for it to all go away. He was moaning softly, listening to the sounds of the giant ape eating. The tentacle end lying across his legs went limp, then was jerked away as the beast finished its meal.

He lay there for a while listening to the slurping, chewing sounds echoing across the lagoon. Squid blood and ink drifted across the surface like oil, and soon the scene became peaceful again, quiet, and when he chanced another glance around the rock the ape was gone, the squid was gone, and it was as if neither had ever been there.

"Shit," Chapman muttered. "Shit." He wanted nothing more than to get back to the crashed Sea Stallion.

SIXTEEN

Weaver was beginning to wonder whether she'd brought enough spare film cartridges. She was using thirty-six exposures, and already she'd filled six of them. She had maybe eight left to spare. Walking from the waterside and into the village, she saw sights she could have used eight rolls on barely without blinking.

The villagers, first of all. They all wore colourful clothing, much of it decorated with patterns and hues that were designed for camouflage against certain backgrounds. Some were jungle tinged, others pale as stone, yet more a muddy, dirty colour like jungle water. Men and women mixed together, seemingly equal. Whatever hierarchy existed here was not dictated by the sexes. Children ran around and played like children do, but even they wore smeared paint across their faces and naked torsos.

The village itself was fascinating. She'd seen similar stilted structures in Vietnam, built higher than potential flood levels, but these buildings were far more complex and sturdy. Their stilts were a mixture of timber and stone, and some of them covered three levels, often built into and around tall trees that might have been a thousand years old. They were also decorated with an array of highly coloured patterns, against which camouflaged villagers could stand and blend in. She wondered whether certain families chose particular colours and shapes.

She snapped photos, recording memories through the lens. The villagers did not react when she aimed the camera at them, neither posing, nor becoming agitated and turning away. They treated her camera like just another stranger. None of them seemed to react outwardly to anything, and she wondered just what they were thinking.

Beyond the village, further along the valley, was the wall.

It was the highest, largest structure they had seen by far, a massive conglomeration of stone and timber that effectively blocked off the valley past that point. It reminded Weaver of a tall dam, except that this appeared to be completely vertical. Huge stone blocks had been used to form the wall, along with timber infill structures in a couple of places that rose high and solid.

Spiked areas—sharpened tree trunks, she guessed, set into stone pockets and protruding outward from the wall's facade—gave the impression of a fortification.

Those same coloured streaks decorated the entire surface. They could not have been for camouflage, and she wondered if perhaps they had some ceremonial or superstitious meaning.

It was magnificent and daunting, and she had never seen its like before. She ached to get closer to make out more detail.

"Did they build that to keep out that thing we saw?" she asked.

"Kong," Marlow said.

"It has a name?" Brooks asked.

"*He* has a name. And yeah, to them he does. But he's not the one they're trying to keep out."

Weaver's blood ran cold. *There's worse than Kong*, she thought, and it was not an idea she wanted to verbalise, or a question she wanted to ask. She and Conrad shared a glance and she saw her fear reflected in him.

"They're petroglyphs," Brooks said, pointing at some of the symbols used on buildings and the wall.

"No," San said, "it looks more like a written language." She started examining the symbols, as if to distract herself from everything that had happened. Weaver wished she had something to offer a distraction other than the view through her camera lens, and the words of this man who had been here forever.

"Did you teach them these building techniques?" Brooks asked.

"Me? Teach them?" Marlow laughed. "That's rich. That's a real riot."

"Who's in charge here?" Conrad asked.

"Nobody," Marlow said. "They're a democratic collective. Pretty neat, really. They don't own property, there's no crime. They're past all that. Thing is, see, with a place like this, whatever lands here stays here."

Several much older villagers approached, dressed in the usual coloured clothes but with jewellery of complex designs hanging around their neck and from heavily pierced ears.

"It's okay," Marlow said to the elders. "These are my friends. They mean no harm."

The elders only stared at him and the new visitors, saying nothing and giving very little away through their expressions. Yet Marlow seemed to glean some meaning from their minimal movements and silence.

"Good, good, thank you," he said. He turned to Conrad. "They say you're welcome to shack up here."

"I didn't hear them say anything at all," Conrad said, and Weaver shared his confusion and suspicion. This mad guy could be making everything up as he went along.

"They don't speak much," Marlow said, frowning as he tried to find words for what he meant to say. If he'd been here so long, perhaps his own language had lost some meaning. "It's kinda nice, really. But once you've been here as long as I have, you get the message."

"You can tell them *we* won't be here that long," Conrad said. "There are more of us out in the jungle, injured. Some dead."

Weaver edged from foot to foot. She felt a stress building, not in Conrad's words but in his demeanour. The others, too, were exuding tension. Nieves and Slivko held their guns down by their sides, but she saw their hands gripping that little bit tighter, knuckles whitening.

"We need to go that way." Conrad pointed at the wall beyond the village.

The villagers reacted instantly. Though their expressions did not change, several of them brought up their spears, and others crouched down as if in preparation for a fight.

"Out there?" Marlow asked, afraid for the first time. "Oh no, they won't let you go out there."

"Won't let us?" Nieves asked.

"Not after you kicked the hornet's nest," Marlow said. "Nope. They won't let you past that wall."

Nieves took a step forward, suddenly more threatening. "Wait a minute, won't *let* us? You're not serious. We can't just stay here, we have to get off this rock. We have lives back home. I have a life. Tell them, we need to—"

"Thank them for their hospitality," Conrad said, stepping forward and cutting Nieves off. Weaver realised that she'd been about to do the same. Nieves was losing it, and it was starting to feel like a mistake giving him a gun.

Nieves looked around and Weaver caught his eye. She shook her head.

"Get out of the office, they said," he muttered. "See the world, have an adventure. Damn it, I need… I need…" He slumped and sat down on the hard ground, nursing the rifle across his legs.

A female villager approached, confident and quiet, and handed him a finely carved stone cup of water.

Nieves looked up, surprised. "Oh. Thank you."

Weaver removed herself from their oddly poignant moment and took a photo of the standing woman handing the seated man a drink. *Every one of these could win awards*, she thought.

"They won't hurt you," Marlow said, looking around at the new arrivals. "They really won't. Come on in, I'll give you a tour of the village."

"I'd rather see more of that," Conrad said, pointing at the shipwrecked *Wanderer*.

"Oh, yeah. There's a lot to see there. Okay, we'll start there. Let's go." Marlow led the way, but Nieves held back, seated with the village woman. He seemed enrapt.

"I think maybe I'll wait here," he said.

Weaver took another picture.

They passed through the village and approached the grounded ship. It looked larger the nearer they got, not quite *Athena*'s size, but close. Weaver could see several rusted holes in its hull, and she wondered whether they had been torn there during the ship's final moments, or had decayed over time since the wreck.

She also wondered what had happened to the *Wanderer*'s sailors and crew.

Marlow led the group—Conrad, Brooks, San, Slivko and a reluctant Nieves—in through one of these openings, up a small slope of wreckage, and into an interior hallway. Lit from several large openings above, the functional passageway had been carved and decorated over the years so that it barely resembled a ship's interior at all.

Weaver used her flash to adequately illuminate the photos she took. She had begun to realise that she was documenting something amazing, unknown, and horrible, all probably for the first time ever. The images she was recording here were unprecedented. They were unique.

All she had to do was to survive and get them off this island.

She photographed Marlow again from behind as he was talking with Conrad. He looked fit and well, especially considering he'd been here for almost thirty years. Yet he still had much of his story to tell. She could sense Conrad's caution, even though Marlow seemed only happy to see them.

"Far as I can tell, this ship washed up about a decade or so before I did," the old pilot said. "Sits on top of a spring. The whole place is hallowed ground to them. Come on through, I'll show you the main spring room. It's sorta… spooky."

Marlow wasn't lying. Even on the approach to the spring room, a strange glowing light emanated from it, speckling the walls with luminescence and catching dust drifting on the air.

They entered the spring room, and for a moment Weaver forgot her camera. Perhaps it had once been one of the ship's holds, or a high-ceilinged rec room, but everything about it had changed. Walls were contoured with crafted wood and dried mud and decorated with obscure shapes and images. The floor had been relaid in blocked stone, smoothed by decades of reverential footfalls. High up, the ceiling was open to the sky, but criss-crossed with heavy vines and hanging plants, making for an artificial forest canopy. At the room's centre sat the well head. Raised a couple of feet from the floor, the well was almost perfectly round, and it emitted a strange phosphorescent glow that permeated the whole room.

While the others examined the well and its strange light, Weaver concentrated on the walls. There was something about the shapes there, the separate planks all painted with patterns, and how the colours interacted with the carvings and moulded mud. Shadow and light conspired. It was not hypnotic, but still the features drew her eye and levelled her concentration. She snapped photos, and in between she simply stared. Blinking slowly, letting her vision settle, she saw it at last.

These were not random shapes at all.

"Look at this," she said, and Conrad and the others came over. After a few seconds they saw as well.

One of the main images showed Kong sitting on a giant stone throne. The seat was made from weirdly-shaped skulls, many of them as large as his. Its feet were bones that had to be thirty feet long. He even wore a crown of jagged teeth.

"Kong," Weaver breathed, and the name itself held a strange power.

"The tribe thinks he's a king, or even some sort of god," Marlow said. "Sometimes I gotta wonder."

"Must have missed that part of Sunday school," Conrad said.

Brooks and San moved from side to side, pointing out new, more awful images. Weaver's blood ran cold when she saw them. She was starting to have an inkling of just why that giant wall had been built across the villagers' valley.

"I used to think this job was a wild goose chase," Brooks said. "Another step in making a decent resume."

"Instead, we're making history," San said.

"Or seeing it," Weaver said.

"Kong keeps pretty much to himself, you know," Marlow said. "But you don't go into a man's abode and start dropping bombs. You can't blame him for what happened."

"Isn't it Kong that killed your friend?" Weaver asked, probing for more of the man's story.

Marlow's face went cold for the first time since they'd all met. "Not Kong," he said, pointing at the other images. "It was them."

The images and shapes across the wall were chilling, and the idea that they were real even more so.

Giant reptilian beasts, one with three heads. A crocodile fifty feet long. Snake-like monsters, slinking from holes in the ground and snapping towards the sun. Web-footed creatures, spikes along their backs spearing bloodied human shapes, diving into the ocean surrounding the island.

"If Kong's god of the island, then the things that live beneath it are the demons," Marlow said. "The villagers won't talk of them, and I've never heard their real name. I just call them Skull Crawlers."

"Why?" Conrad asked.

Marlow shrugged. "Because it sounds neat."

"So why haven't we seen them?" Conrad asked.

"Do we want to see them?" Weaver replied.

"No, you don't." Marlow's voice carried a weight of grief and fear. "They come from the vents, deep down beneath the island. That's why you got Kong so mad. He keeps most of them at bay, down there where they belong, but you don't wanna go and wake the big one."

"Big one?" Brooks asked. He pointed at the horrific images. "What, these are the small guys?"

Marlow moved along the wall and pointed out an image none of them had seen yet. It was the most monstrous of them all, all fangs and claws, and fury.

"It's as big as Kong!" San said.

"Bigger," Marlow replied. "Never seen it, but I know it as the Skull Devil. Kong's the last of his kind, but he's not yet fully grown. Look." He moved along to another image, this one a wide landscape painted on a shadowy corner of the spring room. It showed a lonely Kong, shoulders slumped, standing defiant in a battlefield of dead creatures like him, and Skull Crawlers torn apart by their mighty hands.

"He's still a juvenile?" San asked.

"He's pretty damn huge," Slivko said.

"He'll keep growing, if he survives," Marlow said. "And he'd better. The villagers say if Kong ever went away, the big one would come up and overrun us all."

"And that's why they won't let us leave," Conrad said.

"After the entrance you made? Not likely."

"Our extract team is coming to the north shore of the island in three days," Conrad said. "We have to be there."

Marlow raised his eyebrows. His bushy beard animated his face, and Weaver thought perhaps he'd never believed this possible.

"We're not staying here, turning into..." Nieves said, nodding at Marlow. "No offence, man."

"None taken," Marlow said. "So you really have someone coming to meet you?"

"You're welcome to come with us," Weaver said.

Marlow shook his head. He seemed firm. "Nope. You won't make it to the north shore in three days. No way. Not through the jungle."

Conrad frowned, and Weaver looked around at the others, seeing their disappointment and fear. Then Marlow smiled and continued.

"At least, not on foot."

"You gonna tell me you got your plane flying again," Nieves said, a tone of mockery in his voice.

"Oh, better than that," Marlow said. "Come on. I'll show you."

He grinned at Weaver, and she replied by taking his photograph one more time.

SEVENTEEN

Mills held his breath as the colonel aimed the rifle, and he looked at the target one more time, confused, scared, disbelieving.

The bird was the size of a man, but unlike any Mills had ever seen. It resembled a gigantic vulture, sparsely feathered, leathery winged, its head large and bulging with bright red nodules, its skin lined and creased. It was almost prehistoric, and when it leaned its head back and called, the deep cry did nothing to dispel that notion. Behind it a tall black tree seemed to be its home. They suited each other.

Still, Mills saw no reason to blast it to hell.

They were hunkered down behind a huge fallen tree. There was a big enough gap beneath it for them to walk through, but Packard had called a halt when Cole saw the bird a hundred yards away. It was a good time to rest and take in just one more feature of this amazing, terrifying place.

Packard breathed in deeply, out slowly. "That is one ugly bird," he muttered. Then he fired.

The bird's head exploded and its body slumped heavily to the ground. Even from this distance, Mills heard it. Then behind the bird, something strange started happening to the tree.

Bullet went right through, Mills thought.

The trunk fractured.

Shattered the tree, made of stone perhaps, nothing like—

The branches drooped and then fell, splitting, fragmenting.

Not a tree at all.

The tree was composed of hundreds of those strange birds, melded and clasped together, shocked apart by the gunshot and the death of their companion, and now their strange conglomeration was falling apart, the birds crying out, flapping, drifting and soaring.

"Everyone down!" Mills shouted, but he already knew it was hopeless. If the birds came for them, they were finished. With their combined weapons they might be able to shoot down five more, or eight, but then they'd be smothered, picked apart by angry beaks and cruel claws. The sudden sound was terrifying, a combination of shrieks and the heavy flapping of wings. Mills hugged the ground. Cole was beside him, staring at Mills as if not seeing. Maybe he was praying.

The birds did not attack them. Instead they streamed skyward, spiralling up in patterns which Mills could only admit were beautiful. On the ground they might have been ugly, but once aloft they were graceful.

Packard was already on his feet again, shouldering the rifle as if nothing had happened. "Let's move," he said.

Mills brushed himself down, trying to still his hammering heart and not show his fear. The colonel was already walking away, and Mills and the others scampered out from beneath the massive fallen tree and followed.

"Jesus," Cole said.

"We're in hell," Reles said. "Only explanation. This place is hell."

"Dear Billy," Mills said, "monsters exist, under your bed and signing your pay checks."

They fell into step behind the colonel. He was twenty yards ahead, pushing through the undergrowth and constantly alert. He seemed unafraid.

"Anybody believe we're gonna make it?" Mills asked. He kept his voice low, not wanting Packard to hear.

"Make what?" Reles asked.

"The exfil," Mills said. "If we're not there in a day and a half we miss the flight out, and this freak show of an island becomes our home sweet home."

"We'll make it," Cole said. He spoke with finality. He didn't like the colonel being questioned, but Mills couldn't help that. Normally he'd follow Packard anywhere without question, but the doubts were his now, and this operation was far from normal.

"I dunno," Mills said. "We'd have to beat feet even without the Chapman detour."

"If it was me out there, I'd understand," Reles said. "I'd be okay with you guys getting out. I think." He glanced around at his companions. "Are we sure Chapman is even—"

"The colonel said he's there, he's there!" Cole said.

"Okay, Cole, don't get all bent," Mills said. "He's there. And we get him, and we load out the munitions, and we go find the giant ape and wage war. That about cover it?"

"That's a lot of burned daylight when we've got a hard walk out to the exfil," Reles said.

They fell silent for a few steps, lost in their own thoughts. When Reles spoke again, he said what Mills had been thinking.

"Is he okay?"

"Who?" Cole asked.

"The colonel. He seems a little…"

"Like he's losing it," Mills said. "Like he'd rather kill that ape than get off the island."

None of them replied. Not even Cole, to defend the

colonel he'd follow into a lake of fire and out the other side.

Losing it, Mills thought, watching Packard as he led the way. The colonel seemed taller than ever before, as if a sense of purpose gave him life. Mills only hoped he wouldn't let that hold on life go simply to fuel his aims.

Marlow led Conrad and Slivko past the village and along the riverside towards the vast wall. They walked for a few minutes and the wall barely seemed to come closer, and Conrad realised just how huge it was. It was a staggering architectural and engineering feat. He wondered at the fear these people must hold to force them into a task that must have taken many generations. Its maintenance would be an ongoing effort as well, something that the villagers would commit their lives to performing.

A mile or so past the village, they followed Marlow onto a wooden dock extending out into the river. At last they saw what he wanted to show them.

Whatever Conrad had been expecting, it wasn't this.

"Gunpei and I started building her together years ago," Marlow said. "Finished a couple of years back. Almost finished, anyway. Pulleyed the engine parts from my P-51, the screw from his old Zero. We were gonna head to open sea and civilisation. But that's when one of them got him."

"What happened?" Conrad asked.

"We'd gone down to the beach to salvage more parts from my plane. It's half-buried in the sand down there now, washed way up on the beach by storm surge. We were hoping to tear out some of the electronics so we could rig some sorta ignition switch, and we wanted…" Marlow waved his hand, and Conrad was surprised to see tears in his eyes. "Anyway, on the way back we heard a noise coming from a deep ravine. Sounded like a kid screaming, calling for help. You've seen these villagers, Conrad. You know they don't say much, not even the kids. So we ran to help and…" He trailed off.

"It wasn't a kid," Slivko said.

"Not a kid," Marlow said. "Gunpei had started climbing down into the ravine, while I fed him rope. He always was the stronger one of us. The braver. He was maybe thirty feet down when the strange voice stopped, and then I heard it." He fell silent again, staring out over the river.

"Marlow," Conrad said, touching the man's shoulder.

"Maybe it was laughing," Marlow said. "I dunno. It was like a deep clicking sound, a heavy rattle coming from somewhere inside it. Gunpei looks up at me, his eyes are wide, and I start pulling, because I know we've made a terrible mistake. I hardly even see what takes him. Something whips down there in the dark, reaches out, snags his legs and tugs. And I… I can't hold on. The rope rips through my hands, burning them, and Gunpei is gone."

Conrad and Slivko remained quiet, giving Marlow his moment.

"I didn't even hear him scream."

"That's a good thing," Slivko said, and Marlow glared at him. "Right, Conrad?"

"Right," Conrad said. "A good thing, Marlow. He didn't know what hit him."

"But *I* know," Marlow said. "One of *them* hit him. I spend whole nights lying awake, thinking about how I can pay them back. But…" He shook his head. "I can't. No one can. Not them."

"So let's see this boat you made with your friend," Conrad said, and Marlow smiled.

They walked out along the dock towards the craft these two island-bound enemies had built together as friends.

Conrad inspected the boat, and the more he saw, the more impressed he became. It was constructed from salvaged parts of aircraft and finely crafted timber, all patched onto what looked like the hull of an old World War Two torpedo boat. It wasn't graceful or beautiful, but the engineering abilities used to construct something like this out here were staggering.

"Lovely," Conrad said.

"Does it even float?" Slivko asked.

"Well… she needs work…" Marlow looked around, then leaned in close to Conrad. "But nothing a few extra hands can't fix! We'll have to gather tools and start work after dark. Like I said, our friends aren't keen on anyone splitting town, in case it stirs things up even more."

"You think they'll try to stop us?" Conrad asked. He was aware of the weight of the pistol on his belt, but also keen not to use it. Not on these people. He wasn't sure he could.

Marlow shrugged. "They survive. That's their life."

"So if they see us potentially threatening their survival," Conrad said, but he did not finish his sentence. He really didn't need to.

Time would tell.

Now that the truth was out, Randa felt invigorated. They were within reach of everything they had set out to find. That it had already found them only made things easier.

People had died. That weighed heavy on his conscience, and Packard threatening him with a gun might have been the closest Randa had ever come to death. Now that moment was passed, and they were making their way towards the crashed Sea Stallion, he had time to really appreciate the truths they had discovered.

Everything he'd ever hypothesised seemed to be coming true. If that beast existed, then it stood to reason that the other things he had speculated on were also here, somewhere—the vast underground world that no one had ever seen; the creatures that lived there, separated from evolution for millions of years.

The monsters.

The ape was only the first. Randa believed there would be more, many more. His only hope was that they did not encounter them face to face.

From a distance, though, would be fine. He carried his film camera after all, and once they were away from Skull Island, he would be ready to confront the world and show it that he had been right all along. Brooks and San had always doubted, along with many others in the scientific community. To some he was a pariah, a mad scientist lucky enough to have a monied organisation backing him. Calling someone a hollow-earther had become something of a joke.

He looked forward to seeing their faces when he presented his evidence.

He and the other survivors moved slowly through the jungle, carrying supplies and gear, guarded by the soldiers and following their lead. Packard was treating this like a war zone, and that caution suited Randa. They had seen the destruction and chaos that carelessness could cause.

Randa saw so much here that must have been exclusive to the island. Plant life, insects, several unusual species of small mammal, unique birds of paradise that danced and sang from the tree canopy. The trees themselves were huge and primeval, towering so high up that their heads were often lost in a haze of jungle mist, thrown up by the steaming temperatures and high humidity. A closed ecosystem, this was truly a wild land.

It was also unpredictable. One minute they were pushing through huge ferns, the next they emerged into a wide clearing of knee-high grasses and sparse, thin shrubs. The going was tough, and Randa was soon exhausted. Excitement kept him alert.

"Check it out," one of the soldiers said pointing his gun to their left.

A sheer cliff rose to a ridge line a hundred feet above them. Pressed to the face of the cliff was what could only be a handprint, marked in blood and buzzing with flies and skittering lizards. The ape had come this way.

"Magnificent," Randa breathed, filming the scene.

"It bleeds," Packard said, moving up beside him.

"We did that. And when we reach Chapman, there's enough munitions on his downed Sea Stallion to finish the job."

The column moved out, but Randa could only stare at the handprint. It was like a tribal marking, reminding him of ancient cave paintings from pre-history. There were many theories, but no historian could discern exactly what those long-dead artists had been thinking when they'd made their impressions. There was something about this that was similarly unknowable, as if in pressing his blood to the stone the ape had left something of his unknowable mind for all to see. A statement in blood.

Randa shivered. Cole nudged his shoulder.

"Keep moving, Mr Scientist."

They moved out, and Randa knew that the massive handprint had troubled the soldiers as much as him.

"Man, whatever happened to letting sleeping dogs lie?" Mills muttered.

"They all wake up eventually," Randa said. "The question is, are we ready?"

Walking ahead of Randa, Cole held up his AK-47 like a trophy.

"You know why I carry this instead of an M-16?" he asked. "Took it off a farmer fighting for the NVA. He surrendered after we levelled his village, one of the only ones who didn't fight to the death. He was maybe fifty years old. Told me he'd never even seen a gun until we showed up. Sometimes an enemy doesn't exist until you go looking for one."

"And what happens when they show up at your front door?" Randa asked.

Cole waved the weapon again. "I'll still have his gun."

"Best of luck with that, soldier," Randa said. "You've seen what the enemy here looks like."

"Yeah, but now we know what we're dealing with."

"Sure," Randa said. "It's what we haven't seen yet that really worries me."

The group walked on across the wide clearing and into jungle once more. To Randa, there were eyes everywhere, and all were focused on them.

EIGHTEEN

Mills hoped he never saw another goddamned jungle for the rest of his life. He'd been days away from going home. He wanted out. Out of the jungle, out of the army, out of this crazy mission. He hadn't asked for this, and he hadn't even been told whether they were being paid combat pay for this fun little jaunt.

Man, this was FUBAR.

The landscape of this place was all messed up too. After traversing more jungle they'd started pushing their way through a forest of bamboo stalks. The stems were thick and solid, the leaves sharp, and soon his knuckles were sliced from the leaves' cruel edges. Blood dripped. He thought of that big handprint, and here and there he made sure he left his own mark on the thicker of the bamboo stems.

Something touched his neck. He slapped it away,

the dark shape as big as his thumb scurrying out of sight. "Damn it!"

"What's up?" Cole asked.

"Spider. I hate spiders."

"I'm sure they speak very highly of you."

"They just need to mind their business, is all. Stay away from me, stay unscathed. It's a fair arrangement."

"You ever heard of the mouse and the lion and the thorn?" Cole asked.

"Yeah?"

"There you go. In case we see that thing again."

"You know that story is about a mouse becoming friends with a lion after pulling a thorn out of its paw," Mills said.

"No it's not," Cole said. "The mouse kills the lion with the thorn."

"Man, who told you that?"

"My mother."

Mills raised his eyebrows, but said nothing. Cole was a Sky Devil, but he was also a hard man with a variable-length fuse. He didn't want to diss Cole's mother and light it.

They headed into a thicker patch of tall bamboo. Taking point, Packard began to hack into the stems, carving their way ever forward.

"Man, it stinks in here," Mills said.

"Yeah, like something dead," the soldier to his right

said. They called him Jammers for reasons Mills could no longer remember. Jammers wiped his forehead and lifted his canteen to his lips.

"Not that," Mills said. "Not the smell of the dead. It smells like something *alive*." He looked around, lifting his M-16 and sweeping it in an arc left to right. Nothing. Just bamboo, more and more bamboo.

"What the…?" From ahead, Packard stood staring at the thick stems he'd just hacked through. They were dripping a heavy, dark black fluid, viscous as runny honey. It smelled sweet. One crop landed on the colonel's boot. The stalk he'd cut began to move, and all at once Mills knew.

"Contact!" he shouted, but by then it was already too late.

Just as Jammers lowered his canteen a long, thick stem punched down and skewered him through the throat. He threw his arms out wide, eyes bulging, as the stem burst from between his shoulder blades and blood and flesh spattered the ground around him. He shook, water splashing from the canteen still gripped in his left hand.

Mills looked up at whatever was attacking them, swinging his gun to follow his line of sight, finger already squeezing the trigger. At first his vision was confused by the many bamboo plants swaying around them, heavy leaves seeming to come to life as the shouting and panic fed them. Then he saw the dark mass almost directly above him.

A spider. Huge, horrible, its body the size of a man, long pale legs fifteen feet tall and holding it up above the jungle floor, allowing room for unsuspecting prey to wander beneath.

Now they were the prey. Its wet mandibles clicked together with the promise of food as it lifted Jammers up towards its multi-eyed head.

Mills opened up, the weapon jumping in his hands, gunshots pounding his ears, but already his vision was blurring. He blinked several times, and then something sticky and warm landed across his face, chest, arms. Its touch bore an awful intimacy. He tried to shift the gun but it was like moving underwater, and his breath was stolen just as rapidly as his other senses.

Caught in its web! he thought. The spider had sprayed him with silk, and now it was drawing him up, too. His finger squeezed the trigger again but his mag was already empty. He heard more shooting as if from a distance, shouting, desperate screams as his friends tried to save him from a grisly fate.

"Mills!" Cole shouted, his voice seeming to come from the end of a long tunnel.

Mills struggled, trying to twist and turn his body to tear the webbing, but though impossibly light it was stronger than steel. He heard more shouting from down below, more gunfire, and then he saw…

…the mouth, fanged and dripping with poison. The eyes, each as big as his fist, eight of them all seeming to reflect him. The spiked fur of the spider's grotesque head. He wanted to close his eyes and hide himself from this awful end, but he could not. Even with his eyes closed, no nightmare could ever be worse.

I hate spiders, he thought, and then the world tipped up, he fell to the side, and the ground thumped him hard. He gasped, winded, struggling to draw in a breath as a blade flashed before him and the web ripped open.

Cole was there, reaching for him to drag him free. The toppled spider was struggling, its legs drawing in and extending again as it tried to stand. Bamboo snapped, cruel splinters flying like shrapnel. Mills tried to help, kicking out against the fallen beast as Packard stepped in close, aimed his pistol, and emptied it into the struggling spider's head.

It kicked its legs one more time, then they each curled inward in death, scoring lines across the ground and toppling several of the true bamboo plants it had used as camouflage. Still speared on one of its legs, Jammers was dragged inward and pressed to the spider's bleeding underbelly.

Now, the place really did smell of death.

Mills held onto Cole, unwilling to let go, shaking,

trying to look anywhere else but only able to stare at the dead monster.

"It's okay, pal," Cole said. "Hey, come on, let me help you up. It's okay." Cole eventually disengaged, pulling silk from Mill's shoulders and head with a heavy ripping sound. He freed his arms and legs and finally Mills was able to stand. His legs were shaking.

"Damn," Mills said. Cole raised both eyebrows, finding nothing to say in response.

The others were milling around, reloading their weapons, stunned. They kept watch, looking up now as well as ahead. In Vietnam the danger could have come from a sniper up above, a spike-wielding killer from tunnels below, or VC charging silently from out of the dense jungle. Here, the whole jungle was their enemy once again.

"Shake it off, men," Packard said. "I didn't think for a minute that ape was the only monster here."

Mills was still petrified and traumatised. "Did no one just see that I was almost eaten by a giant spider?"

"I've seen worse," Packard said. "And you're alive, soldier. Let's move out."

All Mills wanted to do was sit down, rock from side to side, hug himself and shake. As the group moved on, he knew that his safest place was with them.

• • •

Weaver knew she shouldn't feel safe, and welcome, and at ease, because this village was one of the strangest places she had ever been, and the threat of monsters from beyond was great. But there was something about these Iwi villagers that settled her nerves. Their silent acceptance of her and the others. Their evident ability to survive and thrive in such a world. The strength in their eyes, and the calm, powerful grace in every action.

Alone, she wandered the village, and her camera was always at hand. She saw children playing in a small circular common area at the village centre, casting coloured stones into a complex grid marked in the dust with scattered chalk. A scoring system seemed to be in play, though she could not discern its details. The children laughed and giggled, but she heard nothing that resembled language. She watched for a while, hunkered down at the edge of the circle, snapping photos of the children at play. They knew she was there but didn't seem concerned.

She walked through the rest of the village, and subconsciously perhaps she always suspected where she was going. When she reached the edge of the village, she had no doubt. The giant wall drew her, its size and splendour a gravity that lured her its way. As she approached and stepped into its shadow she looked around, careful to ensure no one saw her.

The villagers seemed unconcerned when she left the village, and pushing her way through tall grasses and ferns, she saw no sign of any of them following her. There were paths here, trodden down over the years and mostly clear of vegetation. But she didn't think they were well used.

The villagers seemed to be in control. Weaver knew that if they didn't approve of what she was doing, where she was going, they would intervene. She took their silence as assent.

Close to the wall, its true scope and scale really hit home. She'd never seen the pyramids, but she had read and heard all about them. This structure might well be comparable, both in technical achievement and sheer size. Down close to the ground, some of the timbers and stone used in the construction looked incredibly old, with newer areas patched in, an ongoing maintenance effort that must continue for some of the Iwi villagers from birth to death.

When she walked closer and saw the hole, it was as if she'd always known it would be there. It was half hidden behind vines and a heavy dark-green ivy that mostly smothered this lower potion of the wall, and she only saw its dark depths when a flash from her camera illuminated the entrance. Splintered wood around the opening indicated that it had been made after the wall had been built, and some signs of a path revealed that the hole was in use. By humans or animals, she did not know.

Weaver moved closer, cautious and quiet. Birdsong continued around her. Crickets sawed away in the high grasses. Spiders scampered across fern leaves above her head, shadowy silhouettes running and pausing, running and pausing.

She pointed her camera directly at the hole, and the flash illuminated deep inside. It looked like a tunnel, and it was empty.

Weaver took a deep breath and looked around. *If you're watching, and if I really shouldn't go this way, now's the time to tell me*, she thought. Her surroundings remained unchanged, and no Iwis materialised out of the undergrowth.

"If you're not there, you can't get the shot," she said, and taking a small torch from her camera bag, she entered the hole in the wall.

It was cool inside, as if heat from outside could not find its way in. The tunnel was carved through the wall—heavy trunks hacked and splintered, rock chiselled and smashed away—and she could see tool marks in the walls and ceiling. The floor was made from trodden-down mud, hardened over time into a smooth, concrete-like surface. Painted hand marks were pressed to the stonework, and in places they formed complex patterns that made no sense to her.

She was not alone. Lizards scampered across walls and floor, skittering out of sight. Spiders ducked into crevasses. The torchlight swept her path, clearing these animals as effectively as a high-powered hose, and she did not hang around to see what else might be in there.

Daylight welcomed her from the other end, and after a minute walking beneath the great wall, she emerged onto the other side.

She was on a slight rise looking down onto a river valley, the river roaring from beneath the wall a hundred yards to her right. This was the part of the island that the Iwi protected themselves from. The dangerous part.

Though Weaver had already seen some of the danger, she felt suddenly exposed and watched by countless eyes she could not make out. She could see a lot more landscape on this side of the wall as the valley fell slowly away, and in the distance a range of mountains loomed like a giant beast's staggered teeth. *Maybe that's what this is*, she thought. *The island's one big monster just waiting to chew us up and spit us out.*

She started taking photos. She couldn't go far, yet curiosity got the better of her. She also had to be mindful of how many rolls of film she had left. It would have been easy to stand here and take fifty pictures of the landscape itself, trying to catch the wildness and wilderness, but she knew she was going to see more. The future was an uncertain place offering extraordinary experiences, and Weaver was determined to document it.

Something cried out. There was already a distinctive background sound to the island that she was growing used to—birds calling, insects scratching and whistling, frogs croaking, and the constant rustle and scamper of things unseen. This was louder, and obviously from something in pain.

She scurried down a slope, slipping in loose leaves and sliding the rest of the way, camera held in to her chest to prevent damage. At the slope's base she stood and looked around, turning her head when the baying came again to try and discern direction.

Pushing her way through heavy, leathery leaves, boots sinking in soggy ground, she mounted a small hillock surrounded by swamp, and saw what was crying.

The chunk of helicopter fuselage was a shock set against the wild landscape, like a wound in this new reality. It was a large, ragged part of the tail section from one of the downed choppers, scorched along one edge where fire had eaten at it, the oil-blackened guts of the craft's engine hanging out like a mechanical monster's spilled insides. Trapped beneath it was a large water buffalo. It was crushed down into marsh by the weight on its back, one of its long horns chipped and scored from the metallic impact. The creature looked weak and almost ready to give in. Its struggles were slow, its cries wretched.

It saw Weaver and let out another feeble call.

Weaver lowered her camera and stepped down to the edge of the swamp. Water and mud played around her feet, and she knew if she went closer she'd be up to her knees at least. It was no choice at all. She waded in, feeling her boots sink into rotting vegetation beneath the water, swinging her arms and pushing hard as she approached the stricken creature.

Somehow, the buffalo knew that she was coming to help. It ceased its struggles and looked sidelong at her, its eye rolling in its skull with fear or hopelessness. Weaver muttered meaningless words to try and calm it, then started pushing at the fallen wreckage.

It did not shift. Not even a bit. She switched angles and heaved upwards against it from below, trying to shift her feet to gain more leverage, closing her eyes with the effort of pushing. It was stuck fast, too heavy to move—

—and then the whole piece of wreckage lifted up and away from her. She lost her footing and fell against the stricken buffalo, surprised by the sudden movement and crying out when the creature started to thrash and struggle.

The sun was gone. She noticed that at the same

moment that she saw the huge leg beyond the buffalo.

Kong was there. She took a few steps back and looked up, and up, and there he was, way above her, legs stuck down into the swamp like giant tree trunks, his huge body obscuring the sun, one arm held out as he flung the wreckage far into the swamp, the other arm hanging down. His fisted hand was the size of a car. She could feel the heat of him, smell his animal musk, and her skin prickled when her eyes met his.

He was staring right down at her.

Weaver felt her legs weakening in shock. She stumbled back a few more steps, staring up in an effort to comprehend. He could have crushed her with one movement of his leg, one smack of his hand, but she knew that he would not.

It was a shared moment, timeless and endless, during which she understood nothing but Kong. She forgot about where she was, who she was with, even her own identity and memories. For those few moments there was only her and the ape, and nothing else existed.

He turned and walked away. Weaver watched, part of her desperate to run after him. But she knew she could never catch him. Each giant step took him further from her, and a minute later he was gone, her view of him lost behind towering trees and the foliage of this wild landscape.

While she'd been watching Kong, the water buffalo had risen and wandered away. She was alone in the swamp now, and as she caught her breath that place came alive again with sound. The land had held its breath, as had she. Now it was time to live on, and she knew that moment would stay with her forever.

Conrad was waiting for the Iwi villagers to see what they were doing and intervene. At the very least, it would likely prove an awkward confrontation. At worst it might end in violence.

He didn't want either. But right then, he figured that Marlow and his patched-together boat were their best bet for getting to the island's northern shore in time for extraction.

Marlow had been here for a long time and was still alive, and by his own admission that was thanks to the Iwi villagers. There was that to consider, too. Conrad had been in enough war zones to know that a friendly face who knew the lie of the land was priceless.

Still, he had to wonder just how likely it was that this rusted hulk could even sail.

Conrad, Marlow and Slivko were hoisting the engine into place, using a system of levers and pulleys that Marlow said he and Gunpei had designed and built. Most of the pulleys were ungreased, and several of the levers appeared rusted and ready to break.

Nieves sat by and watched, making no effort to help.

Marlow's curiosity knew no limits. He'd been effusive from the moment he'd seen them, but there had still been a shell around him that Conrad had sensed was delicate, and protective. The more he asked about the world outside, the more that shell became fractured. The moment soon came when it broke altogether, and Marlow at last seemed ready to immerse himself in news from beyond his own confined world again.

While they worked, they were filling Marlow in on what he'd missed.

"Hold the phone, Russia was our ally. Now we're at war with 'em?"

"More of a cold war," Conrad said. "No actual shooting."

"So what, you're fighting with nasty words?"

"Something like that." Straining with the weight of the engine, Conrad glared at Nieves. "You do find a way to lend a hand."

"Well, cold war," Marlow said. "No shooting. I guess that's an improvement."

"We also put a man on the moon," Nieves said, coming to help. Reluctantly, from what Conrad could see.

"We did? And brought him back again?"

"Yep, all of 'em."

"Gee whiz." Marlow shook his head. Then he seemed to perk up. "But have the Cubs won a world series?"

"The Cubs?" Slivko said, laughing. "Man, not even close."

"Well at least I haven't missed that," Marlow said. With Nieves's eventual help, they positioned the engine just where Marlow wanted it. "Okay, set her down," the old pilot said. "Slowly. Slowly! This baby's delicate."

They lowered the engine down through the deck and onto its mounting. Conrad was constantly alert for movement on the shoreline or beyond, but the villagers seemed to be staying away. Too trusting, perhaps. Or maybe they knew exactly what he and the others were doing, and were comfortable with the fact it would never work.

"Really think you can get this thing started?" he asked Slivko.

"Pop's a mechanic. If I can't fix this, he'll disown me. If he ever sees me again." Slivko leaned down into the engine compartment and started fiddling.

"Suppose he does get this fixed," Nieves said. "What then? Sail back the way we came? It's the north shore we need to reach, not the south. And that wall seals off the whole rest of the island from us."

"Haven't you seen the river running through it?" Marlow asked, smiling.

"So?" Conrad asked.

"So… there's a hole in that big ol' wall, just at the waterline. High tide, nothing gets through but fish. But at low tide, it's low enough for us to squeeze under."

"I can't believe that's a mistake," Conrad said. "Villagers who could build such an edifice would not have accidentally left an easy access."

"It's not," Marlow said. "Sometimes, the Iwi need to venture further inland."

"Iwi? Weird name."

"It's the closest I can translate what they actually call themselves."

"So when's low tide?" Conrad asked.

"Around daybreak. Which gives us three hours to get to know each other, once Slivko's worked his magic. I camp out in the *Wanderer*. Got myself a nice little loft, even if I do say so."

NINETEEN

Weaver was a listener as much as a watcher. Viewing the world through a lens was one thing, but hearing it was just as important, more so when the people she listened to forgot she was there.

She was setting up a camera tripod to take some creative shots out through the cracks in the spring hall's roof. They were camped out on one of the *Wanderer*'s upper decks, the protective canopy above them split in several places. Through the splits a remarkable display of aurora borealis cast its flickering light, illuminating the night sky above the village and valley.

It was almost peaceful.

San and Brooks sat shoulder to shoulder close by, and Weaver couldn't help overhearing them.

"When I first wrote that Hollow Earth paper, the whole committee laughed out loud," Brooks said.

"Not Randa," San replied.

"Yeah. The one guy in the crowd who took me seriously. Felt good, at the time. Then I thought he was just plain crazy when he said the hollow earth was full of monsters."

"Right," San said. "That, I liked much better as a theory."

Across the deck, Slivko had levelled his portable record player and was lowering a needle into a groove. Crackles, scratches, and then Led Zeppelin strummed into the night.

Marlow was sitting calmly while Nieves helped him shave his extravagant beard. He seemed unimpressed. "What kind of music is this? What happened to swing? Benny Goodman?"

"You're like a time traveller, man," Slivko said. "This is the new sound."

"I hope that thing you call a boat can actually get us upriver and to the north shore in thirty-six hours," Nieves said. "If we miss that window, we're literally up a creek."

"You don't seem like much of an adventurer," Marlow said.

Weaver grinned at that. Brave thing for a man to say to someone holding a razor at his throat.

"I'm an administrator," Nieves said. "And this would be a lot easier with an electric."

"*Electric razor*?" Marlow asked.

Nieves rolled his eyes and carried on shaving. San and Brooks lowered their voices even more. Weaver turned her full attention to the tripod, camera setting, and the shot she was aiming to get.

She didn't see Conrad until he was almost standing beside her.

"The most dangerous places are always the most beautiful," he said, and she nodded, thinking of her encounter with Kong just hours before.

"Going for a long exposure," she said. "But my flashlight broke."

Conrad flicked a lighter open and closed. She flinched back a little, then checked out the lighter he placed in her hand. It bore a Royal Air Force insignia.

"Thanks," she said. "Royal Air Force?"

"You doing that reporter thing on me?"

"Just curious." She smiled.

"My father's," Conrad said. "He tossed it to me from the train as he rolled off to fight the Nazis."

"Did he make it home?" she asked, but when she looked up and saw his face, she knew. "Oh. Sorry."

Conrad looked over to where Marlow was still being shaved and tended by Nieves, chattering all the time, soaking up all the new information he could about the old world he'd left behind for so long.

"Marlow reminds me of him. Could be the jacket.

237

His plane went down outside Hamburg. MIA. I always believed I'd see him again. He was like John Wayne to me, some kind of mythic hero, tall and broad and… In his perfect uniform. Those polished shoes."

"Lose your dad in one war, so you spend the next one trying to bring people back?"

"So you're an analyst as well as a photographer?"

"Just telling you what I see through the lens."

"I guess no one comes home from war," Conrad said. "Not really."

"So is this worth it?" she asked. "All that money they paid you?" Conrad frowned at her, as if disappointed. He knew that she knew it was never about that. "Oh, yeah, I forgot," she said. "You don't get invested in outcomes."

"Almost dying does make you feel alive though, doesn't it?" he said.

"Next you're going to tell me you want to stay here," Weaver said. She felt a pang saying that, as if she was revealing something about herself. Did she want to stay? She didn't think so. But this island was like a drug, and she wanted more and more.

"No," he said. "Not at all. This island belongs to Kong."

"It does," she said, remembering standing in that great ape's shadow. "We shouldn't be here. We have *no right* to be here."

"We better hope this thing can get us away, then," Conrad said.

Weaver turned back to her camera and prepared to take the shot.

Randa was exhausted. Packard had led them on a hard hike through the jungle, with danger all around and death threatening at any moment. And Randa was nowhere near as fit as the soldiers he hiked with. He'd always meant to do something about his weight and lack of physical fitness, and he wished more than ever that he'd done so. His muscles ached, he was soaked with sweat, chafed and bruised and cut, and leaning against a tree, he wasn't sure he could move another step.

Packard was stoking a small fire, readying to prepare some ration packs. Their rest would be brief, he'd said. This was simply refuelling.

"What you're doing…" Randa gasped. "This mission to the crash site… is folly."

Packard glanced up at him then back down at the fire. He said nothing.

"I understand going after your man, but the rest of it? I have a feeling this will not end well." Randa wanted more than anything to be back on mission, gathering evidence and information about the ape and the other incredible creatures on this island, then ensuring that they escaped. That was the absolute priority. Escape, get off the island, and take news of what they had found back to the world.

Back to Monarch.

"You don't like the way I'm handling things, there's the door," Packard said, pointing at the dark jungle around them. He didn't even look up from the fire.

Randa sighed and closed his eyes. He said no more. He needed every moment they were here to catch his breath.

TWENTY

Dawn made the grounded steamer seem less of a ruin and more part of the world. It was as if it had been there always, growing from the rock of the land instead of being washed up decades before, crew already dead or doomed, a place of tragedy and death. Conrad preferred the different interpretation. The grounded ship was almost beautiful, and even where the dawn light probed through holes created by rot and time, it looked like it was meant to be.

He walked along the shore towards the ship, alert for noise and movement around him. Some of the Iwi people watched him passing through the village, their expressions as impassive and calm as ever. He was starting to see a deep knowledge in their eyes rather than the emptiness some of the others suspected. They survive, Marlow had said. To survive for this long in such a place took deep wisdom as well as grit. They carried weapons, but nothing that could hurt the things they had seen, and the other things that lived here. It was knowledge handed down from generation to generation that kept them alive.

He climbed into the ship through one of the holes in its hull and approached that strange central room. Something drew him, and he wasn't quite sure what. He didn't necessarily believe there were answers there, but perhaps the place might prompt the asking of wiser questions.

Besides, Marlow slept aboard the boat, and Conrad had many questions for that old pilot.

Closer to the spring room, he heard the first whispered words. He couldn't quite make them out, because they echoed through the metallic cathedral space, scratching away to nothing. He edged closer and saw Marlow.

Spears of sunlight illuminated the large area, cast down through holes rusted into the ceiling and walls. The well at the centre—a spiritual place for the Iwi, and a hole into depths Conrad suspected contained more than simply shadows—shone with that same strange phosphorescence, moss growing on the rocks glimmering in the fresh day's light.

To one side, Marlow knelt in front of a shrine-like arrangement in one corner. A frayed, tattered Japanese pilot's uniform hung on the wall. A katana sword stood vertically from the shrine, held in place in a carved rock. Sunlight caught it, dazzling, shimmering, almost as if the metal were alive.

Marlow froze, then spoke without turning around. "His name was Gunpei Ikari. We crashed here on July seventh, nineteen forty-four." He stood slowly, aged knees creaking. Still he faced the shrine. "It was the last date that meant anything to either of us. We tried killing each other in the sky, almost succeeded, then we tried again when we were on the ground. But you take away the uniform, and the war, and we were like brothers. That's what we became. True brothers. We swore to never leave the other behind."

Conrad felt a lump in his throat, the burning of emotion the likes of which he hadn't felt for some time. It wasn't that he was an emotionless man, but sometimes it got in the way of the job he had to do. This old pilot had stripped away his defences. Instead of living in the past, he and his enemy had moved on to become what all people aspired to be. Good, honest, loving. Wars were manufactured by empires, and it was down to the single man or woman to end them.

"It's dawn," Conrad said, voice catching. "Let's get you off this island."

Marlow grabbed the sword handle and slowly, carefully, drew it from the shrine. It came out with a whisper like a forgotten voice.

• • •

"You know we really shouldn't be doing this, right?" Brooks asked.

San was staring into the well. Everyone else was down at the dock, quietly preparing the boat for departure. She appeared lost in thought.

"San?"

She blinked, as if stirring herself from some deep introspection. The water in the well seemed to illuminate the huge hold, adding to the sunlight streaming in through rents in the hull. It was a strange place. Brooks didn't like it one bit.

"The year I was born we split the atom," San said. "Just this year we spliced the gene. Everyone believes our knowledge gives us power over nature. That all the greatest mysteries are solved."

"Aren't they in for a big surprise," Brooks quipped nervously. In truth he was *more* than nervous. He was terrified.

San leaned forward and dipped her canteen into the glowing liquid that filled the well.

Where the hell does that come from? Brooks wondered. *Is it even water?* He wasn't about to drink it to find out. In his imagination he dropped into the well and fell, deeper and deeper into the mysterious bowels of this island, his descent lit by the glowing liquid he drifted through, until he reached the bottom and…

He heard a gentle shuffling sound behind him and turned, startled.

One of the village children had entered the chamber and stood watching them, as silent and expressionless as ever. She was a young girl, beautifully dressed, skin already marked with those strange symbols and decorations that camouflaged her against the village surroundings.

She stared.

San slowly screwed the cap onto her canteen and slung it around her neck. Then she put her finger to her lips in the universal sign for silence. *Shhhhh.*

The village girl screamed.

From beyond the chamber and outside the grounded ship, Brooks heard voices raised in response, a strange language he could not hope to understand. It was the first time he had heard the villagers say a word.

"Okay," he said, grabbing San protectively, "now we run!"

Even Conrad wasn't sure whether the boat would work. It was an impressive construction, and he could only marvel at what Marlow and his deceased Japanese brother had achieved during their years marooned here. The boat they'd built—constructed from the ruined gunboat, salvaged parts from their two crashed aircraft, as well as wooden elements from the island and pieces taken from the beached *Wanderer*—was a whole story in itself.

Now, with Slivko finished working on the engine, they were about to find out how that story ended.

Slivko was covered in grease, hands scraped and cut from the many times his wrench and other tools had slipped. He was tightening another of the engine bolts when Conrad heard a sound that made his skin prickle.

The gentle thunder of running feet.

He looked up, stepping past Weaver and Nieves to the boat's railing, and looking towards shore.

Marlow had already seen them.

"Start the boat," Conrad said. He rested his hand on the gun at his hip.

"What is it?" Slivko asked. His head rose above the engine hatch. "Ah, great."

Brooks and San were running for the boat. Behind them, streaming along the shore from the village, were at least thirty villagers. They didn't make a sound, but most of them were carrying spears in a way that Conrad knew meant trouble. These were people on a hunt.

"Oh, goodness," Nieves said. "What's happened?"

"Start the engine!" Conrad snapped at him. He ran

for the bow rope and started untying it. Behind him he heard a mechanical cough, then Slivko shouted in pain from down in the engine hatch.

"Not yet! Gimme a minute here!"

"Sorry!" Nieves said. He was in the cockpit, hand hovering above the engine's ignition switch. Conrad caught Weaver's eye and he nodded towards the stern. She ran that way and started untying the stern docking rope. Even if the engine didn't start, maybe they could push themselves away from shore and float into the river. Problem was, the flow would take them the wrong way.

Brooks and San pounded along the wooden dock and leapt onto the boat. They were both sweating and wide-eyed. Brooks looked petrified.

"What happened?" Weaver asked.

"They saw us taking a sample of water from the well," San said.

Conrad leaned on the railing and drew his pistol, keeping it held down by his leg. For now.

"They know we're trying to leave," Marlow said. "To go back out there."

"Shove off!" Conrad said. "Slivko, we need power!"

"I'm trying!" he shouted from the engine pit. Weaver was at the boat's stern, pushing at the dock with a wooden pole. Marlow did the same at the bow.

The villagers stormed along the dock, and Conrad's heart beat loudly, blood pumping, fear settling in his stomach. He had never been afraid like this before. Usually his enemy was clearly defined—shadows in the trees, screaming men trying to kill him. Here, he did not know his enemy. These people rushing at them with spears at the ready were innocents, and Conrad and his people had invaded their space and abused their trust. His fear wasn't only for himself and his friends, but for these people who had done nothing wrong.

He lifted his pistol and fired three shots into the air above the villagers' heads.

Almost at the same instant, Slivko shouted, "Now!" Nieves pressed the button and the old P-51's engine spluttered into life. Smoke billowed from the engine compartment, and it roared and coughed like an old man waking from a long sleep.

Marlow glanced back at Conrad, his eyes wide and glimmering. It was the first time he'd heard that old engine in decades.

Conrad nodded and kept his eyes on the villagers… but the boat was not moving. There was a central rope securing them to the dock, and it was wrapped around a short post right at the villager's feet.

They stared across at the boat, spears raised, eyes cool and calm. Most of them were looking at San.

Conrad raised the gun again, but he could not bring himself to aim it at these people. He would not, *could* not, shoot first.

Marlow stepped past Conrad and approached the railing, and something about the villagers changed. Conrad couldn't quite make out what it was, but he swore that for a moment the whole world grew quieter.

"Please," Marlow said into the silence. "It's time."

The villagers all focused on Marlow, and after a long moment of silent exchange, they lowered their weapons.

"What's happening?" San asked. She was still clasping her water canteen to her side, the cause of this confrontation in the first place.

"They're letting me go," Marlow said. He drew the katana sword from his belt, lifted it, and smiled at the people who might have been his family for almost three decades. Then he swung the sword down and severed the last rope connecting the boat to the dock.

In their eyes, Conrad saw the villagers smiling back.

"Come on," Marlow said, suddenly excited. "Upriver! Let's get this boat up to speed!" He darted into the wheelhouse and shoved Nieves aside, not unkindly. He was enthused now, piloting the craft he and his friend had made over many years, beaming at them all in the bright dawn light.

The villagers were now moving along the riverbank while the boat chugged towards the wall. The motor was loud, the boat shaking, and Brooks and San were sent below to use the manual pump to try and battle the water gaining ingress through cracks and bolt holes. For now they were keeping the balance, but any more holes would make it a losing battle. Marlow told them it was good for building strength.

Conrad joined Weaver at the bow. She was snapping pictures, as ever, switching between the villagers streaming along the riverbank, to the wall looming ever higher ahead of them.

"I only hope we're going the right way," Weaver said.

"North," Conrad said. "The only way there is."

They continued north, against the gentle flow of the river and towards the massive wall. Entering its shadow gave Conrad a chill.

The villagers were there first, swarming across the wall where it spanned the river and rose high above. The section over the water was wood, great carved tree trunks arching from left and right and meeting in the centre. Conrad could barely comprehend the know-how required to build such a monolithic structure, or the time it must have taken. Centuries, probably. Maybe even longer.

As they neared the wall, he expected Marlow to slow. He and Weaver remained at the bow, and she was using the zoom on her camera to check for the low-tide route beneath the wall that Marlow had alluded to. But there was nothing there.

Just as Conrad began to get worried, he heard a great grinding sound, and a wide spread of the wall's lowest edge began to rise. On the banks the villagers had taken up ropes, two dozen on each, and others were higher up on the wall, hanging onto spurs and turning cogged wheels. The section rose slowly but surely, and as the boat approached he saw Marlow giving one final long, lingering look at the people who had been his adoptive family for so long.

Then the wall swallowed them up, and they passed into virtual darkness.

Conrad felt the sheer weight of the wall above them, almost compressing the air where it pressed down. The water seemed to flow faster here, and when San and Brooks aimed torches at their surroundings they saw heavy spiked structures, thick tree trunks that had been there for generations, with scary shadowy faces formed in the construction.

At last they were spat out the other side. The island opened up before them, river stretching north, mountains and ravines and valleys contouring the land and hiding most of it from view. Much of it was covered in jungle.

Out there also, things that offered only danger.

Behind them the heavy door eased back down. They were in the wild, cut off and on their own once more.

Marlow stood stiffly at the wheel, the captain of this ship.

TWENTY-ONE

Chapman walked.

Part of him had wanted to remain with his crashed Sea Stallion, but it was still smoking, and its impact had stirred up the jungle. Making it back there, he'd been uncomfortable waiting by something so large and so obviously not of this island. Waiting, not knowing if anyone else knew where he was. There were things that might still be making their way to the location to see what had caused the commotion.

And there was the ape, and the squid. Those monstrous things he had seen played on his mind, haunting him with violent memories, and walking went some way to divert his attention from those memories.

An hour out from the crashed chopper, he started talking to himself. He wasn't sure why, because he'd never done it before, but his muttered words were somehow calming. It made his alien surroundings just a little less alien.

"Dear Billy. Sometimes life'll punch you right in the balls." He smiled as he thought of what Billy's reaction would be to those words. He'd be surprised, but he would also laugh. More than anything, Billy was Chapman's reason for surviving.

He heard something behind him, moving back in the shadowy trees. He froze, breath held, listening, watching... nothing. He was skittish and nervous, waiting for something horrific to come for him. So much so that his mind was making ghosts. He didn't want them, didn't need them, and he started talking louder to drown out their chatter.

"Dear Billy, one day—"

His radio buzzed, but when he replied he received only static. He crouched down and tried to adjust the radio, lowering the volume and turning the frequency knobs. He moved over to a fallen log, making himself more comfortable, and placed the radio close to his ear. Ghostly voices came through. Perhaps he didn't really want to know what they had to say.

As he turned the dials, the log beneath him moved.

He froze and looked down. It moved again.

Chapman launched himself from the trunk as it shifted upright, rising high above him, its base digging into the soil as it lifted a heavy weight up into the sunlight overhead.

He staggered backwards, still holding the radio but ignoring the voice crackling through it. Terror took away any hope of understanding. His feet almost tangled in undergrowth, but somehow he remained upright as the giant stick insect lifted itself to its full height.

It must have been twenty feet tall. Its legs were thick and heavily spiked, its head the size of a man, bulbous eyes rolling in different directions as it took in its surroundings. All of its attention rested on him and it faced down at him and hissed. He could smell its breath, and he had smelled death many times before.

Still gripping the radio, Chapman scrambled back the way he'd come. He thought of pulling his pistol, but didn't think it would have any effect on something so huge. The bullets would barely graze its thick carapace. He could not fight this. Panic had gripped him, and flight was the only reaction that made any sense.

The beast kept pace with him easily. Its monstrous legs slammed down around him however fast he ran, and he knew this was a race he could not win.

He tripped and rolled down a slope, smashing against a tree. The wind was knocked from him. *Billy*, he thought. *Oh, Billy, I'm so sorry that I couldn't make it home.*

He grabbed his sealed bag of letters to Billy from his

jacket and pinned it to a tree with a knife. He wrapped a red neckerchief around it, in the vain hope that someone might find it and make sure Billy got to read those words at last. They suddenly meant so much.

Chapman scrambled around to face his fate. Pulling another knife and his pistol, ready to fend off the imminent attack, seemed like a hopeless gesture. But he refused to lie down and die without a fight.

The stick insect punched its legs down either side of his body and leaned in close. Its head was even more horrific this close up, like one of those 50s monster movies given life. Its teeth were long and sharp, and he imagined them piercing him, lifting him so that those powerful jaws could snap him in half with one bite.

He gripped the knife harder. *I'll aim for the eyes*, he thought. *Blind the bastard. Then perhaps—*

The stick insect suddenly froze above him like a fallen tree, almost vanishing into the surroundings again, such was its perfect camouflage.

Seconds later it started backing away.

Chapman kept his breath held. He didn't move. Maybe it couldn't see him when he was still! Maybe it thought he was dead! It backed further away, then turned around and rushed into the trees, gone as quickly as it had appeared.

Moments later Chapman had to question whether he'd even seen the thing at all. He couldn't contain the grin that spread across his face as death stalked away through the jungle, leaving him behind. As if to join in his celebration, the radio buzzed again.

"Chapman, this is Fox Leader, do you read?" It was Packard, sounding desperate.

"Yessir!" Chapman said. "This is Chapman, I copy you, I—"

A shadow consumed him from behind, flowing around the tree he sat against. A coolness washed across him, and he thought it had little to do with the dappled sunlight being shut out from view. This felt like the icy touch of evil.

Chapman turned his head slowly, not wanting to see but compelled to look.

A monster stood behind him. He had never seen anything like it before. It was no known beast, alive or dead, yet it breathed and stared, saliva dripping from its open mouth, eyes wide and unblinking, reflecting his terrified self in their orange glow. Its head was six feet across, much of its vast body still hidden back in the jungle from where it had crept this close to him.

Close enough to touch.

"Chapman?" Packard said.

Chapman dropped the radio and grabbed his dog-tags with both hands.

"Billy," he said.

• • •

Packard sat apart from the rest of his group. Three guards were posted around the small riverside clearing, the rest of them were taking a break and a drink. They all kept their weapons to hand. Since the encounter with the spider and Jammers' horrific death, they could not let their guard down for a second. He tried to keep his voice down low, but now that contact had been made with Chapman, he wished he could reach through the radio and save his friend.

He needed saving. Helpless, horrified, Packard heard Jack Chapman's final agonised screams, and then the sickening crunching sound that marked his end.

He turned away from the group and stared into the jungle as he finally let the signal fade out.

"Sir?" Reles called over. "Anything?"

"Still out of range," Packard said. He packed away the radio and stood, decision made. This would destroy them. And besides, there was still work to be done.

Chapman's death didn't mean that their destination should change.

"Come on, ladies," Packard said. "We got miles to go before we sleep." He watched his men hustle the group together again, efficient, determined, the soldiers he had always wanted them to be.

He was furious. He was grief-stricken. And he knew that their greatest battle was still to come.

TWENTY-TWO

Weaver felt some sadness at leaving the Iwi village behind. Everything on this journey so far had been new, but many of the new images framed in her lens had been terrible or traumatic. The Iwi were not. They were mysterious and enigmatic, and she would have happily spent several weeks staying with them, documenting their lives and existence and building a photographic portrait of this unknown, untouched tribe.

Marlow had lived with them for over three decades, and even he admitted to not understanding much of their history. He admitted that he had always been just a visitor with them, never really belonging.

As the boat worked its way north with Marlow at the helm, she took advantage of the calm moment and checked her equipment. Her used films were sealed in film cartridges, then double-sealed in plastic bags to make sure they didn't get wet. She kept them in a shoulder bag slung tight across her chest. The cameras and lenses were still clean and serviceable, apart from the one lens she'd cracked. She still kept that one tucked away in her bag, just in case it became a last resort.

With a limited supply of film, she had to choose her moment to take pictures. Yet every moment and place on this terrifying, amazing journey seemed picture-worthy. She wandered the boat's deck, framing new moments with each step.

Slivko finally finished levelling his record player, using slivers of wood to prop corners. He lowered the needle on a record, and the first strains of 'Fly Me To The Moon' drifted across the deck.

"Least there's music," Slivko said, glancing up just in time for Weaver to snap his image. He blinked, then looked away. She was used to the guilt of intruding on a moment. Most of the time, she considered it part of her job.

"Slivko," Conrad said. "Remember those things with teeth?"

Slivko looked across the water at the jungle pressed close to the shore and turned down the volume.

"How can you listen to music at a time like this?" Nieves asked. Weaver wondered if everyone found him as annoying as she did. "And why are you carrying that stupid record player, anyway?"

"Calms the nerves, man," Slivko said. "Tunes got me through the Tet Offensive."

Weaver turned away and aimed her camera elsewhere. San approached Brooks and handed him an MCI ration.

"Thanks," he said.

"Thank you. For before. For protecting me when I… you know." She started to open another ration tin.

"Trying, anyway. Lemme get that for you," he said, taking the container. He flipped open a knife and promptly cut his finger as he attempted to open it.

"Allow me," San said, smiling.

"You should see me in the library," Brooks replied, which made San laugh.

Weaver snapped her laughter, and Brooks with his finger to his mouth. It was a moment frozen in time, speaking volumes. The art of what she did was ever-present, but the philosophical impact never ceased to amaze her. People went through life believing that they were constantly on the move, yet she knew that every life was an infinite series of frozen moments. Passing them by with life's riot as a distraction, few people recognised the limitless potential and fascination of these instants.

"Hey, you guys," Marlow said, raising his voice above the music. "So when the man on the moon got up there, did he find the man in the moon?"

"Nah," Nieves said. "Just shadows of lunar dust seas,

higher mountain ranges, that sort of thing. The human brain has a propensity to extrapolate images that don't exist from random images. It's called pareidolia."

"Yeah, well, whatever," Marlow said. "My mother used to tell me the moon was a foolish boy chasing the sun across the sky, forgetting to eat 'til he waned away to nothing."

"That comes from an Inuit myth," San said.

"Myths are the stories we tell to explain things we don't understand," Nieves said.

"Kinda sad when we lose those things to rocket ships and cameras in space," Weaver said, stepping up beside Conrad. She liked him being close. It felt safe.

"Until the myth decides to eat you," Conrad said.

They fell quiet after that, perhaps all remembering the worst parts of their day.

Weaver framed the river ahead of them, jungle on both sides, darkness its destination, and took a picture of their future.

Ever since passing under the wall Conrad had felt nervous. Or rather, even more nervous than before. The others seemed to be enjoying the relative calm aboard Marlow's boat, and the stranded pilot's eccentricities. For a man isolated so long from the world he called home, he seemed largely undamaged. Indeed, rather than just survive he seemed to have flourished. Conrad sensed a deeper sadness in him, but guessed it was more to do with the death of his friend, the man who was once his enemy, than anything else. He'd left a wife and son behind, but this felt so much like another world that their absence was probably remote, like the memory of a fading dream. The Japanese pilot's death must have felt like losing a family for the second time.

Conrad paced the deck keeping watch. Slivko's music played, the scratched records providing a strange soundtrack to their journey. Weaver was at the bow, camera aimed ahead. Occasionally she turned it around to focus on the passengers. She seemed as nervous as him.

"We have no idea what's out there," she said.

"We've got *some* idea. Big bad things."

"Let's just hope we can pass them by."

"Yeah," Conrad said. "The island can't be that big, though."

"Comforting," she said.

Conrad shrugged. It wasn't his job to offer false optimism.

The needle jumped on Slivko's record player. The soldier cursed.

"What do you think will happen when—" Weaver began, and the needle jumped again.

"Choppy waters," Conrad said. He stood and looked

over the bow at the river they were slicing through. The water was heavy with mud from recent rains, but there was very little chop. It was wide and slow here, subject only occasionally to swirls of current.

He looked back at Marlow.

Steering the boat, the pilot was suddenly tense, staring down at the river ahead.

"Hey, try to keep this hulk steady!" Slivko said. "This is Zeppelin, man. You don't want to scratch the Zep."

"The water's not choppy," Marlow said, and Conrad knew that they were in trouble. It was the knowledge in Marlow's eyes that convinced him. They'd hit something.

"Everyone stay alert," Conrad said. "Keep your weapons close."

"Huh?" Nieves said.

The boat jumped, and the record player's needle scratched right across the album. Slivko stood and grabbed his M-16 just as the shape flung itself up and over the starboard railing and curled around his leg. It pulled, he went down, and the boat's forward motion meant that he was instantly dragged towards the stern.

"Help me!" he shouted. He struck the stern railings and his finger squeezed the trigger, sending a volley of shots across the boat to ricochet from the wheelhouse.

"Hard astern!" Conrad shouted. He slid along the deck towards Slivko. Brooks and San were already there, holding the man's arms as the thing wrapped around his leg tried to pull him off and down into the river.

"What the hell is it?" Weaver shouted. She was by his side, having grabbed a machete from a storage locker on deck.

It looked like a snake or a suckerless tentacle, wrapped tight around Slivko's leg and squeezing hard. As the boat slowed its pressure seemed to lessen, but it was still trying to haul Slivko from the deck and down into the water.

Marlow threw the boat into reverse and the engine screamed, smoking as it fought against their forward momentum. The screw bit in and water churned behind them, splashing dark brown and then bright red, and the creature loosened its grip and dropped away. Brooks and San fell back and dragged Slivko with them. He kicked backwards until he was as far from the water as he could get, sat against the wheelhouse, and aimed the M-16 between his feet.

"Marlow?" Conrad called.

"Beats me," he said. "Lots of stuff in this river. Churned it up nice though, eh?"

"It was trying to eat me!" Slivko shouted.

"Nah, don't think so," Marlow said. "Reckon it wanted to pull you in, drown you, then stow your body til it started to rot. Then it'd just pull bits off of you whenever it got hungry. That's how crocs eat, you know."

"What? What?"

"That was no crocodile," Weaver said.

"Sure wasn't," Marlow said. "Keep your eyes peeled, we'll head off any—"

The shapes emerged with barely a splash, several of them leaping up from the river's surface and landing on deck along the starboard side. At first Conrad thought they were long, thin water snakes, a dozen feet long with fine webbed fins and elongated heads ending with small, suckered mouths. Then he saw that they all trailed back into the river.

They met together at a dark mass just below the water's surface.

"Squid!" he shouted. "It's a giant squid!"

That wasn't quite right. The tentacles were strange, not covered with suckers but heavily ridged with muscle. The ragged stump that had first grabbed Slivko was back, spewing blood across the deck.

"Go!" Weaver said, and Marlow leaned down on the throttle.

The creature had learned. This time its limbs were not caught in the spinning screw, but the good hold it had with a few of its tentacles dragged it along with the accelerating boat. Conrad drew his gun and started firing down into the water, then Slivko screamed again.

"Gimme a break!" he shouted, almost manic as he was dragged once again towards the deck's edge.

Weaver started hacking at the tentacle with the machete, careful not to strike Slivko in the leg. The blade seemed to skim from the slick skin, striking the deck and throwing sparks. Brooks held his arm and tried to prevent him being taken, and Conrad looked around for Nieves. The Landsat guy was huddled against the wheelhouse, staring wide-eyed. He'd be no help.

"Where's San?" Conrad asked. "Where the hell is San?" For a second he thought she was gone, and he felt so sad that she'd died without any of them even noticing.

Then she reappeared swinging Marlow's katana sword. It sliced through the tentacle six inches from Slivko's foot, rebounding from the deck with a sweet metallic note and sending the other tentacles into an agonised dance.

Conrad was struck across the face, and he ducked and rolled backwards before the tentacle found purchase around his neck.

"Faster!" he shouted at Marlow.

"I'm giving her all she's got!" Marlow said, and Conrad imagined him screaming it in a Scottish accent. He laughed, almost hysterical, then scrambled to his feet.

Several tentacles were grabbing hold of various parts of the boat, and as they pulled tighter they dragged the body of the beast up out of the water. It broke the surface in a frothing wave, the water churned brown with mud and red with the creature's leaking blood. Conrad grabbed at the railing and looked down, just as the squid—or whatever the hell it was—reared up even further.

He looked it in the eye. Its barbed beak opened as if to laugh at him, or curse.

He shot it in the eye, and the massive fluid sac burst and spewed into the river like a bloody slick.

San sliced at another tentacle and the thing let go, splashing into the water and quickly falling behind them.

"Shit! Shit!" Slivko kicked the parted tentacle from around his leg and watched it fall over the side, leaving a dark red trail behind.

"He sure had the hots for you," Weaver said to Slivko. She stood and nodded her thanks to San, who was still standing with the sword held in both hands. She looked surprised at what she had done.

"Nice swordplay," Conrad said.

"Yeah," San nodded. She stared wide-eyed at the weapon in her hands.

Marlow eased back on the throttle, but didn't slow down too much.

"So what the hell was that?" Conrad asked him.

"Beats me," Marlow said. He shrugged. "Like I said, lots of stuff in this river."

They headed north. Slivko packed away his record player. Their brief moment of respite was over.

TWENTY-THREE

Packard led his men on the hunt for the beast. The fact that not all of them knew that was their mission troubled him a little, but not much. When the time came for him to reveal his intentions, none of his soldiers would object, because they had always followed him into hell, fire and damnation. They always would.

The civilians might not like it. But he was the man in charge, and they had no say. If they didn't like his plan, they were free to leave and make their own way north.

They were all exhausted. The heat sucked energy out of them, soaking them with sweat, draining them of strength, but they forged on. Even Randa, older than the others and less fit, was quietly determined to keep up.

Packard led them, never for a moment letting them see his tiredness. Fury was his fuel. Revenge was his motivator.

When the ground shook, a tingle of anticipation shook him, but he thought, *I'm not ready yet!* If they faced the thing now they would lose. He didn't care whether he lived or died—he was hardly thinking of his own well-being, let alone the others in his command—but he *did* care that the monster died. That was all that mattered in his life.

The beast appeared.

Packard waved everyone down under the trees and behind undergrowth. The giant ape stepped out before them, standing at the edge of the sweeping descent into a wide valley.

He was the size of a mountain. Packard had not been this close before, and he feared the monster might sense his hatred, turn and see him, trample him and his men down into the dirt. He tried to hold it in but it burned, seething behind his eyes and scorching his muscles, urging him to charge shooting and shouting.

I'll bide my time, Packard thought. *I'll have you, you bastard. Just not yet.*

The ape looked down at his feet, examining something on the ground close to where Packard and his group had taken cover. Then Packard saw what it was.

Tracks on the hillside. Deep clawed marks, scratched into the ground by something almost as huge.

The ape snorted and came closer, bending to sniff at the ground. It stood again and followed the tracks to the edge of the valley, pausing for only a moment before performing one huge leap from the ridge line.

Packard ran, leaping over the tracks in the ground and reaching the valley edge in time to see the ape streaking down the side. It held onto trees, swinging its massive weight left and right with a grace that even Packard could not help admiring. It seemed to defy gravity as it descended further down the cliffside, dislodging a pile of boulders that roared down into the darkness.

It paused as quickly as it had begun, crouching low over a crevasse in the ground. Sniffing. Probing with its massive hands.

The ape bellowed, long and loud, looking around as if to find the perpetrators of this carnage.

Packard thought it was one of the seismic charge craters, but there was something else beside it.

The ape stood and edged around a rocky outcropping nearby, bracing its back against the tower and grunting as it started to heave. Its muscles rippled beneath thick fur, chest expanding, and slowly the tower began to topple. The sound was unbelievable, an earthquake echoing back and forth across the valley, as the mountain of rocks tumbled into the crater and the deeper crevasse that had opened beside it.

Sealing something in, Packard thought, and he looked back at the footprints the ape had been examining. He didn't want to know what had made them.

Several loud detonations from down in the valley jerked his head around again, and for a second he thought perhaps one of the choppers had survived after all, and was even now unleashing hell upon the monster. But the sounds came from the monster itself. It thumped its chest, a deep bass rumble that shook trees and reverberated around the valley. Then it started rushing away from them again, pausing now and then to check something at its feet.

Following a trail.

"Let's move out," Packard said. "Next time it might not miss us."

Next time, we'll be bringing the fight to it.

There were no more giant squids or river serpents. Sometimes Weaver saw shapes in the water, but they quickly passed them by. She knew that here, even the appearance of safety was only a facade. Death waited for them beneath every surface.

Following the river upstream led them into a wide marshland, the single route dividing into a dozen tributaries and making navigation more of a case of trial and error. With Conrad steering, Weaver couldn't tear herself away from the bow, because from there she saw everything. Birds she knew and some she did not. Flowers the size of armchairs blooming from lily pads as wide as the boat. Clouds of butterflies no larger than her thumb, flocking together and moving almost like one living creature. Her expertise had always been in conflict—or more accurately, humanity immersed in conflict—but Weaver was quite sure there were as many unclassified organisms here as there were known.

Marlow joined her at the bow. He had taken to strolling the deck of his boat, proud at what he and his friend had made. As he should be. It rattled and leaked, the engine frequently coughed and backfired, and Weaver was convinced that the vessel would fall apart within days, but it was still a marvel.

"So how long have you two been an item?" he asked. It was the last question Weaver had been expecting. She glanced back at Conrad and saw that he'd also heard.

"Eh?" he asked. "We're not…"

"We just met yesterday," Weaver said, saving him from embarrassment.

"Some first date," Conrad said.

"I've got a wife," Marlow said. "*Had* one, anyway. I guess I don't really know which it is anymore. We got hitched just before I was deployed, and she sent me a telegram the day I was shot down. I received it two hours before I took off. She'd just had our baby boy, Hank Junior. I've got a son out there somewhere. A grown man I've never met, who thinks his father died thirty years ago."

Marlow took out a photograph of his wife, delicate now with many years of handling. He held it in his palm and showed Weaver.

"Lemme ask you something, Weaver. Would you wait twenty-eight years for a fella?"

"She probably thinks you're dead," Slivko said from nearby. It was a harsh statement. Weaver glared at him and he shrugged and looked away.

"I don't think so," Conrad said. "People don't give up like that. Mark my words, when you get home, they'll be waiting."

Marlow nodded at Conrad, then stared out over the water again. Weaver saw a perfect shot framed before her—Marlow, the man lost in time; the marshes and jungles, a land that time forgot. She left her camera where it was around her neck and gave him his moment.

"This big flood swallows up a town," Marlow said. "Guy winds up on a roof, water up to his knees, his neighbours come by in a boat and say, 'Hop in, we'll get you outta here.' The guy shakes his head and says, 'No thanks, God will provide.' An hour later and he's up to his neck, when some firemen fly by in a blimp. One of them shouts, 'Grab the rope, we'll save you!' But he shakes his head again and says, 'No thanks, God will provide.' An hour after that and the guy's dead. When he gets to heaven, he's pretty peeved at God for doing him like that. He says, 'I believed in you, I had faith, but you didn't help me!' And God says, 'Help you? I sent a boat and a blimp!'" Marlow laughed softly. "Truth is, I don't expect them to be waiting. Wouldn't blame them either way. All I want is one last chance to see 'em, hold 'em. To me, that'll be as good as Heaven."

"You will," Weaver said. "We're going to make sure of it."

Silence fell across the boat, but it was almost immediately broken by the hiss of a radio.

"Fox Five, come in," Mills said, voice crackling with static. "Is there anyone out there?"

Slivko dived for the radio and snatched it up.

"This is Fox Five, we hear you! We have a boat, we're heading north upriver."

"A boat?" Mills asked. "What kind of boat?"

Slivko looked around, eyes settling on Marlow. "It floats, let's put it that way."

"Roger that, Fox Five," Packard said from the radio. "Sending up a visual from our current position. Stand by."

They watched the skies. Weaver scanned the jungles to either side of the marshland through her telephoto lens, looking from left to right. She saw the flare the same moment as Nieves.

"There!" he shouted, pointing to the left and inland.

"We have visual!" Slivko said.

"Can't get there on the boat," Marlow said. "None of these tributaries goes that way."

"Tell them to hold position," Conrad said to Slivko, steering the boat in to shore. He left the helm and stood beside Weaver and Marlow on the bow. He was readying to move out.

"What're you doing?" Weaver asked.

"I'll go and bring them in. Keep the boat here, moored close to shore. Shouldn't take me more than a couple of hours."

"What if you...?" Weaver frowned. *Something wrong*, she thought. *Something...* The sun had faded. Silence had fallen. Even the movement of the air was strange.

For a split second, everyone froze.

Nieves screamed as a shape swooped down from the jungle canopy at the shore, ripped a taloned claw into his shoulder, and hauled him aloft with a single flap of huge wings.

"Get down!" Conrad shouted, but Weaver and Marlow were already dropping to the deck, Marlow drawing the katana sword.

Conrad and Slivko grabbed their rifles and started firing up into the canopy, their targets shadowy and uncertain. Weaver tried to make out just what had attacked them—she saw wings, claws, vicious beaks, all giving the image of giant vultures.

The thing holding Nieves was tangled in the canopy,

and he was a pale struggling shape, hanging onto a branch as the thing flapped its huge wings and tried to drag him further. The gunfire continued, bullets ripping through leaves and tearing chunks from the trees. She feared that they'd end up shooting Nieves, but then he came apart. That was the only way she could describe what she saw. Part of him went one way, part another, and as the huge winged shape disappeared up through the canopy and away, something splashed into the water twenty feet from the boat.

"Stop shooting!" Marlow shouted. "Quiet!"

The gunfire ceased, echoing away into silence and stillness. Blood was spattered across the deck in several wide arcs. Some still dripped from the heavy leaves overhead.

"What the hell!" Slivko said. "He's just…"

"Gone," Conrad said. He kept his gun ready, cautious and alert.

Weaver could barely believe how quickly it had happened. One second here, the next ripped apart and taken away. A blink between life and death.

It could have been any of them.

"I need to get Packard and his team," Conrad said, reloading his gun. "Get into the middle of the river and moor there, away from the jungle. I'll be back as soon as I can and we'll get out of here."

"You want us to wait here?" Slivko said. "I don't

think so, man. I'm sticking with you."

"Kid's got a point," Marlow said.

"Safety in numbers," San said.

Conrad looked at Weaver, and she nodded. It made sense.

"All right," he said. "Gear up. We're leaving in two minutes."

"Isn't anyone going to say something?" Brooks asked. His voice was shaking, matching his hands. "You know, about…" He glanced skyward. Nobody spoke. Weaver guessed none of them had really known Nieves enough to give him a fitting eulogy.

"He seemed like a good administrator," Marlow said at last.

TWENTY-FOUR

They headed inland. Conrad had taken a compass bearing on the flare, and he paused every few minutes to make sure they were still on course.

He would have much preferred to be on his own. This was his world—navigating through hostile territory, moving in silence, remaining alert in the face of unknown dangers. He had done this many times before. Although the surroundings and perils were different, the methods he used were the same. His bushcraft was his own, developed over years and adapted to suit his own strengths and talents. Bringing the others with him threatened to make all his talents redundant.

He knew, however, that they were safer together. Leaving them alone on the boat might have been to doom them to death. He didn't want that for any of them.

Especially Weaver.

He was already missing the relative comfort of the boat. Heat hung heavy, insects buzzed, plants scratched and irritated bare skin, mysterious rustlings and slower, more measured movement seemed to come from all around. He saw shapes scurrying for cover, and worried that they might be dangerous spiders or disease-laden vermin. Conrad knew more than most how dangerous a jungle could be. This island had to be one of the deadliest places he had ever been, and by far the strangest. Giant apes, giant snakes, giant vultures…

What would come next?

He steered them down into a shallow creek so that they could follow a water course upstream, hoping that the going would be easier. With less foliage to hack their way through, they could move faster towards where Packard and his group were hopefully still waiting for them.

The stream flowed and tumbled along its rough path, splashing from rocks and throwing several small rainbows ahead of them. Conrad remained alert, trying not to get distracted. Dragonflies buzzed across the stream in rough formations, frogs leapt at the marshy edges, and he saw the silvery flashes of fish darting beneath the surface.

Weaver viewed the world through her lens, as usual. He wondered what she'd truly see of this place, and of him, if she was forced to confront it without her glass and plastic safety net.

Something rustled. A bump. He froze, hand held up to halt the rest of the group. There was sound all around—splashing, rustling, bird song and insects buzzing—but something about this sound was different. It was made by something or someone attempting to be quiet.

Conrad lifted his gun and aimed it across the stream at the dense jungle on the other side. A cloud of insects had taken off and were flying in a chaotic, angry mass.

A shape appeared in the shadows. Conrad squeezed the trigger.

The shape became a man, and Colonel Packard stepped out from beneath the cover of trees.

"Colonel Packard." Conrad sighed, remaining alert as others emerged behind Packard.

"You're a sight for sore eyes," Packard said. He almost smiled. "Even you, Miss Weaver."

Slivko and his fellow soldiers greeted each other with shoulder-slaps and banter, relieved to be together again. They still carried the stain of loss in their expressions. Conrad knew that feeling well.

"Thought for sure you'd be monkey food by now, Slivko," Cole said.

"Sorry to get your hopes up, Cole," he replied.

Randa stepped around Packard and splashed across the stream, shaking Brooks's and San's hands.

"I thought you were crazy," Brooks said.

"Yeah, right now I wish I had been," Randa replied. Conrad saw the lie in his eyes. He was delighted at just how right he'd been.

"Me too," Brooks said.

"You aren't hurt?" San asked in Mandarin. Perhaps she thought no one else in the group could understand, but Conrad had spoken the language for years.

"Barely a scratch, dear," Randa replied in the same language.

Marlow had drawn his katana sword at the sounds of rustling, and now he sheathed it and stepped forward towards the soldiers.

"Good to see you, fellas," he said. "New faces sure are a treat."

"Who the hell is this?" Packard asked. He was looking at Marlow like he was something he had stepped in on the sidewalk, and Conrad could have swung for him right then. He'd already marked Packard as arrogant and dangerous. Seemed he was pompous and superior, too.

"Picked up a hitchhiker," Conrad said.

"Lieutenant Hank Marlow, sir. Forty-fifth Pursuit squadron of the Fifteenth Pursuit group out of Wheeler Army Airfield, Hawaii."

"You been here since World War Two?"

"More than half my life," Marlow said.

"I'll be damned," Packard said. "Snap to, Lieutenant!" He saluted.

Marlow snapped a salute back, no longer looking like an old soldier.

"I'm getting him home," Conrad said. "I'm getting *all* of us home. If we follow the river, his boat should take us close to the north shore in time for extraction."

"Good to know," Packard said, nodding and smiling. "But we're not leaving yet."

"Not leaving?" Randa asked. "We need to get away from here, get back home with this information while we still can. It's *important*!"

"I'm not leaving Chapman," Packard said.

"He's still out there?" Conrad asked. "Alive?" He'd assumed that all survivors had gathered together. The idea of one man being out there on his own was awful.

"Last contact was yesterday," Packard said. He pulled out his map and spread it on a rock so that Conrad and others could lean in to see. "He's stayed with his downed Sea Stallion to the west… round about here." He pointed to a spot on the map. Conrad reckoned it was less than two miles from their current location.

"Uh, no," Marlow said. "You do *not* wanna go that way. Trust me on this."

"Why?" Randa asked. "What lives there?"

"Nothing we can't handle," Packard said.

"Like you handled Kong?" Marlow asked.

"The monkey has a name?" Packard said.

"He's an ape, not a monkey. And yes, of course he has a name. Look, if you go there—"

Packard cut Marlow off mid-sentence, advancing on Conrad and talking into his face. "Isn't your job tracking down lost men?" he asked.

Conrad did not back down before Packard's stare. He'd faced men like this before. They were bullies, and deep down all bullies were weak when they were dished some of their own medicine.

But part of what Packard said was right. Conrad could not deny that. He didn't want to leave anyone behind.

"If we reach that position and he isn't there, no wild goose chase," Conrad said. "We make it back here by nightfall. Understood?"

"Loud and clear," Packard said, smiling and turning away. "You heard the man!" he said, louder, and his men started to hustle.

Weaver came to stand by Conrad's shoulder, camera pointed at the soldiers as they shouldered their kit and weapons and prepared to move out.

"Don't forget to remind me that I knew this was a bad idea," he said. Her only answer was to turn and snap a quick photo of his face, close up, as if to record his moment of doubt.

The two groups now one, Conrad felt that they

were one step closer to finally leaving the island that had almost killed them all. Readied, the soldiers and civilians turned to him and waited. He was their tracker, their de-facto leader, and he wasn't the slightest bit comfortable with such a responsibility.

Colonel Packard was on a mission, and nothing would stop him or slow him down. Not even this latest sheer ridge they were being forced to climb.

It was yet another wrinkle in the skin of this freakish island. The going through the jungle was consistently hard, but Conrad always seemed to find the easiest way through. Packard couldn't help but admire the man, even though he would privately admit that there was a tension hanging between them. Whether it was simply a matter of military testosterone or something deeper he wasn't sure. Packard knew he could never trust Conrad completely, but also that was due in some measure to his own ongoing deception. It wasn't Chapman they were going to the Sea Stallion to find. The captain was already dead, his loss as deep and burning in Packard's gut as that of every one of his men who'd died on this island. Packard was a soldier at war, and he needed weapons.

The minute Conrad suspected his deception, Packard knew he'd have a problem. The ex-SAS man exuded an outward calm, even a softness, but that was just to impress the woman photographer. Packard was certain that if the need arose, he'd be the hardest, most brutal killer among them.

As they struggled up the side of the ravine and topped the ridge at last, Packard felt a chill of fear and hopelessness settle in his stomach.

In the valley beyond was a scene of horror. Unlike the rest of the island it was almost denuded of trees, those that remained growing in isolated copses, some of them stripped of leaves and life and standing like lonely gravestones across the landscape. The ground was holed with fissures, and from some of them heavy yellow gases rose from deep down. Here and there the gases were driven upwards with explosive force, intermittent blasts sending siren-sounds at the sky on pillars of boiling steam. In one or two places the glow of volcanic fires scarred the land, open wounds that pulsed with the land's considered heartbeat. Nothing living was visible across the wide valley.

The only things there were dead.

There were many of them, huddled corpses and skeletons large and small, dead creatures piled together in bone pyres, some of them lying or crouching alone in their final moments. Many of the dead were unidentifiable from this distance; smears of grey, white, and brown where skin and hide still clung.

A few were large enough to make out, even from this far away.

Weaver was so stunned that she'd forgotten to lift her camera. They all were. Packard tried to hold in his shock, struggling to shut out the sight, as if to recharge his purpose and refocus on his destination.

"What the hell is this place?" Slivko whispered.

"I've taken enough photos of mass graves to recognise one," Weaver said.

"It's not a grave," Conrad said. "It's a lair."

Packard had been thinking the same. He and the special forces guy swapped a glance, then he took them down from the ridge, eager not to provide a silhouette for anything that might be stalking or hunting them.

Especially not for whatever this lair might belong to.

As they moved down they mounted another small stand of rocks, Conrad steering them through a gap between massive boulders. On the other side he stopped again, staring.

Even Packard experienced a moment of disassociation from the world he knew. The island was strange and dreadful enough, but this was otherworldly, like having a glimpse at an alien heaven never meant to be seen, or an alien hell waiting for them all.

From their new position he could make out two giant ape skeletons. Both seemed larger than the beast Marlow had called Kong, and they had died deaths that even Packard had to admit were sad and mournful. They held each other's skeletal hands.

"Those bones are stripped clean," Conrad said. "They didn't fall here. They were brought here."

"Something's wiping them all out," Randa said.

"Skull Crawlers," San whispered.

"What the hell is a Skull Crawler?" Packard asked.

"Things from beneath," Marlow said. "Devilish beasts, Colonel. You really don't want to know."

"Kong is the last one standing," Brooks said.

"Yeah, well, the crash site should be just beyond this valley," Packard said. *He won't be standing for long,* he thought. *Not if I have my way. I'll leave this island with one more skeleton melting down into its soil.*

"Uh-uh, this place is a real no-no," Marlow said. "We need to go around."

"If we take a longer route, we risk not making it to the northern shore in time," Packard said. "And every moment Chapman's alone is more risk to him."

"We should be going there right now!" the Landsat guy, Steve, said.

"And you're welcome to do that, son," Packard said. "Alone. I'm not leaving Jack out there a minute longer. Who's with me?"

His men glanced around, nervous but not keen to go against their colonel. Reles stared straight ahead across the hellish valley.

"We can make it if we stay together," Conrad said.

Surprised, Packard nodded his thanks to the tracker.

"You heard the man. Stay tight, two columns. Let's move out."

They checked their weapons, then Packard and Conrad led the way down into the valley.

TWENTY-FIVE

Weaver had come to her senses and started using her camera again. It might have been the first time in her career that she'd been so shocked by what she was viewing that she forgot to take a photograph. She was rectifying that now.

As they moved across the hostile, alien landscape, she realised that she needed something to give scale to the images she was recording. She tried concentrating on the people around her, as opposed to simply photographing the remains of these creatures almost beyond imagining.

Brooks and San were collecting samples, tucking rocks into their increasingly heavy rucksacks, filling plastic bags with sand and ash. They seemed unsettled but excited, glancing around like nervous children as they saw things more unusual, exciting, terrifying.

They barely remained in the same place for more than a few seconds.

She framed Randa against a huge skeleton she could not identify and snapped a photo. As she did so, Randa was using his film camera to record the scene. His mouth hung slightly open. She guessed that he was as shocked as them all about how right he'd been.

Conrad paused beside a pile of bones, the remains scattered and splintered. They contained marks that could only have been made by teeth and claws, and in the ground beside him were more claw marks.

Marlow stood beside him and also stared down, terror in his eyes. Weaver assumed they were Skull Crawler marks, and she felt a shiver as she photographed the old pilot.

Cole lit a cigarette. She snapped him with smoke drifting around his face, while in the background a column of coloured steam rose from a vent in the ground. He looked almost serene.

"Cole, what're you doing, man?" Mills said. "Put the cigarette out, we don't have time for that. And what if they smell it?"

Cole stared at his fellow soldier for a moment, then sighed and flicked the butt into a nearby vent.

The explosion was sudden and shocking, a flare of fire blooming from the vent and roaring at the air. Mills stumbled away from the blast and fell onto his back, and Weaver ducked down, catching glimpses of horrific memories—men with burned faces, and children with charred skin.

The fire receded as quickly as it had come, as if sucked back down into the earth.

"Watch those fumes!" Randa shouted. "The whole area's honeycombed with vents, and who knows what's wafting up from below."

Weaver recovered quickly, pleased to see that the soldier was not badly hurt. Shock had thrown him to the ground rather than the force of scouring flames. She snapped a few more shots of Cole helping Mills to his feet, brushing themselves down and checking for any scorched areas. They'd been lucky.

"Listen to the eggheads," Cole muttered.

Weaver smiled and turned away as Conrad led them further across the valley. In places the entire ground was covered in crumbled bones, so that their boots crushed down, crackling over cracked bones and making them even smaller. Perhaps the sand beneath was also the remains of old bones, a generational process that might have been occurring ever since the world began to spin.

She saw a brood of normal-sized vultures resting on a massive skull, heads hunched down as they watched this mysterious group pass. Her camera flashed in the gloom caused by the increasing clouds of steam.

"Mind if I borrow one of those?" Randa asked. His film camera still hung around his neck, but Weaver handed him her flash camera and took out another from her bag. The more photos of this place, the better.

The soldiers moved cautiously, sweeping their guns left and right just as Weaver and Randa moved their cameras. Fear and fascination, weapons and tools.

They passed a long, huge ribcage, Packard leading his men through the hollow space where some unknown creature's insides had once existed. Weaver followed Conrad towards a small lip, the dip beyond hidden until they reached its edge. When she stood beside Conrad she gasped.

They'd seen it from a distance, but close up the giant ape's skull looked even more amazing. It was huge. Much larger than Kong's, she was sure, and she wondered at what might have killed such a massive beast. Past it was the second skull, smaller and scarred by vicious claw marks that might have been the cause of death.

Weaver panned her camera, looking for an angle that would take in the soldiers with the giant skulls behind them. *And there's the book cover*, she thought, clicking off several pictures as the soldiers looked around in wonder and dread.

Something growled. The sound seemed to come from all around, confused by landscape and mist, and Weaver did a quick circle, camera held ready at her chest.

The soldiers scattered, hiding within and around the skulls, gesturing for the civilians to do the same. They aimed their guns into the mist.

Weaver and Conrad ran together, crawling inside the largest skull and peering from a savage wound in its side. The bone was surprisingly smooth and clean, and it smelled of nothing. Whatever might have been left to decay had long since rotted away.

I'm where its brain used to be, she thought, and it was a shattering idea.

Conrad touched her arm and pointed.

A shadow moved against the mist, swirling it into agitated shapes, and then a monster appeared. She had only seen this Skull Crawler before as a wall image, a carved representation with careful colouring in the spring room of the beached wreck. Witnessing it in its full, shocking glory made her skin prickle and her blood run cold.

It was a diabolical merging of newt and Komodo dragon, its scaled skin scarred from ancient conflicts, damp with slime. Spines lined its backbone, several of them snapped off in old battles. Its claws were the length of a human's forearm.

Weaver prayed that Randa did not try to take a picture. The camera she'd lent him had an automatic flash, and she had no doubt it would attract this thing's attention. She could not believe that the soldiers could ever fight it off.

Slowly, its massive mouth unhinged. Its tongue flopped out, long, leathery and scarred. Its stomach heaved, sides sucked in one moment, inflated the next. A heavy drumming sound accompanied the movement as it performed it several more times, and then it brought up the skeletal remains of its last meal.

Two human skeletons, bones ripped apart but skulls and spine stems whole. The skulls were stripped clean, the flesh melted from faces by the monster's stomach acids. A leather belt wrapped some of the bones. A combat boot still contained slick meaty remains.

Weaver slapped her hand across her mouth, biting down on her palm.

The beast shook its head, spattering spit and blood across the ground and the ruins of the more ancient dead. It stalked away, disappearing into the mist with a heavy scampering sound, gone as quickly as it had arrived.

Conrad was already sliding from the skull, knife in his hand and reaching for one of the skulls that had rolled their way.

"What are you doing?" Weaver hissed.

He waved back at her, reached forward, snagged a set of dog tags tangled around the skull's jawbone. He lifted them, paused, then presented them for Weaver's attention.

'Chapman' they read, along with his military number. Weaver frowned, trying to work out what this meant.

"Packard?" she asked.

"Don't tell me you're surprised," Conrad said.

Weaver wasn't sure *what* she was feeling. Could the colonel be lying to them? His major was already dead, consumed, and digested. Their journey towards the crashed Sea Stallion was a wild goose chase.

"Fall in, fall in," Packard said quietly as he and his men emerged from cover. They moved with caution, panning their weapons around them and creating a close perimeter. The colonel stood tall, glaring around to ensure that no one had been lost. His eyes settled on Weaver and Conrad and the human skulls at their feet, and Weaver held her breath. She glanced sidelong at Conrad, but his knife was sheathed, the dog tags already stowed somewhere out of sight.

Packard nodded once, then headed off into the mist. Marlow was close behind, Katana sword still drawn.

Weaver and Conrad followed. She tried to catch his eye, but he was staring at Packard's back, frowning, and giving nothing away.

We've got to confront him, Weaver thought. *He's leading us into danger and we need to know why*. But perhaps doing so whilst making their way through a monster's lair was not the time.

Weaver noticed Randa off to the right, standing

still and scanning the mist for the vanished beast. He had the flash camera she'd lent him raised, panning it left and right like the soldiers holding their weapons. She felt a momentary kinship with Randa, brusque and single-minded though he was. They were both seeking something, committing themselves fully to their quests, and perhaps shutting out the rest of the world in doing so.

"Randa!" Brooks whispered, but his boss didn't seem to hear. He was turning a slow circle, camera at the ready.

"Get over here!" Packard said, louder. Weaver winced at the volume of his voice.

Randa raised a hand in acknowledgment, but as he took his first step, something moved behind him.

Weaver caught her breath. The shape appeared over the top of the smaller of the great Kong skulls, silhouetted against the mist, crawling up and over the skull's curved dome and down towards Randa with barely a sound.

It was the Skull Crawler, its wide reptilian head tilting sideways as if to get a good look at its prey.

Randa turned around slowly and stared right up at it. "Well look at you," he said, and then the monster struck.

It moved fast for such a huge creature, flipping itself over the skull, scooping Randa up in its tail, turning onto its back, and dropping the stunned, silent man into its gaping mouth and swallowing him whole.

San screamed.

As Randa fell he must have triggered the camera's rapid shot function, and he disappeared into the mouth head first, seeing what awaited him. The Skull Crawler's open mouth was illuminated by a flash, and Weaver's last sight of Randa was his legs disappearing between long, cruel teeth.

The camera continued shooting, and the poor man's journey down the creature's gullet was marked with flashes through its translucent skin.

"Get down!" Conrad shouted, grabbing Weaver and pulling her to the bone-strewn ground just as the whole world erupted into a storm of gunfire. After the relative silence it was a shock, and she pressed her hands to her ears, rolling onto her side so that she could still see what was going on.

Conrad was firing his sidearm, switching aim with each shot as the creature circled them in the mist. Only vaguely visible in the haze, the faint flashes that accompanied its shadowy movements must have come from the camera that Randa had been holding. The idea of him swallowed and whole in the creature's gullet, perhaps even still alive for a few seconds more, was both grotesque and fascinating.

Wish I could get that film, she thought.

Several heavy blasts thumped at Weaver through the ground as grenades were lobbed at the circling monster.

"Set up that fifty-cal!" Packard shouted. Weaver saw a flurry of movement as one of the soldiers set up a machine gun atop the cracked skull of what might once have been a triceratops. Bullets seared the air and ricocheted from rock and bone. Tracer rounds probed the mist for the elusive beast, but during occasional pauses in gunfire they all heard the unmistakeable growls, scampering of feet, and crushing of old bones indicating that the Skull Crawler was still out there.

Now that it knew they were there, it would not be leaving.

Conrad and Weaver rushed for cover against one of the Kong skulls as the .50 opened up. Its heavy, devastating fire punched holes through the smoke and mist, the gunner pausing and turning slightly when another camera flash came from elsewhere.

Marlow ran across the clearing, katana sword held in both hands, and it was as if the Skull Crawler was drawn to him. The mist parted and it darted towards the airman, mouth open and teeth dripping a bloody saliva.

Marlow slashed and dived, twisting out of the beast's reach and leaping into an ancient, giant ribcage where San and Brooks were also sheltering. As it turned for him again, a burst of gunfire lashed along its ribcage, wounds bursting open and spraying blood. It writhed and twisted, lashing out with its tail and knocking the .50 cal machine-gunner from his perch. Then it went for Marlow once more, giant mouth snapping open and closed, old rib bones shattering—

—and Marlow leapt forward with the sword held high, slamming it down into the monster's eye.

For a moment the scene froze. Gunfire ceased and faded into echoes, the creature grew still, and the only noise was the sound of broken bone falling around Brooks and San.

Deeper, into its brain! Weaver thought. Marlow caught her eye and she nodded, urging him on.

Then the Skull Crawler opened its real eyes, two feet back along its head from whatever feature Marlow had impaled, and a steady growl rose deep within its throat.

"Gills," San shouted. "It has gills!"

"Write the paper later!" Brooks said, shoving her from the shattered ribcage and away from the monster. Marlow tugged the sword free and went with them as the Skull Crawler thrashed in pain, its head shoving Marlow along so that he went sprawling, stood, and ran again. Old broken bones flew, and a haze of bone dust rose like slow smoke.

"Come on," Conrad said to Weaver. "Stay close!" He skirted around the Kong skulls and she followed, keeping the raging beast to their right as they worked their way around to where the soldiers were gathering. The camera flashes had ceased, and she thought of

Randa deep in the belly of the beast. Surely he was dead by now? Suffocated, or chewed in half as he went down? She hoped so. To still be alive in there, feeling its stomach acids already eating at his skin, knowing what was to come, would surely be the greatest form of torture.

At least he'd died knowing that he'd been right all along, even if one of his theories had come to swallow him whole.

From her right she heard Packard yelling, "Engage! Engage!" and a flash of boiling heat seared her right arm and leg as a flamethrower spewed fire at the Skull Crawler. It shrieked and jerked away from the flames, and she saw the brief look of triumph on the soldiers' faces. But then the monster charged *through* the flames, whipped its tail around, and the stream of fire flipped and roared at the sky as its bearer was pummelled into one of the Kong skulls. The gas canister on his back ruptured and exploded, shattering the skull and sending bone shards whistling through the air like shrapnel.

Weaver dived for cover, landing beside Conrad on a bed of broken bones. Someone screamed. Someone else's scream was cut off by a gurgling, strangled cry. As Conrad pulled her to her feet, she grabbed her camera and snapped off a few blind shots.

The scene was one of chaos: soldiers ran and fired,

but the Skull Crawler appeared unhurt; fires had broken out across the ground and among the skeletons of dead giants. Brooks and San were nowhere to be seen, but Slivko was writhing on the ground with a shard of bone protruding from his torso.

Packard and his men were so focused on battling the beast that they did not see what was happening behind them. The fire from the flamethrower had spread across the half-rotted carcass of some great beast, and out poured a stream of vulture-like birds. They were all talons and fierce beaks, wings beating at the flames, feathered bodies smoking, furious and vicious.

Instead of fleeing the scene of destruction, the birds turned their rage against the soldiers.

"Marlow, your sword!" Conrad shouted. The old airman lobbed his blade, Conrad caught it, and as he lashed out at the attacking bird creatures, Weaver and Marlow followed close behind.

Weaver edged towards Slivko, realising that the bone shard had actually pinned him to the ground. Shouts and shots continued around them, the Skull Crawler somewhere behind.

"Help me!" she shouted, and Marlow was already by her side, holding Slivko's arms as she readied herself. Conrad continued slashing out at the birds whenever they came near, and feathers and blood spattered all around.

"I got you," she said to Slivko, grabbing the bone shard, "but this is gonna hurt."

"It's mainly my jacket," he said. "I think it might have—"

She pulled. Slivko screamed. The heavy splinter of bone she tugged out was smeared with blood, but it looked like a flesh wound across his hip. They'd have to patch it later.

"—just nicked me," Slivko said.

Conrad lowered the bloodied sword and started shooting over Weaver's head.

Weaver ducked and turned to see the Skull Crawler charging towards them. Bullets rattled into its heavily scaled body, some of them finding home and spouting gouts of blood, others ricocheting from scales with sparking puffs of dust. It went on, intent on adding to its meal with the four people before it.

"Get down!" Conrad shouted, shoving Weaver on top of Slivko and Marlow, pulling his father's lighter from his pocket, igniting it and throwing it.

Useless, pointless, Weaver thought, fearing that in his final moment Conrad had resorted to foolish defiance in the face of oncoming death.

Then she saw the lighter spinning towards the small vent in the ground just ahead of the sprinting Skull Crawler, and she understood.

She crouched over Slivko and covered both of their

heads with her arms, just as the vent's gas ignited with a ground-shaking, ear-shattering boom. Heat pulsed across the open ground, singeing the hairs on the back of her neck and legs, and the explosion was accompanied by a high, pained shriek that seemed to split the air in two.

Weaver risked a look and saw the Skull Crawler sprawled across the ground less than thirty feet away. The searing burst of flame had caught it across the side like a blowtorch, blazing into its torso and splitting it open. Superheated insides were spilled across the ground, much of the mess cauterised black. It writhed and groaned, head scraping this way and that, claws scratching messages of pain into the dirt. It was almost pathetic, and Weaver felt a moment of sorrow for this dying beast. It was a hunter and killer, and that was all it knew.

Its movements lessened and she stood and started taking pictures again.

"Nice throw," Weaver said, as she and Conrad helped Slivko to his feet. "Your dad would have been proud."

The shooting had ceased and a spooky, uneasy silence hung over the scene. The dead Skull Crawler's fat spat in the flames. Weaver lifted her camera to take some photos, but then she saw the extent of damage the surge of fire had wrought upon the beast. Its gut was wide open, heavy scaled hide ripped and ruptured ribs scorched to blackened spurs. She had no wish to see what might have been revealed inside its stomach.

The recent meals it had eaten.

Turning away, she closed her eyes and breathed deeply to try and swallow down the puke that threatened. She smelled burning meat and death. It was a smell she had always been at home with, but now it seemed harsher than ever before.

"Rally up, we need to keep moving," Packard said. His remaining soldiers obeyed his orders, keen to be doing something meaningful rather than simply looking at the results of the recent, shattering battle.

There was no time to dig graves for their comrades. Packard collected the dog tags himself.

Weaver took a moment to look around at the scene of devastation and catch her breath. They were all very lucky to still be alive. Conrad had saved them, and she was pleased to hear a few grateful comments from the Sky Devils. Even Packard gave him a curt nod.

The Skull Crawler would add one more, final skeleton to its own valley of bones.

TWENTY-SIX

Packard had seen two more of his men die, but all for a cause: to kill the thing that had first taken them down. To end King Kong. It was his driving force, the fuel that fed his interior fire, and the stench of more death in his nose did nothing to lessen his determination. He had smelled it many times before. This mission had become personal, and the outside world was now very far away. His war had never ended. It had simply shifted focus.

They climbed out of the valley of bones, and on the slopes they entered the jungle once more. Though his troops were traumatised, they still moved with true professionalism, alert to dangers and covering ground silently. Which was more than could have been said for the others.

He heard Marlow stomping towards him from fifty feet away.

"Look, this is crazy," the old pilot said, drawing level with Packard. "You may outrank me, Colonel, but I've been here a helluva lot longer and I'm telling you that thing that just shredded us was the first. And we're on their turf now. We need to turn back toot sweet!"

"Not with Chapman stranded out there," Packard said with true passion. He had almost begun to believe his own lie. "No man left behind."

"He's not," Conrad said. His comment brought the group to a standstill on the wooded slope, sun dappling through the trees, insects buzzing them. The atmosphere was loaded. Packard wondered whether he should have brought the ex-SAS man in on his plans from the beginning. That, or killed him.

"That thing we just killed got him." Conrad held out a set of dog tags on their chain.

Mills took the tags, looked at them for longer than was necessary. Then he passed them on.

"This doesn't change a thing," Packard said. We're still going to that crash site."

"What's at that crash site that you want so badly?" Conrad asked.

"Weapons," Packard said. "Enough to kill it."

"Kong didn't kill Chapman," Conrad said.

Packard pulled a handful of dog tags from inside his jacket and held them out. "But it did kill these men. My men! All dead!"

"No," Marlow said, shaking his head. He looked like someone had just threatened to kill his momma. And Packard had almost started to respect him. "No way," Marlow continued. "You can't kill Kong. He's just trying to protect this island from those things."

"He's right, Colonel," Brooks said. "We can't kill Kong. Those other creatures are the real threat."

"The Skull Crawlers," Marlow said.

"Right," Brooks nodded. "There are more down there. *Lots* more."

"And Kong keeps them in check," San said.

"Take away a species' natural competition and they'll proliferate out of control," Brooks said.

"And they have gills," San said. "Marlow stabbed that thing there when he thought it was an eye."

"Is this a goddamn biology lesson?" Packard asked. He was quickly losing his patience, but he had to be seen as in control. Not raging. Not mad.

"It means they could get off the island," Brooks said.

"Then we'll end them, too," Packard said. "*All* of them. After we bring down that beast you call Kong."

Marlow unsheathed his katana sword with a whisper of leather on steel, and levelled it at Packard's face. "I can't let you do that."

Packard remained still and silent while his men aimed their guns at Marlow. They did so without fuss, but every single one of them meant it. He knew that each trigger was being squeezed to half of its limit. It would take only a twitch from Marlow for a fusillade of shots to be fired, and he would be torn apart.

"Hold it!" Conrad said. "Hold your fire!"

Packard stared from Marlow to Conrad and back again.

"When I was a kid," he said, "it was always the ones that shrunk and ran or stared down at their shoes that got it from the older boys. Maybe that's who you are. Me? I'm the one with a rock in his hand. Ready. And this is one war we will not lose."

"You're nuts," Marlow said. "This is *nuts!*"

Packard moved quickly, ducking down and swinging his rifle around, pounding Marlow heavily in the ribs. Marlow gasped and buckled in pain, dropping his sword and pressing his hands to his stomach as he tried to catch his breath.

Mills darted in and grabbed the blade.

"Please," San said, stepping forward towards the gun-wielding soldiers. "You need to listen to us."

"You're making a mistake," Brooks said, supporting his friend and colleague.

"Your lies got my men killed," Packard said. He clenched his jaw, resisting the urge to lash out at these people, these fools. "*You're* the ones who made a mistake. I'm just putting things right." They'd let their passion for science blind them against harsh realities.

That's why he was here. He was the realist.

"You've lost your mind," Weaver said.

Packard spun and advanced on her, but Conrad had already grabbed her arm, staring at Packard as he said into Weaver's ear, "Not our fight."

Packard stopped and stared them down. He knew that Conrad meant business, and if it came down to it, he would offer a hell of a fight. But now was not the time, and that wasn't what Packard wanted.

What he wanted was still out there somewhere, hiding in one of this damned island's dark places.

"Whose side are you on?" Packard asked Conrad.

"You'll find your Sea Stallion up that ridge," Conrad said, pointing past Packard and neatly avoiding the question. "I'll lead these civilians back to the boat. We'll wait for you there."

Packard couldn't trust the captain, but he could also see no lie in the man's eyes. Conrad wanted these civilians safe, and knew that where Packard was going, what he was doing, was far from safe. Besides, it would get the ex-SAS man out of Packard's hair. That would be a blessing. If they remained together for too long, Packard knew they'd end up fighting for real.

He nodded to Conrad, then turned to his men. "Let's send it to hell."

• • •

As the soldiers followed their colonel, Conrad helped Marlow to his feet, handing him the sword that Mills had dropped. Marlow plucked a handful of leaves and cleaned the blade, then sheathed it, holding onto his bruised ribs. He didn't seem shaken. Conrad wasn't sure a man like this *could* be shaken after everything he'd been through. Not by a human, at least.

"We need to stop them," Marlow said.

"Feel free to try," Conrad said. "He seemed pretty open-minded and friendly. Or let them go, come with me, and maybe we get off this rock."

"You told Packard we'd wait at the boat," Weaver said.

"We do that and *none* of us gets out of here alive." The implication was obvious. It wasn't a decision that Conrad was comfortable with, but it was the only one that made sense.

"You're sure you can do that?" Weaver asked.

"We really don't have much choice," he said. "Packard's gone all Ahab on us, and I don't think anything will change his mind. Come on. Let's move out."

"But Kong—" Marlow began. Conrad cut him off.

"I think Kong can look after himself."

Taking a heading and leading the small group back down the valley side and towards the river, Conrad's doubts began to grow. The giant ape might have spent his life fighting and defeating monsters, and he had the scars to prove that.

He had only just encountered the greatest monster known as Man.

Packard led, and Mills and the others followed. Mills would have followed his colonel pretty much anywhere, and over the past few years they'd been to hell and back together, several times. Now was the first time he was having doubts.

Packard was as cool and calm under pressure as he'd always been, but there was something about his actions that screamed obsession. Logic and good sense had taken leave. As his unit was slowly being whittled down, it was obvious that Packard needed to restrategise, to take into account the fewer soldiers at his command. So why didn't he? Whatever drove him also seemed to blind him. Mills was troubled, but for now he kept his concerns to himself.

They moved across the rugged terrain, making their way up towards the ridge line where the Sea Stallion had crashed. The going was difficult but consistent, with the group making headway through dense undergrowth and beneath the shadowy jungle canopy. They remained alert for dangers known and unknown. Recent events had shown them they had to be prepared for anything.

Mills wondered whether any of them were destined

to make it home. That idea had crossed his mind many times before, but usually when facing an enemy they all knew and understood, to some extent at least. Contemplating his own death was part of what it meant to be a soldier, but he'd always succeeded in keeping those ideas remote from his actions, not something that might interrupt or distract. This was different. Thinking about their possible annihilation by some unknown creature, in an unknown place, was horrific.

No one would ever find out what had happened to them. In the cruel jungles and fields of Vietnam, at least the news and circumstances of your death would be transmitted home. You died with honour. Here, he might cease to exist without his death impacting the world at all.

They remained quiet, with communications kept to a bare, whispered minimum. When the slope became steeper and they had to use their hands to pull on roots and trailing plants, several men at a time would remain motionless, weapons trained above and below them. Then they changed position, those who had climbed now standing guard while others scrambled up. They made good progress that way, and soon they were nearing the long ridge line.

Close to the ridge line and the crashed Sea Stallion, Mills saw a white object pinned to a tree slightly away from their trail. He worked his way across to it, glancing back at his fellow soldiers and making sure he wasn't straying too far. Cole caught his eye and Mills nodded, acknowledging that he wouldn't be long.

He knew what they were before he touched them. He pulled the knife from the tree and plucked the impaled pages from the blade. He held up the letters for Cole to see. Cole raised an eyebrow, then turned away and continued up towards the ridge.

"Dear Billy," Mills said to himself, "your father was one of the best." He followed Cole and the others, shoving the letters into a pocket inside his shirt and slipping the knife into his belt. "I'll get these letters back to you," he whispered.

They moved on and Mills took up the tail position. He glanced back every few seconds, making sure no one or nothing was following them. He hated bringing up the rear, but knew it was a position they had to share.

In Vietnam he'd been on a reconnaissance patrol with nineteen other men. Five days out, with heavy rain blurring their vision and supplies running low, their captain was trying to lead them to a pre-arranged LZ. As night fell Mills was in the middle of the line of troops, helping to carry an injured man on a stretcher. It was hard going. By the time they reached the LZ the following morning and heard the Hueys coming in to take them out, Mills was the last man in the patrol, and everyone behind him had vanished.

The jungle had swallowed up seven men. They were never found.

He refused to let that happen to him now. This jungle was more dangerous than any he had ever encountered. A tree trunk might be a creature's leg. A rustling in the shadows could manifest into a swarm of flesh-eating flying monsters. Anything could be hiding just out of sight, and something probably was. He held in his fear and kept his senses alert.

Mills smelled the crash site before they saw it. The stench of leaking aviation fuel was almost overpowering. Luckily there had been no fire. If there had, the amount of armaments on the Sea Stallion would have blown out the side of this hill, taking with it everything they had come here to retrieve.

Pieces of the wrecked aircraft were strewn around the main fuselage. Trees had fallen, others bore scars from detached rotors. The crash site was large, and the remains of the successfully crash-landed helicopter was a sad testament to Chapman's final moments on this earth.

Mills approached the helicopter and saw the dead co-pilot's body, still strapped into his seat. He was already stinking of decay. Something had eaten his eyes.

"Over here," Cole said. He was looking down at his feet thirty feet away. Another body. "Must've been thrown out in the crash."

"Bury them," Packard said. His voice was strained with grief and rage. "We bury our dead, then kill the beast that killed them."

Mills helped. They dug shallow graves and heaved the bodies inside, trying to ignore the damage done to their hardening flesh by creatures of the jungle. When they dragged the co-pilot across to the grave, a black scuttling shape fell from the open wound in his chest and tried to run. Cole stomped on it. It took three more stamps to burst the spider's hard body. He ground it into the soil.

They shovelled dirt into the graves and then stood back, sweating and sad in the heavy heat. They'd buried too many men in shallow graves on the jungle floor. Reles planted two rough crosses made of tied sticks above the graves and hung the dead men's dog tags around them.

Packard stepped forward with another cross and pushed it into the ground between the graves, hanging Chapman's dog tags from it. His body nowhere to be found, it was as if the captain shared these graves with his crewmen.

"These men didn't die in vain," Packard said. "Nor will their deaths, or those of the other men lost on this island, go unanswered." He spoke quietly, but Mills and everyone else heard the passion in his words.

They stood motionless and silent for a while, silently saying goodbye to their friends.

It was Packard who broke the silence.

"Let's kill the monster," he said. "Rescue as much ordnance as you can. Pile it up. We'll see what we've got, then formulate a plan."

Mills, Cole, Reles and the others approached the downed helicopter and started delving inside. Dusk was falling, and the light quality was fading. They had to hustle.

"What do you think about this?" Mills asked quietly as they worked. The aircraft's contents had been disturbed in the crash, but the loadmaster on the ship had done his job well, and most of the weapons were still safety stowed.

"Old man's got a plan," Reles said. "We follow it."

"Cole?" Mills asked.

"You're asking me like you want me to disagree with him," Cole said, tugging at one of the napalm barrels. "Ain't gonna do that."

Mills helped Cole with the barrel.

"So what about you?" Reles asked.

"We've never faced anything like this before," said Mills. "If the colonel suggested we'd win this war by jumping from a cliff, would you? That's what this is."

"He's always been there at the bottom to catch us," Cole replied.

"Yeah," Mills agreed.

Half an hour later they stood in a rough circle

around the pile of weaponry they'd extracted from the wreck, and Mills felt the hairs on the back of his neck prickling. Even he hadn't realised just how much heat they were carrying. There was enough shit here to take on and defeat a small country.

Packard looked grim but satisfied as he surveyed the neatly stacked equipment.

"Those seismic charges seemed to get the thing's attention last time," he said. "Mills, Cole, prep that ordnance."

"Where are we going to set the ambush, sir?" Cole asked.

"That lake we passed in the valley bottom," Packard said. "Flat ground, good cover, decent vantage points. Any thoughts?"

Nobody spoke. No one offered any criticisms. If any of them were doubting what they were doing, they kept quiet.

Mills and Cole set to work preparing the seismic charges for setting and priming. Mills had followed orders his whole life, and he believed that was what made him a good soldier. Whatever doubts he might harbour over what they were about to do, Reles and Cole were right. Now was not the time to start questioning their colonel.

A good soldier didn't do that.

TWENTY-SEVEN

They moved everything down to the lake. It was difficult work, even though it was mostly downhill. The napalm barrels could be rolled, their descents controlled with ropes, but the evening heat was intense, and the work was backbreaking. Their food rations were dwindling, and Mills didn't feel he could trust any of the berries or nuts they'd seen growing on the island. The animals here were inimical to man, it only followed that the plant life would be too.

"Night's falling!" Packard said. "Hurry it up. We don't have long."

They went to work setting their traps. They were experienced at setting booby traps, but not for an enemy so large. They worked on the idea that all the basics were the same, all it took was more firepower.

With everything done and the sun dipping to the

horizon, they settled into their assigned positions, checked their weapons, and waited.

"You think he's losing it," Cole said from Mills's right. It was not a question.

"It's not up to me to doubt the old man's orders," Mills said. They only ever called Packard 'old man' when he couldn't hear. He wasn't even that old, but he had at least twenty years on all of them.

"Still," Cole said. Silence fell for a while.

"So what do you think?" Mills asked at last.

Cole shrugged. He didn't reply.

Mills looked across the clearing by the lake shore at Packard, sitting quietly between two large piles of fuel-soaked sticks and branches. *Losing it?* he thought. *I think it's already lost. But I'd follow him to the ends of the earth.*

Looking around, the idea settled that they were already there.

Conrad couldn't bear admitting it to himself, but he was lost. Somewhere in the past half an hour they'd left the route he'd intended taking, and now there was a steep slope rising up on their left, a fast-flowing stream to their right. He didn't recognise either of them. It stood to reason that following the stream would take them back to the river and Marlow's boat, but that was easier said than done. Not far from where they stood, the stream turned into a torrent, entering a narrow canyon with no safe way through. The water became so violent that it threw up a mist that drifted back to soak them, diffracting the setting sun and making false rainbow promises of hope and beauty.

"Get off this rock alive, huh?" Weaver asked as she stood by his side. At least she was good enough to keep her voice low.

"Sarcasm isn't a survival skill," he gave back. He looked around them, spotting what might have been an easy route up the steep slope. Once up there he'd be able to take a bearing from the setting sun and determine which way they needed to go.

"Stay here," he said to the group. "I need to get up top." He remembered the last time he'd done something like this, the snake he'd come across. Such encounters would not always end in his favour.

Most of them nodded, seeming only too pleased to take a rest. As he headed into the mist and started climbing, he sensed someone behind him.

"Wait up!" Weaver said. She held her camera in one hand, using the other to grab onto branches and roots. As he glanced back at her she took a quick snap of him from down below. Probably not his best angle.

Conrad smiled. He was pleased for her company.

They headed up the slope, and as dusk fell it became

even steeper. What had looked like a low ridge seemed to grow the higher they climbed. A fall would not be too dangerous, because the slope was so heavily overgrown with hardy trees and shrubs, but the plant growth made the going hard and slow. Their physical conditions didn't help. Conrad was thirsty and hungry, and he knew that if he was tired, then the others would be close to exhaustion.

He and Weaver helped each other up the slope, and eventually they reached the ridge line above, falling on their backs and breathing heavily with exertion. After a couple of minutes Conrad tried to look down below to see how the others were faring, but they were out of sight behind the sloping mass of trees. Even if they'd lit a fire he didn't think he'd be able to see it from this high up.

Weaver nudged him, turned, and pointed out over the landscape. To their right the setting sun was bleeding across the primeval horizon, and the moon was already out, casting a silver snake across the land perhaps a mile to the south.

"There," Conrad said. "The river. Not far to go now."

Weaver started snapping pictures.

Conrad froze. He opened his mouth to breathe out, trying to figure out just what he'd sensed, heard, or smelled on the air.

Weaver raised an eyebrow. He held up one hand. *Wait*.

A stillness settled around them, a heavy silence, as if all jungle sounds were being absorbed by something close by. Something huge.

Kong's head rose before them, breath misting the air, his eyes fixed on them both as he pulled himself easily up the other side of the ridge line.

Conrad had never seen anything so magnificent, nor felt so miniscule. Beneath this creature's gaze he was a whisper of his former self, all memory and experience wiped away as he faced the undisputed king of this island.

Weaver stumbled back and he caught her arm, felt her galloping pulse as he pulled her to his side and they shared comfort in contact. *We're really seeing this*, he thought. He could smell the giant ape and feel his heat. He was more real than anything Conrad had ever seen or known before.

Kong moved closer as he stared at them, frowning as if in concentration. Closer, closer, his breath washed over them. Conrad could feel the beast's warmth, and hear his booming heartbeat. He had a sudden shocking image of the ape's mouth yawning open and him sucking them in, drawing a breath that would drag them from their feet and down into his monstrous stomach. He remembered Randa slipping down the Skull Crawler's throat, the flash of his camera marking his progress through the monster's thin amphibian skin.

Would he and Weaver know the same feeling? Would they survive long enough to be squeezed into Kong's gut with the remains of his last meal, a stew of acid and diced flesh?

Even as his fears traced cool fingers down his spine, everything changed.

Weaver took a step forward, reached out, and touched Kong. Her fingertips brushed the heavily textured, knotted skin of his nose. She pressed her hand flat against him. Her breath was held and for a while it was just her and Kong, beast and woman, a connection across aeons of evolution. The rest of the world seemed to revolve around them, and Conrad felt very small and far away. Time ceased making sense.

In the distance, a heavy boom thumped through the air. Conrad knew that noise. He'd heard its like far too many times before, and Kong's reaction only confirmed his fears.

He dropped down and back, moving almost silently for such a massive beast. One moment he was there, the next he was gone, vanishing back and down into the evening mist shrouding the valley.

Weaver was left with her hand out and fingers splayed, still touching the memory of Kong.

Another explosion sounded from far away.

"They're trying to draw him out," Conrad said.

"They don't know what they're doing," Weaver said,

her voice almost dreamy. She lowered her hand and turned to look at him. "Conrad, they have no idea. We can't let them. We can't!"

"We won't," he said. "Come on." He turned and headed back down from the ridge, Weaver following him. They scampered quickly, barely thinking about hand- or footholds, grabbing onto trees and roots, vines and wild shrubs, clambering over rocks and jumping across cracks in the steep valley wall. Conrad felt his heart pounding with wonder and dread at what he had seen, and what he knew was about to happen.

He felt more explosive impacts through the ground, the noise shielded by the mass of the ridge, but the shockwaves travelled across the island, ripples calling Kong to his possible doom. Packard and his soldiers had failed to take him down that first time with the helicopters, but they'd been unprepared, caught off guard.

This time might well be different.

"Conrad," Weaver said when they were a short way from the camp. She grabbed his arm and held him back, pulling so that he turned to face her. They stood face to face. It felt like they'd known each other for years, not days. "I feel... changed," she said.

Conrad nodded. He knew what she meant. Going up that hill had been an attempt to find out where they were and navigate a safe way off the island. Coming down again, everything felt different.

"We've got to help," she said. "That's what you do, isn't it? Help people?"

"I've killed a few, too," he said. He wasn't sure why he'd spoken so frankly. It felt harsh, but Weaver didn't seem fazed.

"A few?" she asked.

"More than a few."

"And that's why you save people now."

"I do it because I'm good at it. But... I don't save everyone. There was this girl, Jenny. We rescued her, and we were bringing her out when she was shot in the head." He found it difficult to continue. He'd never talked to anyone about Jenny, not the friends he still had in the services, not the women he occasionally spent one night with, talking into the early hours knowing they'd never see each other again.

"You blame yourself," she said.

"Of course not," Conrad said, feeling the lie burn on his face. It was such an obvious lie that to admit the truth would have felt more so. "What about you?"

"Me?"

Conrad nodded past her up the hill they'd just descended. *Why do you need to save him?* he wanted to ask.

"My father," Weaver said. "He was a good man, but never someone I could impress. I think... he was trying to make me the person he wished he'd been, but

I could never live up to that."

"So you remove yourself from the world so you can't fail anymore."

"Partly," she said. "And I follow all the bad stuff because…"

"It makes you feel like a good person."

Weaver shrugged. "I don't think he'd be proud."

"So stop trying to please him," Conrad said. "Start to please yourself."

"We *have* to help Kong!"

"We will," Conrad said. Neither of them had a choice.

They moved off to find the others. Conrad eased back as they approached, knowing that they'd be on edge. As they emerged from the shadows, Brooks lowered a big branch he'd been wielding, relief evident on his face.

"Did you see the river?" he asked.

Conrad tried to speak but could not. Everything before him—the people, the place, the fear on their faces, the shadows crowding in—seemed so false set against what they had so recently witnessed.

Out of all of them, Marlow understood. "They saw Kong," he said.

"What's he talking about?" Brooks asked. "Which way are we going?"

"You three need to get back to the boat," Conrad

said, pointing up the slope they'd just descended. "That way, over the top and down to the river. It's getting dark, but you have to keep moving. Use your torches. Treat every shadow as a threat, and take it slow. Wait for us until dawn. If we're not back by then, you go."

"You don't have to twist my arm," Brooks said.

"Where are you two going?" Marlow asked Conrad and Weaver.

"We're going to save King Kong," Conrad said.

Marlow shook his head. "Not without me, pal. Not without me."

Conrad nodded. Marlow knew what he and Weaver had faced, understood what they were feeling. Besides, he knew this island better than any of them.

In the growing darkness, with distant explosions reverberating like thunder, the three of them set out into the heart of the island.

TWENTY-EIGHT

This is it, Packard thought. *This is my moment. This is my time. This is my world.*

He sat shrouded in shadows, motionless and alert to movement and danger, while in the darkening distance fires burned and explosions flowered and faded once again. He was a man used to conflict. He could already smell the faint trace of smoke on the air, and it settled his nerves and calmed his galloping heart. Violence was his drug, fire his fuel.

He waited, knowing that everything was drawing closer. Kong. The fight. The end; for one of them or the other.

He could hardly wait.

"Fox Leader to Fox Two," he said into his radio. "Ignite secondary charges."

Several more explosions erupted closer to his

hiding place, flashing across the canyon and the lake at its base. The echoes reverberated back and forth, sounding like a living thing voicing its displeasure. As the explosions and echoes faded away, Packard held his breath as he waited to see whether it had worked.

Come on, monster, he thought. *Come to me, Kong.*

He looked around the clearing at the places where his men were hiding. He knew where they were but could see none of them. They knew their business.

In the distance he heard another dull impact.

"Fox Two?" he muttered into his radio. "That you?"

"Negative. All our charges are expended. That's not us."

"Then it's him. Get ready, everyone. Target approaching."

Another boom echoed in, then another, and a shadow danced on the canyon wall on the far side of the lake, thrown by moonlight and the guttering fires from seismic charges. The shape was humanoid, hunched and huge. He had taken the bait.

Packard hefted the torch he'd made and sparked it with his lighter. It flared alight and he squinted against the sudden glare. He touched it to the piled branches on either side and flinched back when they both ignited, fuel-soaked timbers spitting and crackling as the flames consumed them.

He stared ahead across the lake, just as several trees

close to the shore were sent splintered and torn into the water.

And there he stood, the mighty Kong, come to try and finish what he had begun.

"I'm ready for you this time," Packard muttered. "Come to me, you son of a bitch."

Kong roared and pounded his chest. The sound it made was as loud as the seismic charges, and Packard saw moonlight dancing across the lake as its impact drove ripples across the water's surface. His hand tightened on the flaming torch, but his resolve did not waver. The ape was doing exactly what he'd intended.

He charged into the lake and started splashing his way across, sending six-foot waves in confused patterns to surge against every shore. The water came up to his ankles, then his knees, as the animal moved incredibly quickly through the water.

Packard stepped forward as if to meet the charging beast. He could feel his men around him watching, and with his free hand he signalled for them to stay low and hidden. If Kong sensed anything of an ambush he might back off and come for them another way.

They hadn't planned for that.

As it was, Packard's plan worked perfectly. As Kong reached the centre of the lake, Packard swung his hand back and hefted the torch overarm, out across the water.

Kong paused, and perhaps for a moment Packard saw understanding in his eyes. He hoped so. He hoped the monster had some inkling of the agony about to engulf it.

The napalm spread in the lake erupted into white-hot flames, encircling the giant ape. He screamed and thumped his chest, smashing his huge fists down into the water in an attempt to douse the flames. It succeeded only in spreading the fire further across the surface and splashing it up into his fur. His shadow performed a jagged dance as the fires cast his silhouette in a dozen directions, and Packard grinned as he saw flames licking against the ape's fur.

"Kill it," he said.

His remaining men—Mills, Slivko, Reles, Cole, and Landsat Steve—started shooting at the huge beast, concentrating their fire on his head. When their mags were empty they reloaded and fired again, Cole using his grenade launcher to fire grenades out over the blazing water. The cacophony of sound was a concerto to Packard's ears, and Kong's roar of pain made it sublime.

The colonel added to the maelstrom of hot lead, firing his rifle at the beast's head, picking his shots, aiming for the eyes. Kong's hide must have been inches thick, his flesh and blubber more than dense enough to swallow a million bullets, but if they could put some rounds through his eyes and into his brain…

The ape stormed forward, wading through burning water, brushing flames aside, coming for the shore.

Packard paused, doubting his plan for the first time. Then he continued firing.

Kong emerged from the lake with blazing napalm sticking to him in a dozen places, flickering across his body like dancing clothing. His roar was rage and pain as he flailed towards Landsat Steve, and Packard watched in awe as the ape fell forwards and crushed the man from existence. Kong landed on his front, the impact knocking the other men from their feet, uprooting trees, and sending a huge wave back across the lake, burning napalm rolling in complex, beautiful patterns.

They found their feet again and drew close around Packard, guns trained on the fallen giant. But he was not dead yet.

His breath was laboured and uneven. His panicked heartbeat pounded at the ground. Fires still sizzled across his body, fur as thick as tree branches shrivelling and crackling. The stench of burning flesh was almost overpowering. It reminded Packard of 'Nam.

"Men, you're looking at a relic of a bygone era," he said. "We brought it down and now we have the privilege of finishing the job. Place those charges. It's time to kill Kong."

The surviving Sky Devils started to move in, cautious

and afraid, carrying the charges that would blow holes in the fallen giant's shivering body. Reles carried the final three seismic charges, and he lobbed them from a distance, his aim true. They landed beside Kong's head where it rested on the ground. The ape blinked slowly, eyes watering heavily. If he had any inkling of what these objects meant, he did not show it.

As the other men stood guard, Reles unwound a wire as he backed away from Kong. He reached Packard and handed him the wire. The colonel nodded his thanks, started connecting the wire to the detonator, and already he was seeing the effect of the explosions in his mind's eye. He would leave another dead enemy behind, and over time Kong would rot and his skeleton would stand as testimony to the brave men who had killed him.

"Packard, don't do it!" The voice came from behind and he recognised it instantly. Conrad. He should have expected the ex-SAS man to appear at some point. Packard hadn't trusted him from the start.

As he turned around, his Sky Devils all spread and aimed their rifles at Conrad. He was pointing a pistol at Packard's torso. The colonel smiled, feeling relaxed and in control. He was at the centre of things, and that gave him the perfect edge.

"Conrad," he said. "I'll give you three seconds."

"I asked you people nicely, last time," Marlow said.

He'd approached silently, and now he was standing behind Reles and pressing the tip of his sword to the man's back. If Packard had ever doubted him, Marlow had now revealed himself to be just as much of a fighter as the rest of them.

Cole and Mills turned their weapons against Marlow. Reles, eyes wide, kept his aim on Conrad, along with Slivko. It was a stand-off, and Packard knew that he had the balls to see it through.

"We don't want a fight here, Packard," Conrad said.

"That thing brought us down," Packard said. "Killed our men!"

"You brought the war to Kong," Marlow said.

"It's not a war at all," Conrad said, aim never wavering. "Kong was just defending his territory. Your job, Packard, is to bring these men back home."

"Not without its head," he whispered, his words carrying to everyone.

"You're not thinking clearly," Conrad said. He took a step closer and the tension built, weapon barrels fixed on targets, Marlow's sword twitching and eliciting a sharp intake of breath from Reles.

We're one eye-blink away from violence, Packard realised, and that was always the time when he felt most alive.

"We're soldiers," he said. "We do the dirty work so that our wives and children don't have to cower scared.

They shouldn't even have to know that a thing like this exists."

"You've lost your mind," Conrad said.

Packard glared at him for a moment, then continued wiring the detonator.

"Put it down!" Conrad snapped.

"You're gonna have to shoot me, Captain."

"Stop!" The voice came from behind him and Packard rolled his eyes. He should have known that where Conrad was, Weaver would be close behind.

But it was not the group of men she approached. She sprinted past them towards the fallen ape, standing less than ten feet from his face and the explosive that would soon blow it off. His eyes fluttered open and a heavy, low rumble came from somewhere deep in his chest.

While everyone else watched the woman, Packard pressed the last wire between his thumb and the point on the detonator. One twist of his hand and it would go off.

"If you kill him, you kill me," Weaver said.

"Get her out of there," Packard said to Reles. Eyes wide, Reles glanced across at Weaver, while Marlow still pressed the sword against his back. One move and he could be gutted, if Marlow had it in him to do so. None of them could predict. He'd been marooned here for so long, the sun might have fried his brain.

"Packard, last warning," Conrad said. "Put it down!"

"Soldier, I am ordering you," Packard said to Reles. He looked at Weaver. "Move. I don't want to kill you, but—"

"I've shot nothing but destruction and dead bodies for the last six years," Weaver said, backing even close to the ape's head. "I know you've lived in it, Packard. But there's more. It existed before us and it'll be here long after we're gone. Don't do something that accomplished nothing. Don't kill just because you can."

"Put it down, sir." That was Slivko. And even before Packard turned his way, he knew what the soldier was doing.

Aiming his rifle as his commanding officer.

"Son," he said, but then he looked around at his other men and saw uncertainty working beneath their expressions, too. Reles was the first to lower his gun. Cole followed. Then Mills, his face showing vague disgust.

"Come on, Colonel," Conrad said. "It's over."

Every sinew of Packard's body, every instinct he had, urged him to fight against his men's betrayal and strive to achieve his aim. One twitch of his hand and the beast would die, the woman would die. And so would he.

He knew that a moment's hesitation could change his

world, and so it did. His soldier's mind was convinced, but his natural fear of the void held his hand still.

The surface of the lake rippled and the ground began to shake as something broke the water's surface far out. A screech ripped the sky. A chill went through Packard as deep as his soul, like something unseen drawing a claw down his back and parting the skin.

"The big one," Marlow said. "The Skull Devil. It knows he's down!"

"Fall back!" Conrad shouted. "Go. Go!"

The fearful men and the woman ran, but Packard stood his ground. He hadn't come this far to run. He hadn't gone through everything to simply fail. He stared out over the lake, detonator still clasped in his right hand.

"Colonel! Sir!" Conrad shouted, but he ignored him. *Let them run*, Packard thought. *They don't deserve to die here with me.*

A geyser of water erupted from the lake and powered into the sky, burning napalm splashing up with it and lighting the heavens. Rising beneath the geyser, as if pushing it up into the sky, rose the glistening mass of a creature the likes of which Packard could have never imagined. It was huge, its mass even greater than Kong's. Snake-like, reptilian, its head was the size of a small house, body long and supported on several strange, flexible limbs. The Skull Devil's eyes burned, perhaps reflecting the fires, perhaps bearing some diabolical light of their own. Its mouth was surely the gateway to hell.

Sensing movement to his right, Packard turned towards Kong. The ape was lifting his head, glaring at Packard and then past him at the monster rising at the centre of the lake.

Packard lifted the detonator as if to show it to Kong. *My last act is to take you to hell.*

"You mother—"

Before Packard could react, Kong's fist fell, shutting out the sky and the stars, the lake and the fires, and then finally ending everything.

"Packard," Weaver said, but there was nothing of the man left. She could not mourn his loss. He was an obsessive driven by blood and conflict. Like many such men he'd died ingloriously, ground into the soil beneath Kong's fist.

What she could do was wonder at Kong's strength and resilience. Here was pure power in physical form, machine-gunned and set aflame, now rising again to combat his one true enemy. He pushed down, levering himself upright and turning at the same time towards the looming Skull Devil. They faced each other, Kong on the shore, the monster in the lake surrounded by floating fire, like two mountains drawing each other with a terrible gravity.

Weaver lifted her camera and framed the shot just as the beasts rushed each other, collided, and crashed together with a ground-shaking impact.

Conrad grabbed her arm and tugged her back into the tree line, and for a while Weaver staggered back and tried to bring her camera to bear.

"We have got to go!" he shouted into her ear, even his raised voice sounding small beneath the sounds being made by the fighting beasts.

Weaver turned, nodded, and ran into the trees. With every step she could feel the ground vibrating, and she remembered the steady *thud, thud* of Kong's heartbeat as he'd been lying on the lake shore. She'd believed him close to death. How wrong she had been.

Rushing through the trees, she hoped with every part of herself that he would survive.

TWENTY-NINE

In the west, across the heart of the island, the sky was growing light. It was a beautiful sunrise, smearing the rugged horizon and piercing the trees that smothered distant ridge lines and mountaintops. At any other time Brooks might have spent time taking it all in, but he didn't believe he had any time. It could be that they were already too late.

"What's taking so long?" he asked for the tenth time.

"The window's going to close," San said. "We're running out of time." That sentiment had been repeated several times, too. They were both struggling to hold onto reasons to remain where they were. But as the sun rose and a new day began, the reasons were harder to find.

We can't just leave them! Brooks thought. Neither of them were saying that anymore. Speaking the words shamed him, and guilt was already building, even though everyone else might already be dead. *We can't!* He could feel himself wavering. A decision loomed.

San held up her hand, head tilted to one side. Brooks frowned, listening.

He heard a sound like thunder in the distance, even though the sky was clear and cloudless. Then a roar.

A claw of fear scraped down his back, sending ice through his veins.

"They told us to leave at dawn," San said.

"I know."

"It's dawn."

"I know."

Another roar echoed out to them, startling aloft a flock of birds from the trees along the shore. There was no telling where the sound had come from. It had sounded far away, but if the thing making that noise was as big as most of the monsters here, maybe it would be able to reach them in the blink of an eye.

"So what are we going to do?" San asked. She and Brooks stared at each other for a beat, because they both knew what had to be done. They'd known since the first smear of colour in the western sky.

Brooks nodded once, and San started the boat's engine.

• • •

If he'd had any sort of plan to begin with, it was in tatters now, so Conrad just ran. Weaver was close behind him, still hefting her camera in one hand. She'd probably die still taking pictures. He didn't like that thought. If the situation didn't change rapidly—if he didn't come up with a plan that involved more than simply running blindly into the jungle—death might visit them all far too soon.

Behind Weaver came the surviving Sky Devils Cole, Mills, Reles and Slivko. Marlow brought up the rear. He was probably fitter than all of them from his many years on this strange island. However fit they were, however fast they could run, there would be no outrunning the Skull Devil.

Conrad also knew that time was ticking. Dawn had come, and although that helped them navigate through the trees, it also meant that their window for getting to the extract point was beginning to close. If San and Brooks had any sense, they'd have already started the boat and sailed north.

Unsure of the direction they were taking, aware that they were throwing caution to the wind in their headlong rush away from the battling creatures, still he did his best to peer through the trees and tangled undergrowth ahead of them. With terrible danger behind them, he didn't want to run them off a cliff or into a giant rodent's nest. At least the threat behind was known.

Machete drawn, he hacked through vines and hanging plants, always checking to make sure he wasn't slicing at the legs of some waiting creature. Spiders scuttled away, but they were only as big as his hand. Snakes coiled around branches around them, but most seemed a normal size. It stood to reason that the island's ecosystem would not support hundreds of giant beasts, and that those that existed must be rare and long-lived. He had no wish to meet any more.

Spying a clearer space ahead of them, Conrad increased his efforts. Reles and Mills helped him, hacking at hanging vines until they burst through the last of the trees into a wide open space.

"Yes!" Reles shouted, and other voices were raised in delight.

But Conrad's heart fell. At first glance they appeared close to the ocean, but between them and the sea was a wide, level spread of marshland, stretching left and right for at least a mile. Planted at its centre, halfway between where they stood and open water, was the skeletal remains of a shipwreck, half-buried in the marsh and rusted and rotted away. It lent the whole scene the air of a graveyard, and Conrad wondered how many sad human remains spent a lonely eternity beneath the surface.

"It's marshland," he said. "We'll sink and drown, or get caught and…" He didn't need to say 'and what'. They could all hear the fight behind them, and they knew

344

that the warring beasts were coming their way. The ground shook, rippling the surface of a nearby pool of brackish water. Their furious roars serenaded the growing dawn. Trees cracked and snapped, sounding like bomb detonations echoing through the jungle.

They didn't have very long.

"Terrific, now what?" Weaver asked. She was panting but still in control, and if she was feeling panic she didn't show it.

"Reles, your flare gun," Conrad said. The soldier handed the gun and its ammunition belt over without question. Conrad assessed their situation again, taking in everything he could about the location. It was barely a plan, but it was all they had. Conrad checked the gun over, then handed it and the belt to Weaver.

"Get up on those rocks and fire these," he said, pointing ahead to where a rocky promontory jutted out into the marshland. "With any luck, the extract ship will see us."

"What about you?" Weaver asked.

Behind them, the battle was drawing close. The tree line shook with increasing impacts, and Conrad knew they had only minutes to act. The soldiers and Marlow were preparing to make a stand, even though rifles and a sword would do nothing against such massive beasts.

Conrad tried to shake the idea that this was all hopeless. Only once in his life had he given up hope, when he'd seen the dead girl Jenny lying at his feet. Never since. He wasn't about to start now.

"Just run!" he said to Weaver. "We're armed, you're not, and you're probably faster than all of us!"

Securing her camera around her neck she nodded once and then ran for the rocks.

The Skull Devil smashed through the tree line. It seemed even bigger than it had before, none of it hidden beneath a waterline and with dawn's early sunlight revealing the whole of its grotesque, horrific body. Much of it was snakelike, but with thick legs and heavily clawed feet. Its head was almost amphibian, but scaled and spiked, its mouth wide enough to swallow Marlow's boat with all of them inside. Its tail whipped from side to side, scoring deep scars across tree trunks. It stood and stared at them, sweeping its head from left to right as it took in the scene. In its gaze Conrad saw an awful malevolent intelligence.

Mills started shooting first, and the others quickly joined in. Even though Conrad knew it would do no good, he started firing as well, aiming for the monster's eyes.

It stormed towards them. If the bullets did penetrate anywhere, they did not seem to bother the beast. It roared as it came, displaying vicious teeth and a long, forked tongue that whipped at the air, sensing, tasting them. They would hardly constitute a meal.

Conrad had one grenade on his belt. If it came to it, he'd pull the pin seconds before being swept into the monster's mouth.

He glanced back at Weaver and saw her running along the single spit of land that protruded out into the marsh. She reached the rocky promontory and started scrambling up, looking back over her shoulder but not slowing down. The flare pistol was stuck in her belt. They had to give her as long as possible to give them all a chance.

But Conrad felt hope slipping away. How could they fight such a monster? With bullets and bombs that would barely scratch its thick hide? Even if they still had the flamethrower or the .50 cal, or the barrels of napalm, head-on combat with this beast would be brief and with only one possible outcome.

"Back," he shouted to the others. "Back!" They ceased firing and ran towards the sea, and already Conrad could feel the soft ground beneath his boots. Areas of higher ground might offer some hope, and yet the beast had come from beneath the lake, and it would surely be as at home in this marshland as anywhere else.

He wouldn't give up. He *couldn't*. Not here, not now. Not while he had a single breath in his body, a single desperate thought in his mind.

"This way!" he shouted, leading them out into the

marsh. If they worked their way across the marsh and towards the sea, maybe they could hold it off until the ship arrived.

He glanced across the marsh at the old shipwreck and discarded any notion of heading there. It would offer them scant protection, and once inside they would be trapped. He wondered what had grounded the vessel, what had happened to the crew. Maybe a monster had dragged it ashore, like a spider trapping a meal...

"Cole!" Mills shouted. "Whatcha doing, man? Fall back!" Conrad paused and looked back at the soldiers, only to see Cole standing on dry land and facing down the charging monster.

Cole looked back and locked eyes with Mills. "Live your life," he said. He turned back and hefted the grenade launcher from his shoulder, crouching and firing in a single movement.

Conrad allowed himself a moment of hope as the grenade smoked towards the advancing beast. One in the mouth would be lucky. One in the eye would be even better. Such an impact might not kill it, but could give them a chance to escape, and might even deter the Skull Devil from attempting to attack them again.

The grenade exploded against the creature's chest. It reared up, shook its head, then fell onto its front feet again, the foot-long claws sinking into the ground and splashing stinking marsh water into the air.

It roared. Its breath reached them all, stinking like rotten meat and death.

"Come and get me, you bastard!" Cole shouted. He pulled two grenades from his belt, bit out the pins, and ran towards the Skull Devil as it came for him. His aggressive attack brought the monster up short, and for a moment it seemed to pause in puzzlement at this tiny enemy charging it down. Then it lunged for Cole.

It opened its mouth to bite him in half as the first grenade exploded. Cole was blasted to pieces, his head and part of his torso spinning to the right. When the Skull Devil flinched away from the blast and instinctively snapped at the flying piece of meat, the second grenade clasped in the dead man's hand detonated.

This time Conrad saw the blast light up the monster's mouth, smoke enveloping its head and shrapnel tearing chunks from its teeth and gums. It roared in agony, but even its mighty voice could not drown out Mills's shout of despair.

"Noooooo!"

Conrad grabbed him by the shoulder, squeezing hard. They had to take every chance Cole had given them.

"Come on!" he shouted. "We have to move!" They ran across the marsh, finding fewer areas of dry land, moving slower, but still putting distance between themselves and the stunned Skull Devil. As they splashed up to their knees in foul-smelling water, their feet released clouds of stinking methane from the rotting vegetation beneath the water's surface. At any moment Conrad expected to go in up to his waist or deeper, and then that would be the end of him.

Conrad kept firing. He'd seen a hundred men die in explosions, and he'd been close enough to death—had dealt it himself, many times—to wonder at the moment between being and not being. Seeing Cole blown apart had only made him wonder more.

He turned to face the attacking monster just as it made its killing lunge. The face in his mind at the moment of death was Jenny, not lying dead with her brains blown out, but crying as she reached for him, as if she had lost him and not the other way around.

A boulder smashed into the Skull Devil's head, knocking it sideways and sending it sprawling into the marsh.

Conrad gasped and stepped back, saved from falling by Marlow who caught him under the arms.

"Look!" the pilot shouted. "*Look!*" He pointed to their left as Kong thundered from the jungle. The ape ran on all fours, one giant fist clasped around another huge rock. His fur was still smouldering in places, and here and there it was burned away entirely, revealing raw, open flesh. The wounds did not seem to have lessened him at all.

Kong's face was filled with rage.

He reached the Skull Devil as it was finding its feet, raised the other boulder above his head, and brought it down into the monster's side with sickening force. Thick hide split and spewed dark blood. The creature howled, high and piercing.

As Kong raised the rock a second time, the Skull Devil twisted its huge snake-like body, whipping its tail around and slamming it across the ape's chest. Kong staggered back and tripped, falling back into the tree line and releasing the rock. The ground shook as he fell.

The attacker roared in triumph and advanced on the fallen giant.

Conrad knew that he and the others should be using this opportunity to flee. Yet the fight was both awful and fascinating, and he couldn't help but watch. His feet were rooted to the spot.

Kong grasped a huge tree and hauled himself upright, grabbing the trunk in both hands and tugging it from the ground. He used his momentum to swing the uprooted tree around and smashed it across the Skull Devil's head. Leaves and mud flew, branches splintered. It fell again, more dazed than before, clawing with its huge feet to drag itself away from Kong and along the shoreline.

Conrad searched for Weaver. She had reached the top of the rocky spit of land, and she did not hesitate for a moment. She pulled the flare gun and fired, launching a bright red light high on a column smoke.

"Come on!" he shouted. "While we can, come *on*!" The soldiers and Marlow followed him out across the marsh, running parallel to the rocky promontory where Weaver now stood. Conrad could not help glancing back over his shoulder with every few steps, because the balance had changed. He allowed himself hope once again.

Kong was winning. Still grasping the uprooted tree, he was beating the Skull Devil across the head and back, slamming the trunk into its body and driving it further across the marsh with every blow. He took a step between each impact, kicking at the writhing body and pushing it closer and closer to the old shipwreck. Bloody and filthy water surged across the marsh and splashed down like rain. The trunk splintered, turning from a massive club to a deadly spear in the giant's hands.

"Go on!" Conrad shouted, and it was strange feeling a moment of elation amongst such horror. For the first time he recognised the true wonder in this magnificent beast—a brutal, furious, primeval wonder that he had never witnessed before. He hoped that if they did escape he would never see its like again, but knowing

Kong was here would perhaps open up his mind to the world and its stunning potential. Discovering King Kong must be like finding God.

But the devil was here also, and though beaten and bloodied, he was far from down.

The Skull Devil righted itself and rushed Kong, slamming its head into his chest and driving him back and down, both bodies crushing the shipwreck's remains in a scream of tortured metal and roars of animal pain.

Oh, no, Conrad thought. The monster reared up over the fallen Kong, lifting its tail and poising it above its head like a scorpion's stinger. Kong tried to roll, but the Skull Devil butted him again, slamming him back down into the shipwreck.

The monster's tail was long, strong, and tipped with a cruel ivory barb the length of Marlow's boat. Smashing it down into Kong's face would surely provide the killing blow.

Machine-gun fire shattered the scene, and .50 cal rounds strafed across the Skull Devil's midsection, blood flowers bursting from its hide. It shrieked and fell aside, crawling behind the shipwreck and the fallen ape to shield itself from the fusillade of bullets.

Marlow's boat powered along the coast, San at the helm, Brooks propped behind the mounted .50 cal gun. Conrad didn't think he had ever been so glad to see anyone.

"Come on!" he shouted. "Get to the water!" He looked up at Weaver and waved, but she was already starting to climb down from the rocks.

"It's back up!" Mills said.

The Skull Devil was on its feet again, and preparing to rush them. Weaver's rock was now between it and the boat, so even though Brooks still manned the gun, he didn't have a clear line of fire.

As the monster took its first step, Kong grabbed its tail and hauled it back. He stood again, letting go and backing away as the Skull Devil turned on him one more time. For a few seconds they circled, sizing each other up and readying themselves for the fight they both had to continue.

The Skull Devil lashed out with its tail, Kong ducked and launched himself forward, and they clashed.

Conrad splashed on as the boat powered in as far as they dared, and soon all but Weaver were within hailing distance of Marlow's vessel.

"Nice to see you, fellas!" Brooks shouted, still positioned behind the .50 cal and looking for a clear shot.

"Feeling's mutual!" Marlow shouted. "Hope you're looking after my boat."

"Weaver, hurry!" Conrad shouted. He wasn't sure whether she heard, but she continued scrambling down the rocks, leaping from boulder to boulder with dangerous abandon. She had no choice; Conrad knew that, and she did too. Kong stood between them all and certain death, and this was a race against time.

As Slivko and the others waded out and started climbing aboard the boat, Conrad saw Kong give the Skull Devil a massive kick that sent it reeling. Its tail whipped out and Kong ducked the sharp, pointed end… but then its long mass wrapped around his waist, squeezed, and threw him to the ground. He smashed down onto the shipwrecked boat once again, roaring in pain when he landed. He flailed his arms to right himself, but the ship's rigging and an anchor chain were tangled around one arm and his legs.

Kong paused for an instant, taking in the scene.

The monster's sharp tail lashed out again and scored Kong across his hip and stomach. He screamed and tried to grab onto the tail, but it slicked through his hand, flicking out and slashing him across his palm. Blood flew in a rainbow arc.

"Brooks!" San shouted on the boat, and a second later Brooks opened fire with the heavy machine-gun. Bullets streaked across the marshland and stitched the Skull Devil's back, and as he shifted his aim up towards his head—

—the weapon jammed.

The Skull Devil whirled around and faced the

boat. It snarled and hunched down, every inch the devil, blood flowing freely from many wounds, teeth dripping with it, and Conrad knew it was seconds away from its final charge.

"Uh, Marlow, little help?" Brooks said.

Marlow scrambled across the boat to the gun and started tinkering.

"She always was a little temperamental. Hey, Reles, gimme a hand!"

Conrad clung onto the boat's railing but didn't pull himself up. He looked across to Weaver, almost at the base of the rock formation yet still too far away. She'd never make it in time.

The Skull Devil was paused now, looking back at the defenceless Kong, then out at the boat once again. It was weighing its options. He sensed that awful intelligence again as it decided which enemy it wanted to destroy first.

It seemed to lock eyes with him as it made up its mind.

"It's coming," he said, more to himself than everyone else. He made a decision. He wasn't certain that it was brave. He'd never considered himself a brave man, but rather someone good at getting the job done. As the Skull Devil splashed through the marsh towards the boat, Conrad let go of the railing and dropped back into the water. He swam as far as he could, crawled quickly back onto the marshy land, and ran away from the boat. He fired several shots at the beast as he went, eager to draw its attention.

It shook its head as bullets pricked above its eyes, then turned to look at him.

"I'll keep it busy!" he shouted, still running. "You go!" He didn't hear any response, and did not risk glancing back. He only hoped they'd be wise enough to take the chance he was offering them.

He continued shooting as he went, short, careful bursts that each found their mark. He aimed for its eyes. If he hit them, it did nothing to slow the monster down. It was coming for him. That had been his intention, but now he had seconds to live. He scanned the ground ahead of him, seeing nowhere to hide. He stepped into a deeper area of marsh and went down, gripping the rifle as he went under the stinking water. It flooded into his mouth and he gagged, puking as he struggled to his feet again, running, spitting vomit and rank marsh water aside as he went, firing his pistol back over his shoulder and holding the rifle in his other hand.

He risked one glance back to see the boat cutting through the water away from the shore.

Then a spark of light lit up in the distance, and a flare arced in and struck the Skull Devil on the back of its head.

It skidded to a stop, throwing up a wave of mud and water. As it shook its head and turned around, Weaver fired a second flare that wavered through the air and hit it on the right leg.

Conrad fired a long, sustained shot into the back of its head just below what might have been an ear. His M-16 ran dry and he threw it aside, firing his pistol again.

Past the monster he could see Weaver, halfway between the rock and the shore, feeling across her belt for more flares but finding nothing there. They were both out.

The Skull Devil looked back and forth between them, confused about which one to go for. With so many enemies now almost helpless, it was spoilt for choice.

Conrad fired his last three rounds and it came for him, tail raised and ready to slam him into the ground. He grabbed his last grenade.

From his left, a great shape rose out of the marsh. It was Kong, ripping himself partly free of the wreck, tugging on a heavy chain that still held him down, and then swinging it up and around, the rusted propeller tangled in its end performing a perfect arc into the Skull Devil's side.

It slashed the monster and flung it sideways across the marsh, smashing into the rock pile Weaver had just left. Its tail flipped around, and Conrad's breath caught in his throat as he saw Weaver struck and sent spinning fifty feet into the sea.

Her body struck the waves and went under.

"No!" he shouted as the same wave knocked him down. There was nothing he could do. He was too far away, and he couldn't tell whether anyone on the boat had seen what was happening.

Finding his feet, Conrad started making his way back towards the shore. She would drown before he got there. That, or some unseen beast would rise from the depths and take her away beneath the waves.

All he could do was try.

Kong had also noticed, and Conrad was shocked by the change in the giant ape. His fury seemed to seep away in a flash, and he took a first huge step towards where Weaver had disappeared beneath the surface. He remembered standing atop that ridge and Kong appearing before them from down in the valley, Weaver reaching out and touching his face, and even then thinking that some sort of contact had been made. That connection seemed even more obvious now.

With Kong's attention distracted, the Skull Devil grabbed the advantage. Ignoring its terrible wounds, it pulled itself upright and charged the ape.

Conrad looked across at the boat, bobbing now closer to shore, and the men trying to fix the machine-gun on its deck. While Marlow struggled to fit a new ammo belt, Reles snatched up a big hammer and gave the gun two heavy whacks that echoed across the marsh.

They paused, then Reles opened fire once again.

The rounds slammed into the charging Skull Devil, driving it back and down. Wounds upon wounds, it seemed at last that the gunfire was having an effect. The monster writhed in the marshy ground, struggling to turn away from the volley of gunfire but succeeding only in presenting its other flank. Reles was a good shot, and very few bullets missed. Conrad could sense that much as the Skull Devil wanted to flee this stinging fusillade, the fight with Kong was a greater draw.

Meanwhile, Kong had taken full advantage of the Skull Devil being incapacitated. With two huge bounds he was at the water's edge, bending down, reaching into the sea.

Conrad could only stand and watch; amazed and terrified.

The gunfire ceased. Marlow was at the helm now, swinging the boat around and heading back to shore close to where Conrad stood. He was up to his thighs in stinking marshy water, and if the Skull Devil had come for him then he'd have been trapped and helpless.

But he still couldn't bring himself to move.

Kong brought his hand out of the sea, fist closed. He stood to his full height and opened his fist, staring down into his hand at whatever he held there.

Weaver, Conrad thought. *Please let that be Weaver. And please don't let him eat her.*

The ape seemed mesmerised by the shape in his palm. He was so tall that Conrad couldn't make out Weaver, but he did see slight movement—an arm raised, perhaps, and the swing of wet hair as she rolled onto her side. Kong brought his hand closer to his face, and it was as if the rest of the world no longer mattered.

That was when the rest of the world bit back.

The Skull Devil charged, screeching and vicious, shedding blood from its countless bullet wounds yet appearing strengthened by them, not weakened. Pain drove it on. Fury gave it an edge.

Kong closed his fist protectively around Weaver and braced himself. Then he ran towards his approaching enemy.

Just before they met, the Skull Devil reared up ready to bite, its long, wicked tail whipping around to slash at the great ape.

Kong had other plans. He brought his heavy fisted hand up and around and slammed it straight into the monster's mouth. He swung his shoulder, using all his immense weight to shove his fist deep into the creature's gullet, deeper, further, until his arm was buried in the Skull Devil's innards right up to his massive bicep.

Kong roared as he withdrew his arm and fisted hand, the beast's teeth scoring deep lines in his fur.

The Skull Devil swayed on its feet, blood pouring from its open mouth. Then its eyes dimmed and it dropped into the marsh, one last, heavy rattling breath leaving it before its flexing torso grew forever still.

The silence was startling. Kong stood still for a moment, breathing heavily as he stared down at his vanquished enemy. He shoved the carcass with one foot, and again, testing to see whether the monster was feigning.

The Skull Devil was dead.

Kong's shoulders drooped a little as he stepped over the huge corpse and approached Conrad.

Conrad had to force himself not to step backwards. It would have done no good, but instinct urged him back, the same instinct that would have brought his arms in front of his face if a building were falling upon him. From the corner of his eye he saw the boat bobbing less than fifty feet away, and he was aware of the survivors watching Kong, and him.

He didn't look. He could not tear his eyes away from the massive beast now standing close to him.

Kong dropped to his knees with a booming splash, sending tremors across the marsh. He placed his blood-soaked fist on the ground, and uncurled his fingers to reveal Weaver lying there, safe and awake in his palm. His fur was caked in blood and gunge from the dead Skull Devil's insides. His hide was ripped and bleeding, and blood dripped and washed around Weaver. But she appeared untouched. He tilted his fist and she slid to the ground, grunting as she landed and sitting up. She was soaked to the skin, trembling from her cold dip in the sea, but she did not appear scared. She left her hand on Kong's. As he went to stand and pull away, Weaver held on. Only briefly.

Kong stood. They were in his shadow, perhaps forever. He stared down at them, and they looked up at him, locking gazes for a moment that might have been the longest of Conrad's life. Then he turned, swaying slightly, and started walking away. He was limping. His vast body was covered in open wounds, and there were also older scars there, marks where the fur had not grown back that illustrated older, more mysterious battles. Conrad wondered at what these battles might have been, and whether the dead beast now sinking into the swamp was responsible for some of those wounds.

None of them had any idea how old Kong might be, or what ancient combats he might have fought. His was a history that remained shrouded in the mists of time, and Conrad believed that was as it should be, just as with any god, or any legendary king.

Conrad ran over to Weaver and grabbed her hand, helping her to her feet. Neither of them spoke. There were no words.

They watched Kong splashing across the marsh and then approaching the tree line. Weaver pulled away and grabbed at her camera bag, drawing a camera out and checking it, wiping the lens, aiming it at Kong.

He paused close to the trees and turned back, looking at them one more time.

What's he thinking? Conrad wondered. *Is he as amazed at us as we are at him?* He doubted that. He thought perhaps King Kong was the most amazing creature on their planet, known or still hidden away.

Weaver lowered her camera without taking a shot.

"No Pulitzer?" Conrad asked.

"Maybe some things are better left as myth," she said, echoing his thoughts. Her voice sounded shaky. He took her hand again and squeezed, and they both took comfort from the contact.

They watched Kong as he walked into the jungle, trees shaking at his passage and then closing behind him. They could make out his route for a while, and then all grew quiet. Even then they continued watching. To move would be to move on. Despite all the horrors, neither of them wanted wonder to leave them behind.

THIRTY

Later, they finally left the river estuary and headed out into the open ocean. The boat was hardly seaworthy, but it held together reasonably well. They took turns operating the manual pump, and Marlow stood proudly at the helm. Weaver thought he looked like someone going somewhere special, as well as leaving something behind. He'd be forever existing in two worlds. Perhaps they all would.

Weaver sat alone on deck, looking ahead but thinking back to those moments when she'd believed she was going to die. The Skull Devil's tail had sideswiped her and sent her spinning through the air, consciousness wavering from the impact. If she'd landed on land she would have died, and even landing in the sea had felt like hitting solid ground.

A heavy impact, the breath knocked from her, and the gagging, cloying taste of sea water filling her mouth and rushing down her throat.

From there, it felt like a dream. She was sinking, darkness closing around her as shadowy shapes wavered at the edges of her perception. Perhaps they had been long sea weeds, or maybe the eager, welcoming embrace of a creature on the seabed waiting for this imminent taste of something new.

Then darkness closed around her and pulled her up and out of the water. She hardly remembered any of what followed. From what Conrad had told her, she was glad. It was the sunlight that welcomed her in again, as Kong's hand opened to reveal Conrad standing twenty feet away, the blue sky above him, Kong's warm, protective hand beneath her.

She hadn't wanted him to let her go. She'd held on. But Kong had known the truth—they were from two different worlds, and even though he'd saved her, they belonged far apart.

Sailing away from the island, she realised the deep truth of that. It was difficult leaving something so amazing behind.

She looked around at the other survivors—San, Brooks, Mills, Slivko, Reles—and saw the same look in their eyes. They had all been offered a glimpse at something remarkable. Through the horrors they had witnessed, despite the death that had circled them and taken many of their friends, they all understood how privileged they were.

At the helm, Marlow was holding the tattered photo of his wife. Conrad rested a hand on his shoulder. Two good men, and as Weaver raised her camera and framed a shot, Conrad looked down at her.

"What do you see?" he asked.

"A face tells a story," she said.

He smiled. "So, did you get the shot? The one that's going to change the world?"

"One image of Kong and this place would be overrun by government and soldiers. This world, this one here, doesn't need changing. The one out there is another story."

"Word will get out," Conrad said, quieter, looking around at the other survivors. "It always does."

"Not from me," Weaver said.

Ahead of them the storm loomed, surrounding the island and all but hiding it from the outside world. They were heading for a break in the storm, and she knew that there were rough seas ahead. She also knew that they would make it through. They had all come too far, and seen too much, for the sea to take them now.

While Marlow braced himself at the helm and prepared to ride the first of the waves, Weaver put her hand in her camera bag and felt the film cartridges.

They were all ruined, damaged by sea water despite their packaging. She wasn't even sure why she was keeping them. At any other time the loss would have devastated her, but not now. Now, she didn't mind. She'd already decided that the ring of storms they were approaching was there for a purpose.

Skull Island was a wild place set apart from the rest of the world. It and its inhabitants, both human and inhuman, deserved to be left alone.

Weaver would not be the person to break its secret.

EPILOGUE

Conrad was so exhausted that his eyes felt heavy and his limbs were not his own. All he wanted to do was sleep. The powers that be, however, seemed to have other plans for him.

Even before arriving back at port, he and Weaver had been helicoptered off and whisked to a private facility for debriefing. The others had been taken on different helicopters, and he assumed that they were also here somewhere. Probably in very similar rooms, having answered identical questions. He wasn't fazed. He understood what was going on because he'd been in similar situations so many times before.

But he *was* pissed off. They hadn't even been given clean clothes. Coffee, yes, and food. While his stomach was comfortably heavy, the coffee he kept topping up was the only thing keeping him awake. He stank.

Weaver stank, too. They'd gone beyond joking about it.

They both carried wounds that had been tended and dressed. The deeper scars would be kept for themselves. Maybe they'd even help each other tend them. He hoped so, and he thought Weaver hoped so too, but recent events made such considerations seem petty. After what they'd been through together, going out for a drink seemed so… mannered.

"Why are you still keeping us here?" he asked the one-way mirror. He suspected there were at least a couple of guys and a camera behind there, recording every sigh, every nod of the head, and every look he and Weaver shared.

"We've told you everything we know," Weaver said. She didn't sound as tired as she looked. "We want to go home. We want to…" She sniffed her shirt. "…*change*."

"We get the point," Conrad said. "We really do. We never went to any island."

"What island?" Brooks asked. He and San had entered the room behind them, and Conrad was angry at himself for not hearing, but only for a second. He was too tired to be really angry, and he'd allowed himself to relax too much to care.

At least Brooks and San had been given the opportunity to get cleaned up. Showered, dressed in civilian clothing, they still carried bruises and abrasions from their expedition. Deeper in their eyes, Conrad saw marks that would not be so easily washed away.

"Sorry for the cloak-and-dagger stuff," Brooks said. "Bigger budgets mean more fingers in the pie. You know how it is."

Conrad only shrugged.

"Welcome to Monarch, by the way," Brooks said.

"Little drab," Weaver said looking around. "Might need someone to come in and decorate, brighten the place up."

"So come work here and hire one," Brooks said.

"You're doing the hiring now?" Conrad asked.

"Randa might be gone, but we're continuing his work."

"We know you're tired," San said. "We know you've been debriefed. But if Brooks and I can have one last moment of your time?"

Conrad and Weaver exchanged a glance. He saw her concern as well, and he marvelled yet again at how attuned they were. Perhaps that drink wouldn't be so petty. Maybe it would lead on to greater things.

"Good news never follows that sentence," Conrad said. "So what have you got?"

San dropped a folder on the table and slid it to them, still closed. It was marked with the Monarch logo—two triangles with their points touching.

Conrad flipped open the cover and saw the first of many pages of text, communication extracts, poor photographs, and other information. He feared that they hadn't come as far from that island as he'd believed, and he remembered the stink of the marsh, the alien regard of the Skull Devil's eyes.

"Skull Island is only the beginning," Brooks said.

"There's more out there," San said.

"What do you mean, 'more'?" Conrad slid the folder across to Weaver, but to begin with she didn't seem eager to look at it. She realised as well as him that to do so would be to change their lives.

"This world never belonged to us," San said.

Brooks flicked on a projector. "The only question is, how long until they try to take it back."

He began to cast images onto the plain painted wall. They were of ancient cave paintings, eroded sculptures, timeworn hieroglyphs showing fantastic and terrifying creatures of all shapes and sizes. Some of them were recognisable—he saw a Kong-like figure battling a giant winged beast. Others were more mysterious. A huge lizard on its hind legs, at war with a giant dragonfly. A hammer-headed beast in combat with a many-tailed, skeletal bird.

More. Much more, all of it terrible.

Conrad gasped. Weaver went to say something, but her voice broke. There really was nothing to say.

All they could do was look, and let the fear settle around them.

• • •

Several days passed before they set him free. To some he was a hero, an amazing survivor from a war that was already fading into history. They even talked about arranging for him to meet the president one day soon. To others he was a celebrity. His story had leaked out, and there was talk of book deals, the offer of a movie of his life, and more.

He had only told them a small part of his story. When they probed, he feigned forgetfulness, giving them bizarre and surreal tales that eventually forced them to accept the fact that his time on the island had driven him mad.

He was fine with that. He'd prefer madness to fame and perceived heroism. From the first moment they had emerged from out of the storm and back into the world once again, there was one place he'd wanted to go.

Now he was there, and Marlow had never been more afraid. Sitting in the cab a few doors down from the house, he remembered Gunpei Ikari, his greatest friend.

They hold each other by the throats, knives raised, blood burning in their eyes and murder on their minds, and then Kong rises before them, lessening them with his gaze and making nothing of their reasons for fighting. Like that, their fury fades away.

Seven years later, he and Gunpei are sitting around a camp fire in the wreck of the *Wanderer*. That day has been a hard one for them all—a Skull Crawler surfaced and took away three village children, and Kong chased it halfway across the island before battering it to death. They are quiet and contemplative, sipping some of the Iwis' ale and sharing a comfortable silence, as is so often the case.

"What's your most frightening moment?" Gunpei asks. He speaks English, and Marlow speaks Japanese, and their talk is usually a flowing merger of the two languages.

"Today took the biscuit," Marlow says. "You?"

Gunpei is silent for a long time, staring into the flames. He's quiet for so long that that Marlow thinks he might have forgotten the question and let his mind wander, and he's fine with that. It happens to them both. With so much time to fill, their imaginations have become fertile ground.

"Our first day here," Gunpei says at last.

"When we first saw Kong," Marlow says.

"No. My most frightening moment was the one just before he appeared, when I almost murdered my best friend."

• • •

Marlow remembered his surprise at Gunpei's comment. It wasn't like Gunpei to be so personal, or so vulnerable. Up until now, it was the nicest thing anyone had ever said to him.

He opened the cab door at last and walked along the Chicago street. It was autumn, and leaves whispered along with him on the gentle breeze. He liked the idea of having seasons again.

They were expecting him, but that didn't make this any easier. His wife could have moved on for all he knew, and his son also had a son of his own. He'd flown out of their lives, and now he was stepping back in. No one could guess how things might change.

Come on, Marlow, he thought. *You've fought monsters. This should be easy.*

He reached the door, but before he could knock it opened. A young man stood there. He was tall and strong and proud, and Marlow felt his vision beginning to blur.

The young man reached out and took his hand, and said the nicest thing. "Dad."

THE END

ABOUT THE AUTHOR

TIM LEBBON is a *New York Times*-bestselling writer from South Wales. He's had more than thirty novels published to date, as well as hundreds of novellas and short stories. His latest novel is the thriller *The Family Man*, and other recent releases include *The Hunt*, *The Silence*, *Coldbrook*, *Alien: Out of the Shadows*, and *The Rage War* trilogy.

He has won four British Fantasy Awards, a Bram Stoker Award, and a Scribe Award, and has been a finalist for World Fantasy, International Horror Guild, and Shirley Jackson awards. Future releases include the *Relics* trilogy from Titan Books, and fantasy novel *Blood of the Four* (with Christopher Golden).

A movie of his story *Pay the Ghost*, starring Nicolas Cage, was released in 2015, and several other projects are in development for television and the big screen.

Find out more about Tim at his website www.timlebbon.net